D0463618

F
Norman-Bellamy, Kendra.
More than Grace

MORE THAN GRACE

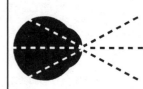

This Large Print Book carries the
Seal of Approval of N.A.V.H.

More Than Grace

Kendra Norman-Bellamy

THORNDIKE PRESS

An imprint of Thomson Gale, a part of The Thomson Corporation

Detroit • New York • San Francisco • New Haven, Conn. • Waterville, Maine • London

GALE

LIBRARY OF CONGRESS CATALOGING-IN-PUBLICATION DATA

Norman-Bellamy, Kendra.
  More than Grace / by Kendra Norman-Bellamy.
    p. cm. — (Grace series ; #3) (Thorndike Press large print
African-American)
  ISBN-13: 978-0-7862-9806-8 (alk. paper)
  ISBN-10: 0-7862-9806-5 (alk. paper)
  1. African Americans — Fiction. 2. Physicians — Fiction. 3. Large type
books. I. Title.
PS3614.O765M67 2007
813'.6—dc22   2007024426

Published in 2007 by arrangement with Harlequin Books S.A.

Printed in the United States of America on permanent paper
10 9 8 7 6 5 4 3 2 1

MORE THAN GRACE

PRELUDE

Slam!

That last one was just to release more brewing anger. Sherry knew her husband couldn't hear the explosive thud of the door she'd just closed. She'd already heard the screeching wheels of the Lincoln Town Car when Derrick pulled out of the driveway of their condominium. He seemed to press the gas pedal of the car with the same force that she'd used to close the bedroom door for the third and final time.

"You're the one who's wrong, Derrick Jerome Madison!" she screamed aloud, with tears burning in her eyes.

It was the third consecutive night that the two of them had endured the same argument and in Sherry's book, it was getting old. They'd had this discussion for a year leading up to their marriage, so she had no remorse for standing firm on the conclusion that Derrick had wholeheartedly agreed to over seven years ago.

For almost a year now, her husband had been hinting at the topic of their having a second child. He seemed to get the itch shortly after their godson was born. After watching his best friend, Greg, bond with his little boy, suddenly, the daughter that he and Sherry had wasn't enough. Now, Derrick needed a son of his own to feel complete. One child was what they agreed to having and as far as Sherry was concerned, the case was closed, the lock had been snapped and the key had been long ago become scrap metal.

"When men start having to go through the pains of childbirth, you can have as many as you like!"

No one could hear her as she spoke the words, laced with residue anger, towards the closed curtain, but saying them seemed to make Sherry feel better. She'd been in love with Derrick since they were high school seniors and there were very few things that she'd deny him, but this one was high on the short list. Memories of the misery of her pregnancy, including the fifty pounds she had gained when carrying the now almost five-year-old Denise were not serving as objects of enticement. Though she'd always been a full-figured woman, ten of the pounds that pregnancy had put on her still lingered and that wasn't the worst of it.

Sherry's pregnancy was long and lonely. Derrick had seemed oblivious to her discomfort and her need for understanding. Both of them were excited when they got the news of the pregnancy and he'd made a solemn promise to be by her side and at her beck and call throughout. That promise was short lived as she recalled. Today, he was a doting husband and father, but during those nine months of sick mornings and sleepless nights, she remembered him being distant.

"Fool me once, shame on you," she mumbled as she stepped into the hot stream that gushed from her shower-head.

Sherry didn't even finish the cliché. Ten minutes later, she stepped from her cleansing, feeling a bit more relaxed, but with her mind still racing. She and Derrick had never disagreed this passionately about anything in their marriage. They'd had their share of arguments and had occasionally even gone against her late mother-in-law's wedding day advice to them.

"I don't care what y'all do, don't y'all never go to bed at odds with one another. God don't like that and neither do I. Y'all hear me?" Julia Madison gave the instructions while peering at them over her glasses as the wedding reception came to a close.

Stifling laughter at the seemingly far-fetched words that came across more as a threat than advice, in unison the newlyweds replied, "Yes, ma'am."

That vow had been broken years ago, but still Derrick and Sherry had a loving, solid relationship. The level of intensity that the topic of a new addition to the family had brought on had never before made an appearance in the Madison household. Tonight, upon packing a small bag and heading for the front door, Derrick hinted that he was going to sleep elsewhere. For them, that was a first.

"Go ahead and sleep somewhere else. See if I care! You don't ever have to come back!"

As soon as the words escaped her lips, tears welled in Sherry's eyes once more. She didn't mean them, but she was too stubborn to take them back. Sometimes she could be as mulish as her husband was known to be.

Not even in the frame of mind to say her usual nighttime prayers, Sherry crawled under the covers and buried her face in the pillow. Their king-size bed had never before seemed so big nor so empty.

CHAPTER 1

It had been a long day to end an even longer week. Situations in the life of Dr. Gregory Dixon had changed substantially over the past year and a half. More specifically, they'd changed over the past six months. In one sense, the alterations were advantageous, but on the other hand, the new experience didn't give him the high that other surgeons in his place would likely have gotten.

Taking a much needed moment, Greg locked the hotel room behind him, dropped his attaché and umbrella on the floor beside the bed and lowered his back flat onto the comfortable mattress. Covering his face with the palms of his hands, he exhaled deeply, trying to propel from his body all the tiredness that had settled in on the cab ride from Lenox Hill Hospital.

"Some vacation," he said, through a halfhearted chuckle.

It took effort, but after a few moments, he managed to stand and walk to the safe beside the door and reached for the knob that kept his private belongings private. Greg knew his combination so well that even his tired mental state couldn't fog the numbers. Five right, twelve left, ten right — they were the numbers representing the months of the births of his wife, his son and himself.

From the fireproof metal encasing, he retrieved a journal that he'd been keeping since shortly after the birth of his son, Julian. He'd always been grateful for every blessing God had given him, but Julian's birth, coupled with the second successful life-saving surgical procedure that he'd performed on his own wife had made Greg even more appreciative. Now, he took nothing for granted.

This extensive time off from his permanent job had been taken especially with the people closest to him in mind. Greg had vowed that he'd make more time for his family, yet here he was, nearly two-hundred-fifty miles away from them.

Opening the leather-bound book, he began thumbing through the pages, but his thoughts were still in Washington, D.C., where in reality, his wife, Grace had spent the last two weeks caring for Julian as though she was his sole parent. What had started out as enthusiastic journal entries thirteen days ago, now read like writings on a prison wall.

Immediately, when his vacation from Robinson Memorial began, Greg got the call that he remembered praying for when he began his career as a neurosurgeon intern. Back then, he longed for the day when he'd be so skilled at his craft that prominent hospitals all over the world would recognize him by name. He'd seen his mentor, Dr. Simon Grant, be called away on several occasions to assist in surgical procedures at other medical facilities wherein the hired staff were for some reason unsure of themselves. After six years, Greg finally knew what it felt like.

He didn't want to appear ungrateful, but what had begun as a three-day assignment had now stretched into one far longer. After an eight-day stretch, Greg was able to fly home in time to spend Mother's Day with his wife and son before heading back to New York to start the routine all over again. Tomorrow, he'd catch the first nonstop flight out again to spend another weekend at home. Time with his family, that he'd once taken for granted, now seemed like moments to cherish.

Greg finished his journal entry for the day. It was shorter than most of his previous notations, but he was just too tired to continue. Unmotivated to get up and lock it away, he placed the book on the stand beside his bed and reached for the telephone. It was late, but not too late to call home.

"Hello?" Her voice was almost a whisper.

"I'd like to speak to Mrs. Jessica Grace Dixon," Greg teased.

"Well, hello, Doctor." Jessica's voice was still lowered, but Greg could tell from the sound of it that his call had brought a smile to her face.

"Hi, Grace," he responded, referring to her by her middle name as he always did. "Did I wake you?"

"No," she said. "Julian just drifted off about twenty minutes ago and I just don't want to talk so loud that I wake him."

"He's sleeping in our bed?"

"Well, you're not here," Jessica responded. "So, I thought I'd find another man to take your place."

She laughed following her lighthearted comment, but Greg didn't find it quite as amusing. The meaning behind his unresponsiveness finally sank in and Jessica sobered.

14

She broke the moment of silence that followed. "Greg, I'm only kidding. You know that, right?"

"Yeah, I know," he said through a heavy sigh. "I just want to be there, that's all."

"We know you do." Another quiet moment followed before she spoke again. "You're still coming home tomorrow afternoon, right?"

"Tomorrow night, actually," Greg corrected her. "My flight doesn't leave until five. It'll be six-thirty, at least, by the time I get home. I'm going to go in tomorrow and make one more round before heading to the airport."

"How's the police officer coming along?"

"He's improving," Greg told her. "My prognosis remains the same. He'll recover well, but it's highly probable that he's going to have limitations to the use of the left side of his body. Physical therapy is in the future of his recovery, so that'll improve his chances of having a wider range of motion in his left arm and leg."

Sergeant Evan McDonald was the reason that Greg was working in the acute-care hospital that was located on Manhattan's Upper East Side. Like Robinson Memorial in D.C., Lenox Hill Hospital was famous for the exceptional attention given to

15

critical-care patients. But with more than 650 beds, Lenox Hill could house a few dozen more people than the hospital where Greg worked daily.

Sergeant McDonald had been brought in at a time when Dr. Joseph Armstrong, the head neurosurgeon, had chosen to leave the country on an extended retreat. As capable as the remaining staff was, they were all apprehensive of the tedious surgical procedure that the undercover veteran officer would have to have if his life was to be spared. Even after being briefed upon his arrival, Greg was taken aback when he saw the unconscious officer, whose head had been bashed in on one side with a blunt object during a drug sting that didn't go according to plan.

"He's the one I need to check on before leaving tomorrow to make sure he's getting the care he needs," Greg informed Jessica. "We don't need a setback like the one he had last week. Once I'm sure he's still stable, then —"

"Then you're gonna come and take care of me, right?" Jessica interrupted.

It wasn't quite what Greg was going to say, but he liked the sound of the words she spoke. "Yeah," he said. "Most definitely."

"I was kidding, silly," Jessica said with a

16

childlike giggle.

"I wasn't," Greg told her.

Jessica knew his tone. She felt the color flush from her face as she held the phone to her ear and gently stroked the soft hairs on the side of Julian's head.

"Are you ready?" he broke the lingering silence.

"For what?" she asked knowingly. Her tone remained soft and her voice still sounded calm, but Jessica's body was aflame on the inside and she knew that her husband wasn't ignorant of the position in which he had placed her.

"For me," he answered without hesitation, prompting another pause on the other end of the line.

"Yeah," Jessica finally spoke. "I have to make up for nature's bad timing on last weekend."

Not that he needed reminding, but her words took Greg back to a whole weekend of only being able to hold her and imagine what might have been. The thought of not having any restraints in place on this visit turned the tables and it was Greg's body's turn to be awakened.

"Hold that thought," he said, not wanting to aggravate the loneliness any more than he already had. "We'll continue this conversation in a few hours."

"I'll be here," Jessica assured him.

"If you're not, I'll find you," he said. "I love you. Kiss Julian for me."

"I will," she promised. "I love you too."

Greg hung up the phone and proceeded to prepare himself for bed. The spacious penthouse accommodations of the On the Ave Hotel where Lenox Hill had graciously placed him offered almost all the comforts of home. He could have meals delivered to his door, the sizeable bed was more than cozy, and the forty-two-inch plasma flat-screen television offered so many channels that Greg could find a show to watch for whatever mood he was in — be it sports, drama or his favorite, *Jeopardy!*. Even the bathroom was equipped with an eight-inch plasma television of its own. Still, with all of its luxuries, the distinctive hotel was no match for the comfort of the lively laughter of his son or the tender touches of his wife.

As he tucked away the clothes he'd earlier shed, his eyes fell to the screen on his cellular phone. A message had been left during the time he was taking his shower.

"Hey, Greg. I was hoping to talk to you for a second before I dozed off. Nobody's sick or anything, so don't worry about trying to call me back. It's not that important. I just wanted to chat a minute. Missed you around the dinner table last weekend. Love you. Oh, yeah . . . you missed a really good fight between your mom and Ms. Mattie. 'Bye."

There was something about the sound of Sherry's voice that concerned Greg. They talked quite often, but she never made it a habit to call him at such a late hour. For a moment, he contemplated returning her call, but replaying the laughter he heard after her last statement erased his uneasiness. Besides, exhaustion had taken its toll and talking to Sherry would call for more energy than he was willing to dispense right now.

Slipping his freshly showered body beneath the crisp white bed linen, Greg picked up the journal from the nightstand and reopened it to the halfhearted entry about his day at the hospital that he'd scribbled earlier. Finding new inspiration, he picked up his pen and resumed.

Journal entry continued: 12:22 a.m. Despite my fatigue, God is faithful in all. I am now two-thirds complete with a temporary assignment that I should have finished many days ago. I don't know why God still has me here, but I have to believe that there is a purpose. I miss all those things that I had access to on a daily basis just a few weeks ago. Because of my late flight out, I'll only have a few hours to spend at home before returning to the Big Apple and I'll have to divide my time wisely. Of course, I'll make time for Mama and Ms. Mattie. If I don't, I'd never live to tell the story. Then there's my homeboy, Rick. I've got to play at least one game of one-on-one with him. I promised Sherry that I'd have dinner with them, so that will give me a chance to spend some time with Dee as well. So many people, so little time.

But first things first. I've got to see, taste and touch Grace. I'm sometimes in awe when I think of how much intense love and passion this one woman has brought to my life. Even more astonishing is that a few years ago, the notion that I could share the innermost part of my heart with anyone else other than her was for me, unbelievable. Until recently, it seemed that everything I did in life was either for Grace or because of Grace. Then came Julian, the most beautiful boy in the world . . . and I'm not just saying that because he looks like me. I have so many hopes for him, so many dreams. What my father couldn't do for me, I want to do for Julian. It almost seems strange to say that it's not just about Grace anymore.

My love for her still runs deeper than words could say, but with my son, I realize that now, it's about more than Grace.

Good night.

CHAPTER 2

Jessica took a quick peek over her shoulder at her husband's pride and joy, who sat snug and safe in a child-restraint car seat behind her. Julian stared with contentment at the white mesh sunblocker that covered the window beside him. Apparently, no longer interested in the cup of juice that his mother had given him, he dangled it in one hand, while using the other to reach for the Disney characters that decorated the shade.

Thank God for spill-proof cups, Jessica thought. *And thank God for grandmothers.*

Greg had called nearly an hour ago from J. F. Kennedy Airport in New York to let her know he was boarding his plane and was on his way home. If she had calculated correctly, she only had a few minutes to finalize her last-minute plan to give the two of them some much-needed alone time.

As Jessica pulled up into the driveway of the home that her mother and mother-in-law shared, both women were standing at the door awaiting her arrival. She had had no second thoughts when she dialed them immediately upon ending her brief conversation with Greg. Asking them to keep Julian for the night would be no infringement on their plans. The two women were chronic homebodies who loved keeping their grandson and he enjoyed every minute of attention that they showered on him during his periodic overnight stays.

"There's Grandma's baby!" Mattie called as Jessica unlocked his seat and hoisted the twenty-pound, seventeen-month-old in her arms. Just the sound of his grandmother's voice made the toddler's face light up with merriment.

"Yay!" he cheered through giggles, nearly dropping his cup in the midst of trying to clap his hands.

"Thanks, Mama," Jessica said, placing a kiss on Mattie's cheek while transferring the child to her mom. "Thanks, Ms. Lena," she said to her mother-in-law, who leaned her face in for a smooch as well.

"Where you running off to?" Lena laughed as Jessica turned away after handing her the child's diaper bag.

"Greg will be home in just a few minutes," she answered. "I want to be there before he gets there."

"Well, you shole better hurry," Mattie said, " 'cause you know that son-in-law of mine drives like a bat out of hell sometimes. And he ain't never late for nothing."

"Tell him to call me when he gets home," Lena said.

"I will, Ms. Lena."

"You in a mighty big hurry," Lena added. "Y'all getting ready to make us another one?" She patted Julian's arm as she spoke.

The unexpected comment stopped Jessica in her tracks and brought to her face an uncontrollable blush. She didn't know why it surprised her. Nothing that her mother or mother-in-law said should catch her off guard, yet sometimes it did. They were known to speak their minds and generally did so shamelessly.

"If y'all do," Mattie added, "get that girl this time, hear?"

Laughing at the women and their forwardness, Jessica got inside her car and returned Julian's wave as she backed out from the driveway. Quickly putting them out of her mind, she headed home and was relieved that she'd gotten there ahead of her husband.

For Greg, the traffic seemed to stand as still

as time itself. Everything about the trip, from the long security lines to the flight had seemed to take forever. Now, of all days, an accident ahead had traffic tied up and moving slowly.

"I can't believe you took this route without listening to the traffic report first!" he scolded himself. Realizing that getting frustrated wasn't going to make it any less aggravating, Greg tried to calm himself by turning the radio to his favorite jazz station and cranking up the volume. Oddly, the song playing was the same one he'd heard through his earphones just before stepping off the plane after it landed at Ronald Reagan Washington National Airport.

His mind floated back to the seemingly endless flight. Fifty thousand feet above the ground, time always seemed to pass at a slower rate than normal, especially when there was an agenda planned. The entire trip had only been about ninety minutes long, but it seemed so much longer — even in the comfort of first-class seating, where he got more attention and service than he wanted. One stewardess told him that he looked like a younger, more handsome version of Malik Yoba. Another one seemed to search for reasons to stop by his seat.

"Would you like a cocktail, Doctor?"

Greg's window stare on the flight had been repeatedly interrupted by the attractive stewardess's varied offers, some of which were subtle and unspoken.

Melaina was her name and the sound of it seemed to roll off of her tongue when she introduced herself. She was from Milan and gave validity to the belief that Italy produced some of the world's most beautiful women.

"No, thank you," he'd always reply. Once, to make her feel useful, he'd requested a glass of water.

"Certainly." She seemed happy to oblige.

A smile crept across Greg's face in spite of himself. Years ago, his now deceased godmother had called his dashing good looks "a blessing from God that the devil would try to turn into a curse." Over the years, Greg had grown accustomed to the attention that he received from women. In more recent years, he'd even learned to appreciate it as the compliment that it was. At the end of the day though, he knew that there was only one woman for him and that was the woman he'd made his wife nearly five years ago.

When the flight was complete, Greg, like the other passengers, gathered his carry-on bag and prepared to descend from the confines of Delta Flight 1285. Taking his turn to disembark, Greg's eyes once again met those of the friendly airline attendant.

"Thanks for flying Delta, Doctor," Melaina said. "Enjoy the rest of your evening."

Greg flashed a smile that displayed a single dimple in his left cheek. "You do the same," he responded.

And enjoying the rest of his evening was just what he was looking forward to doing. On any given day, the twenty-six-mile ride from the airport to the house Greg shared with his family would take no more than half an hour. But this night, an accident ahead had tied up the evening traffic and what should have been an eventless drive was anything but. The soothing voice of Anita Baker that oozed through his car's sound system was unsuccessful at easing Greg's nerves as tension mounted and his patience ran thin for the slow-moving cars ahead.

"I could park this thing and walk home faster than this," he voiced in exasperation.

The flashing lights of emergency vehicles could be seen in the distance as the root of the problem came within sight. The reality of seeing it all caused Greg to reevaluate his thought process. The three-car accident was far more than a fender bender. One vehicle, a pickup truck, had overturned in the center lane. The cab of it was almost flattened from the impact. One of the cars had been hit with such force that it had been sent into the grassy area several feet from the highway. The other, with all of its windows smashed in, had apparently been sent spinning out of control and came to a stop facing oncoming traffic head-on.

A fire truck was still on-site. Policemen stood in the center of the road with flashlights and directed traffic into the one open lane. The medical examiner's car parked beside the fire engine indicated that not all of those involved had been fortunate enough to escape what was certain to have been a horrible death.

As a child riding in the car with his mother in years past, Greg used to watch Lena briefly close her eyes and whisper a quick prayer for the victims of accidents that they would see. It was a practice that he'd adopted and did instinctively during moments like this one.

By the time he parked his car in his garage, only the porch light kept the house from appearing to be in complete darkness. Pulling his suitcase from the trunk for the second time in as many weeks, Greg started up the steps that led to the side entrance of the living room. Total quiet blanketed the house. He laid his case at the side of the sofa and immediately walked into his son's room, hoping to catch a glimpse of him, even if he were asleep. Assuming that the empty crib meant that Jessica had once again allowed him to sleep in their bed, Greg turned off the nursery's light and anxiously walked into what his mother-in-law called "the honeymoon suite."

Despite the obvious fact that he'd arrived home nearly two hours after she would have expected him to, Greg was disappointed that his wife hadn't waited up for him. She generally didn't turn in this early, but through the darkness, he could see her nestled beneath the covers. Fighting the urge to wake her, Greg turned and walked into the bathroom and closed the door behind him. He was feeling very selfish in his desire to carry Julian to his own room and then awaken Jessica with creative love-making techniques. Imagining that she'd had a full and busy week working and caring for their son without him there to help, Greg stepped into the shower and tried to wash away his desires with the hot water.

The sudden motion of the shower door startled him. With cloth in hand, Greg turned around just in time to see Jessica step from her satin gown and into the stall with him. For a moment, it seemed he was dreaming, but when she reached forward and touched his bare chest with her hand, Greg knew that it wasn't his imagination.

Pulling her closer to him and into the downpour of water, Greg watched as her short curled hair quickly flattened under the drenching moisture. With his hand, he whisked away strands of hair that stuck to her face and then wasted no time covering her wet lips with his. The washcloth that was no longer needed was dropped to the floor beneath them as Greg freed both his hands for exploration purposes.

Jessica moaned and he felt her knees weaken as they often did when the passion of his kisses reached the height that they now had. On most days, Greg would wrap his arms around her for support. This time, he continued to smother her lips with demanding mastery. Lifting her slightly from the floor, he then guided her weakened body and positioned her perfectly against the wall of the stall. Seconds later, another moan — his this time — was followed by Jessica's gasp.

The waters that pounded against Greg's back seemed to give him a rhythm by which to pace himself. Several minutes later, with their strength drained, Jessica sank to the floor of the stall. After shutting off the water, Greg joined her and pulled her wet body close to his. Silence reigned for several moments.

"You know, a simple 'hello' would have done," he finally spoke, still breathless.

Jessica laughed aloud while using her hands to smooth her saturated hair behind her ears. "I'll keep that in mind for next time," she said.

Greg quickly rethought his position. "You'd better not."

"I thought you'd change your mind," she teased.

"Shhh!" Greg said.

They both sat quietly and listened through the stillness. Jessica looked around in confusion, wondering what it was they were listening for.

"What?" she whispered.

"I thought I heard Julian," he told her. "The last thing we need is for him to wake up and walk in here on us."

"That's impossible."

"Not with all the noise you were just making," Greg pointed out.

"I wasn't making *that* much noise," she said with a playful nudge to his arm. "Anyway, Julian is with our moms."

"He's not here?"

"You sound disappointed," Jessica noted.

"I am," Greg admitted. "I was hoping to spend some time with him. I haven't seen him in days."

"You haven't seen me in days either."

"You sound jealous." Greg laughed.

"Well, maybe I am," Jessica admitted. Her tone was serious, causing Greg to take notice. She shrugged her shoulders and then continued. "I mean, I'm glad you miss him. But I made arrangements for him to be there because I just thought you'd be happy to have some time alone with me first."

Greg took a moment to search Jessica's face for any indication of teasing, but found none. A small part of him wanted to laugh out loud at her childlike insecurities, but somehow her words touched a chord in his heart. Knowing that she missed him in his absence and realizing that as much as she loved their son, there were still times when she longed for solitude with only the companionship of her husband was undeniably appealing.

Shifting his weight, Greg came to a standing position and then reached out his arm for Jessica to join him. He turned the shower back on and retrieved the earlier abandoned cloth. Quietly, he lathered both their bodies and then pulled Jessica close to him while allowing the water to rinse them thoroughly.

No words were spoken between them, even as they stepped from the stall. Greg reached for the towel and proceeded to dry himself first and then transferred the soft, damp cotton fabric to Jessica. He moved his hands at a snail's pace, taking the opportunity to explore her body as he wiped away the excess water.

Minutes later, they were both nestled beneath the bedcovers, exchanging quiet, deep kisses that seemed to linger and sweeten every moment. Jessica's arms tightened around him and Greg could sense her hunger for more.

"It's just me and you, baby," he whispered. "Whatever you want. We've got all night."

CHAPTER 3

When Clara died unexpectedly fifteen months ago, it seemed as though the entire D.C. area went into momentary shock, which was immediately followed by extended mourning. For a while, there was fear that the Fellowship Worship Center, one of the most popular churches in the District of Columbia, would lose its beloved pastor, Luther Baldwin. Each time he stood in the pulpit on any Sunday morning following his wife's death, he would barely be able to begin his sermon before breaking into tears. After weeks of that, one of the younger ministers began filling in on a regular basis and there was talk among members of the board of directors that he should perhaps take the reins permanently.

"Reverend Parker is all right," Lena said on more than one occasion in the board meetings. "But he ain't no Pastor Baldwin. The devil is a lie!" she exclaimed with a pound of her fist. "That ol' bowlegged, beady-eyed, slew-footed snake wants us to lose our pastor, but we gonna pray him through this. Y'all hear me? We gonna pray him through!"

Mother Clara Baldwin had been the pastor's one and only love since they'd met as teenagers in an open field where neighborhood black children were allowed to play football. Pastor Baldwin had always said that they'd be one hundred years old and still in love. Instead, just weeks before turning sixty-nine, the minister had been forced to say good-bye to the woman who'd given him eight beloved children and more than fifty years of love and devotion.

Mother Baldwin's death had gripped her husband's heart to massive degrees. During the early months following her fatal stroke, he grieved heavily, even to the point of having to be hospitalized for hypertension and severe chest pains. Pastor Baldwin's recovery from her demise was gradual, but prayers and perseverance brought authenticity to Lena's words. One Sunday in February, the preacher walked onto the pulpit and brought a message that seemed to set the church on fire. Pastor Luther Baldwin was back and now at seventy years young, he was showing no signs of turning back.

Since accepting his assignment in New York, Greg seemed to take on celebrity status with his family members and friends. They didn't get to see him as often as they had been accustomed to, so when he made his weekend appearances, those closest to him vied for his attention. This Sunday morning, he and Jessica edged their way into the seats that their best friends had saved for them and quick embraces were exchanged before they joined in the praise and worship service that was already in progress.

Julian got first dibs on Greg's arms and Jessica smiled as she watched her mother swat playfully at the toddler who had so quickly abandoned her at the sight of his father. When the song ended and they all took their seats, four-and-a-half-year-old Denise squirmed from Sherry's arms and forced Julian to share his father's lap. Greg was delighted to accommodate both the children.

"Let the church say amen," Pastor Baldwin said in his distinguished bass pitch.

"Amen!"

"Every head bowed," he instructed. "Let us pray."

The audience came to a complete silence in preparation for the impending powerful chat with the Lord. Pastor Baldwin was a dedicated pastor and what Lena often called a "prayer warrior." Even those who didn't deem themselves Christians or believers would come to him when they were in trouble. Those who knew Pastor Baldwin, knew that he was genuine in his walk with the Lord and they believed that if anyone could get a prayer through to heaven, he could.

"Our Father, our Father, our most righteous Father," the preacher began. "We come before you as humbly as we know how. Lord, we just want to thank you."

"Thank you, Lord," the congregation echoed.

Jessica kept her head lowered, but she opened her eyes and succumbed to the smile that tugged at her lips. Pastor Baldwin's prayers were often long and detailed, but no one ever complained. In fact, a sense of relief came to those who were fortunate enough to have him interject their names in the blessing on any given Sunday. It was as though they felt just a little more confident that God's eyes would watch them because the aging preacher had given heaven the specifics.

That was the feeling that Jessica experienced when he included Greg's name and his extended assignment in today's prayer. As much as she missed his daily presence at home with Julian and her, Jessica was proud that Greg had been chosen to temporarily walk in the shoes of the absent New York surgeon. Inwardly, she wished that the pastor had also called the names of their friends. Though she hadn't shared the details with Greg, Jessica was fully aware of the strain that had crept its way into Derrick and Sherry's marriage.

Twenty minutes into the sermon, both Denise and Julian were asleep in Greg's arms. Sherry lightened his load significantly when she relieved him of her pleasantly plump daughter. Throughout the remainder of the service, Jessica stole periodic glances towards her husband and observed Greg admiring his son while he lay cradled in his arms. Instinctively, she'd known before the seed of life was ever planted that one day, her wonderful husband would also make a wonderful father. But Jessica had to admit that her anticipation fell short of reality. He was far more attentive and adoring than she'd ever imagined he would be.

At that moment, Greg glanced in her direction and caught her watchful admiration. Jessica smiled and quickly turned away. A short moment later, she felt his hand grasp hers and then watched him bring the back of it to his full lips, brushing them gently across her skin before returning her hand back to her lap.

Can we have the benediction, please?

The exaggerated cough from Mattie, who sat beside her, brought Jessica back from the less-than-spiritual place that her mind had just traveled to.

"Amen," Jessica quickly said, having no inkling what Pastor Baldwin had just said. Mattie grunted, not fooled one bit by her daughter's feeble attempt to pretend she'd been paying attention to the message all along.

Jessica managed to bring her focus back to the scripture lesson for the day. Even at the ripe age of seventy, Pastor Baldwin's wisdom far exceeded his years. As a student of divinity at Morehouse College in Atlanta many years ago, he'd gotten what he referred to as his "learner's permit from man." He always followed that reference by making it known that it was God who had given him his "license." Thirty minutes later, and with an emotional crowd standing and begging for more, a sweat-drenched Pastor Baldwin took his seat in dramatic fashion while the ushers scurried to attend to those who needed their assistance.

The service had gone on longer than usual. Since Greg sometimes worked at Robinson Memorial on Sundays and often took a break to join his family in morning worship, Jessica wasn't unaccustomed to seeing him periodically glance at his watch. Today, though, he did it more often than normal. She knew that in his mind, he was contemplating how few hours he would have to spend with family before preparing for New York once more.

Everyone seemed to share his thoughts. Once the benediction was finally given, the section of the row where they sat passed on the usual after-service fellowship and, instead, headed for the nearest exit door and congregated in the parking lot.

Derrick, Greg's lifelong best friend was the first to embrace him. The men, both tall, dark, handsome and successful had faced a few bouts of adversity in their similar lives, but their bond remained stronger than ever.

"So what's the plan for today?" Derrick asked, still standing close to his friend. "You gonna be able to fit a brotha in your schedule?"

His attempt to whisper failed. Both Sherry and Jessica overheard him and exchanged knowing glances. It was clear that he wanted some time alone with Greg, no doubt to fill him in on what had transpired over the past few days.

Greg knew his time was limited, but something about the look in Derrick's eyes caught his attention. It reminded him of the late-night voice-mail message from Sherry. Searching his friend's face, he could see that something was pressing on Derrick's mind, but Greg couldn't readily determine what it was. Derrick's tone had been close to normal, but his eyes were almost pleading for an affirmative answer. Briefly glancing towards their wives and noting both their demeanors, Greg knew his instinct wasn't misleading.

"Yeah, Rick" — he nodded, giving Derrick the answer for which he was begging — "of course, I'll make time for my road dog, man!"

Greg's lighthearted answer did nothing to ease the obvious tension that surrounded the small grassy area where the four of them stood.

"Our moms cooked dinner," Jessica said, taking Julian from Greg's arms. "Why don't you and Rick ride together over there? Me and Sherry will bring the kids with us."

In her four-inch heels, Jessica stood face-to-face with her six-feet-one-inch husband. Leaning in close to him, she placed a light, but meaningful kiss on Greg's lips and affectionately scaled her hand from the top of his shaved dome to the base of his neck. The look in Greg's eyes conveyed an unspoken message that Jessica read well. Feeling flushed, she backed away and turned her attention to Sherry, who stood in silence behind her, staring listlessly into the distance.

"You ready?" she asked.

"Sure," Sherry said.

Even as they turned to walk towards her friend's car, Jessica could feel Greg's eyes burning into her back. She knew he was watching her every step, admiring her long legs and the sway of her hips. Just for confirmation, she turned and glanced behind her. She was right.

Chapter 4

Greg had only been working the job in New York for a couple of weeks, but it seemed that in that short time, the situation with Derrick and Sherry had turned inside out. He knew that the consistent vibrating of the phone clipped to his belt was an indication that his mother was repeatedly calling him to find out their whereabouts. Greg knew that Lena was probably on the verge of getting in her own car and combing the streets. She never did like it when he was late for dinner. Today, though, as he stood in the coolness of Derrick's office, other matters took precedence.

In a way, his heart went out to Derrick as he listened to him purge himself of details of the ongoing dispute that had him at wit's end. Having Julian and experiencing the joy that the last year and a half had brought to his life, Greg understood his friend's desire to try for a son. On the other hand, he also could see Sherry's point of view.

Greg remembered how unhappy she was for most of her pregnancy. Not only that, but he also recalled Derrick's constant complaints about the change in Sherry's demeanor and how short-tempered and miserable she had become. She hadn't been the glowing expectant mother that Derrick had read about in the pamphlets given to him by the doctor. He wanted more than anything for the day of delivery to arrive so the whole "ordeal," as he referred to it, could come to an end.

Somehow, in the midst of his ranting today, Derrick seemed to have forgotten all of that. All he was able to focus on was his desire to have a son to carry on the Madison name and perhaps carry on the thriving law practice that he had started a year ago.

After nearly seven years at the law offices of Manhattan, Brown & Madison, Derrick made the well-thought-out decision to venture out on his own. Representing a sixteen-year-old by the name of Travis Scott nearly two years ago, had changed Derrick's life and his future in law forever. He'd always had a heart for young black men who were wrongfully charged with crimes and placed behind bars, but bittersweet memories of his relationship with this young man in particular had made Derrick take a step back, rethink and regroup.

Six months of planning brought the unveiling of his independent business, Madison at Law. In the foyer of the business, the walls were decorated with framed pictures of some of the most prominent past and present-day black leaders and African–Americans. On one wall were photos of Dr. Martin Luther King, Jr., Thurgood Marshall, Nelson Mandela, Shirley Chisholm and Reverend Jesse Jackson. Displayed on the opposite wall were images of Malcolm X, Kweisi Mfume, Mary McCloud Bethune and, to the amusement of most first-time visitors, Michael Jordan. As out of place with the theme as Michael's picture seemed to be, Greg understood the hype. He had one just like it hanging in his office at Robinson Memorial.

Inside Derrick's private office, where they now both sat, the only photo that hung on his wall was one of Travis Scott. It had been almost two years since the boy's brutal, senseless murder and the photo gave Derrick daily inspiration to keep fighting for the rights of others just like him.

"It's just nine months," Derrick said, getting up from his chair and walking towards the window.

His words brought Greg back to the conversation they'd been having since they pulled out of the parking lot of Fellowship Worship Center. Realizing that his friend needed more time to talk than the drive from the church to his mother's home would allow, Greg had made a detour to the office. It was a decision he knew he'd have to give account for once his mother had a chance to corner him.

"Look, Rick," Greg began.

He wanted to choose his stance with caution. Greg and Sherry had always been very close and he didn't want it to appear as though he was taking sides. At times, Derrick was known to be sensitive to the knowledge that his wife and best friend confided in one another and Greg was mindful of that.

"I know where you're coming from," he told Derrick. "I mean, Julian has brought more to my life than I can tell you. Although he has some features of Grace, every time I look at that kid, I see a mini me."

"See, that's all I'm asking for," Derrick interjected, happy that his friend seemed to see it from his position. "I want a chance at a son that I can say that about. There ain't hardly one drop of me in Dee-Dee. She's just like Sherry in every way. She's not even

46

a daddy's girl anymore. I need a son that will worship me like Julian does you. I need somebody to leave this business to one day, man."

Greg had to smile, in spite of Derrick's obvious pain. Julian really did adore his father and clung to him at every opportunity. Greg's passions about the future his son would choose, though, didn't mirror his friend's. He couldn't care less whether Julian chose the medical field or not, as long as he chose a profession that was honorable and fulfilling.

"Who says Dee can't be a lawyer?" Greg suggested, with a hopeful look in his eyes.

Derrick's position was unfazed. "You know what I mean, Greg. Dee probably will want to follow in Sherry's footsteps and either be a teacher or a beautician. You know — something that appeals more to females than the courtroom. I need a son so that I can be an influence on him to walk in my shoes."

Even when Greg challenged him on the what-ifs, Derrick didn't skip a beat. In his opinion, if the child ended up being a second daughter for him, he'd love her just the same. For him, it was the willingness to give it a try that meant the most. Sherry should at least give him the opportunity to have a son. Greg's attempt to come from another angle was cut short.

"Man, you got a son, so you can think up all these scenarios. You got what you wanted."

Greg corrected him. "Need I remind you of how much I wanted a daughter? But when Julian was born, I was more than content. Man, when I think about how I almost lost Grace in the process, I wouldn't *dare* ask her to go through another pregnancy."

"So you're not having any more kids?" Derrick could hardly believe his ears. Both Jessica and Greg had voiced their desire to have a fairly large family.

"I'm not ruling out the possibilities, but we won't have another one due to my suggestions or demands, that's for sure." Greg counted with his fingers as he continued. "The mood swings in her third trimester and the distance it caused, coupled with the aneurysm and the subsequent cesarean and brain surgery . . . man, it's still way too fresh in my mind. Grace is too important to me to risk something like that happening again. I'm content with having Julian for a son and Dee for a goddaughter."

Silence blanketed the room for several moments. Derrick shoved his hands in the pockets of his suit pants and stared into the sunlight from his office window. Though he seemed at a momentary loss for words, Greg knew what his best friend was thinking. He was figuring that Greg thought that way because Jessica's life was on the line at the time of Julian's birth. He was sure that Derrick was thinking that if the death scare had never occurred, Greg and his wife would probably already be expecting their second child. Greg was fully prepared for Derrick to make those points, but he wasn't prepared for what he actually heard.

"It's not just Julian, man. I mean, yeah, that little tiger would make any man want a son, but it's not just him."

Slowly turning from the window, Derrick avoided eye contact with Greg as his sight rested on the sixteen-by-twenty-inch framed portrait of Travis. Walking closer to the image of the smiling teenager, whose life had been cut short by a single bullet to the head, he took his finger and ran it from one corner of the rosewood casing to the other.

"This boy was more than a client to me, Greg."

It was no secret to anyone in Derrick's inner circle the magnitude of his attachment to Travis Scott. He had only known the boy for a few weeks, but they had bonded and

Greg knew that in some way, Derrick saw an opportunity to mold the young boy into a respectable man.

Travis was a suitable substitute for a biological son. Experiencing injustice and watching Derrick's passion in defending him, the high school junior had already decided that he would pursue a law degree upon completing high school. Back then, when the gang members killed Travis, they also killed a little part of Derrick.

For the third time, Greg's cell phone vibrated against his hip. He knew he couldn't keep avoiding his mother's calls, but right now, Derrick's heartache was more important than eating Sunday dinner.

"Gone and answer it, man." Derrick shrugged. "I'm too hungry to talk anymore anyway."

Lena was not at all amused that the two men had kept the family waiting. Greg had managed to weasel his way out of a lengthy tongue-lashing over the phone, but both he and Derrick were forced to endure it once they reached the home shared by Lena and Mattie.

"Boy, I know I raised you better than that."

Heeding the instructions given to them upon their arrival, Greg and Derrick joined their wives on the living room sofa and waited to be called into the dining area. A wall divided the living room from the kitchen and adjoining dining room, but the few feet of separation didn't hinder Lena from continuing the scolding that started when she opened her front door to let them inside.

"You know you ain't got but a little while to be in town as it is before you have to go on back to New York. Seems like you would've been anxious to get over here and spend some time with your mama. We ain't seen you in forever."

"Sorry, Ma," Greg called in response to his mother's embellished words.

For the moment, his apology held no merit. Over the clanking of pots and glasses, the displeasure in Lena's voice could still be heard.

"Sorry, nothing. You knew we were over here waiting for y'all. Even got the man of God sitting around hungry 'cause of y'all. Now we got to reheat the food just 'cause you decided you wanted to run the streets with that old scoundrel Derrick. Ain't you learned nothing after all these years? Every whipping you ever got as a child, he was the reason. By now, seem like you ought to have gotten it through your head that he ain't nothing but trouble."

Pastor Baldwin held the Sunday edition of *The Washington Post* to his face to hide his stifled laughter, but the shaking of his body was a dead giveaway. Even Greg and Derrick struggled not to burst with laughter as Lena spoke. She kept on scolding, not once caring that Derrick was right there and could hear her every word.

"Um-hum." Mattie didn't even know the men as children, yet she mumbled in agreement, all the while helping to place the food in serving bowls.

By the time they were all seated and Pastor Baldwin had extended the blessing, Lena had recovered. Ever since Ms. Clara's passing, the church's leader had been given an open invitation to share in whatever meal that Lena and Mattie had prepared for the family on Sunday. It was evident that being surrounded by familiar people who loved him was heartwarming for the widower, but he tried to limit his acceptances so that he wouldn't become a burden or be viewed as a charity case.

Chatter flowed around the table as usual, but Greg and Jessica couldn't overlook the obvious fact that as much talking as Derrick and Sherry were doing, they weren't talking to each other. Surprisingly, none of the others showed any sign that they had picked up on the Madisons' avoidance of one another.

"Mother Dixon, Mother Charles, the two of you outdid yourselves once again." Pastor Baldwin patted his full stomach, having cleaned his plate.

"Thank you, Pastor," Mattie said.

"What you thanking him for?" Lena asked. "Pastor Baldwin, aside from the dinner rolls, that whole meal was prepared with these hands right here." She held up both her hands to be sure that there was no mistaking which hands she was referencing.

Mattie looked at her friend and shook her head in disgust, replying, "I hope he remembers that when his belly starts to aching tonight."

Two hours later, the pastor had retired to his own home. The women worked together to clean the kitchen while the children entertained one another in the playroom and Greg and Derrick played an intense game of one-on-one in the backyard. Noises of Julian and Denise fighting over a toy drew Jessica from the kitchen to take on the challenge of referee. When she returned a few minutes later, her earlier thoughts that her mother and mother-in-law had lost their keen senses of discernment were proven untrue.

Jessica's heart went out to her friend, who was now standing in a corner with her arms folded while the two women who, though of no biological relation to Sherry, acted as though they were the official stand-ins for her mother, who lived in New Jersey. Somehow, Lena and Mattie had in fact noticed the friction between Sherry and Derrick and now they were digging for answers.

Sherry held out as long as she could, but to no avail. After several minutes of enduring their questions, she finally told them of the unresolved matter that had caused the four-day mutual silent treatment. Finally having the answer they'd been asking for, Mattie began pouring fresh cups of coffee. That was an undeclared cue for all of them to have a seat at the table for what Greg liked to call a "mother-to-other" discussion.

"I just don't understand y'all new-age women," Lena said, taking a sip from her cup before deciding that Mattie hadn't added enough sugar. After testing it again to be sure it was just right, she continued. "Lord knows if Phillip hadn't of died, Greg would have a whole bunch of brothers and sisters. When I was young, we saw babies as a gift from God and if a woman couldn't have any, people looked down on her. Now, y'all see babies as some kind of curse that God placed on Eve back in the garden and the fewer you have, you think you're better off."

"Ms. Lena, it's not that I don't think babies are a blessing," Sherry defended herself, adding more sugar to her cup as well. "I do think they are a blessing. I have Dee and she's enough for me. God has more ways than one of blessing a woman and I'll take all my other blessings in some other form, thank you very much."

"Don't get sassy, Miss," Mattie said before Lena could.

Jessica pushed her cup aside. She'd never liked coffee, so her mother placing it there was futile. Though she'd dare not chime in with her thoughts, Jessica fully understood Sherry's stance. Her reasons were different than her friend's, but the final ruling was basically the same. Having another child was not something her body was aching to do either and she was thankful that Greg wasn't demanding that they give pregnancy another try.

On the other hand, she could also see her mother-in-law's point of view. Jessica had grown up an only child and so had Greg. Both of them knew the sentiment of wanting a sibling to share their home with and neither she nor Greg wanted Julian to have that longing. Still, her childbirth experience had been too traumatic for either of them to soon forget.

Both her midwife, Dr. Mathis, and Dr. Grant, the head neurosurgeon at Robinson Memorial, had assured Greg and Jessica that her aneurysm had in no way been directly related to the pregnancy. But it was still a chance that neither of them was ready or willing to take, despite the fact that like Lena, they too had initially planned to have a much larger family.

"When I had Jessie, I was by myself," Mattie was saying to Sherry. "You got a husband who is gonna be right by your side up 'til the very end. Being pregnant is such a temporary discomfort, baby, and you got yourself such a good husband. I don't understand why you denying that man another child."

"Ms. Mattie, I'm not *denying* Ricky anything. Before we got married, *we* agreed that we'd have one child. That wasn't my rule; we both were on the same page. I'm just making him honor the agreement that we made together."

"A man's got a right to change his mind, Sherry," Mattie told her.

"And a woman's got a right *not* to change hers."

Lena placed her hand on top of Sherry's in an attempt to calm the annoyance that she could see was brewing up inside her.

"Derrick is the husband and that makes him the head. The good Lord made it so he gets a little bit of an edge over you."

Those words only added to the fuel. Sherry slipped her hand from under Lena's and stood up from the table, facing both the women who spoke primitive words that were more foreign than Greek to her ears. With her hands on her hips and her neck rotating her head in circular motions, Sherry had visibly lost all will to contain her emotions.

"That's fine and good, Ms. Lena. But when God gives Derrick the ability to carry a baby in his *head* instead of me doing it in my stomach, then I will be all for it."

"Girl, you must done lost your mind, taking on that tone with me." Lena's voice level was controlled, but her tone was stern as she slid her chair from the table and stood her five-foot-five-inch frame directly in front of the slightly taller Sherry as if daring her to speak another word.

Lena had known Sherry since the days when her relationship with Derrick was strictly platonic. For years, the Queen Latifah look-alike had been known as the pudgy, tomboyish third wheel in the tricycle friendship of Gregory, Derrick and Sherry. Lena had delivered a few swats to Sherry's behind in her younger years and felt as connected to her as a second mother would. Sherry's words, in Lena's opinion, were disrespectful, and disrespect had no place at 555 Apple Road.

Jessica had been quiet for the duration of the discussion. But she felt that now was as good a time as any to step in and break up what had the makings of being a much uglier battle than the one Dee and Julian had been involved in just minutes earlier.

"Come on, you guys," she said, choosing her words quickly, but with care so as not to offend either party. "Sherry, you've known Ms. Lena a whole lot longer than I have and you know that she wants nothing but the best for you and Rick. Nothing is getting solved like this. And Ms. Lena, Sherry has to make up her own mind about whether or not she's going to have another child. Having a baby shouldn't be done out of force or guilt. This is a matter that clearly won't be settled today, so let's just let it simmer. I'm sure everything will be just fine."

It was a long shot, but it worked. Jessica's

words calmed the situation that had become overheated. Both women seemed to be embarrassed by their actions and slowly returned to their seats.

"I'm sorry, Ms. Lena."

Sherry had barely gotten the apology out of her mouth when the back door opened, and through it walked two perspiring men who had taken obvious pride in the way they had played their game. Throughout the duration of the dispute between the women, the children remained satisfied, playing with their many toys. But at the sound of Greg's voice, Julian began banging on the closed door. Muffled sounds of him calling for his father could be heard above the chatter between the men.

While Greg ducked into the restroom to wash his hands and face, Jessica opened the playroom door and hoisted the child in her arms. Denise followed, bypassing Derrick and making her way to the kitchen and onto her mother's lap. His eyes expressed his disappointment, but Derrick said nothing.

A bit more refreshed after his semicleansing, Greg freed his struggling son from Jessica's arms and hugged him.

"Be-ball, be-ball, be-ball!" Julian repeated, pointing at the round object in Derrick's hand.

"Yeah." Greg laughed. "Daddy whipped up on Uncle Rick with that basketball too."

"I wouldn't call a six-point win a whipping," Derrick defended.

Like the game they'd just played, the battle over whether or not Sherry should give her husband the child he wanted was over — for now.

CHAPTER 5

Lenox Hill Hospital had over thirty separate clinical departments. Prior to his assignment, Greg had never visited the medical facility. Therefore, it had taken him a few days to get accustomed to the layout of the building. While he genuinely was ready to get his last week of duties complete so that he could feel as much of a constructive father and husband as he did a doctor, Greg couldn't deny that working at Lenox Hill had its rewards.

Dr. Armstrong was highly respected among his peers, and with Greg there to fill in, the staff gave him the esteem of the absent surgeon's equal. When Joseph Armstrong went on vacation, he'd cleared out most of his personal belongings from his office, making it an easy decision for the Director of the Division of Neurosurgery to allow Greg to make the space his temporary headquarters.

The office was more spacious than the one Greg occupied at Robinson Memorial. The window was wider, the closet space was roomier and the desk was larger. Even the sun seemed to shine brighter as it glistened through the security blinds that Greg had opened upon his arrival. On the walls was an eye-catching selection of artwork that stimulated the imagination. The London Bridge, the Eiffel Tower, the Grand Canyon and the Leaning Tower of Pisa were all masterfully captured on canvas in vibrant colors that almost gave the oil paintings the appearance of enlarged digital photographs.

"No wonder the good doctor likes to travel," Greg mumbled as he picked up his clipboard and prepared to make his morning rounds.

He didn't know whether it was intentional on his part or not, but Greg had not gotten to know most of the staff members on a personal basis. Today, like most days, he walked down the hallways and nodded his greetings to most of them in passing. Like at Robinson Memorial, Greg was the object of affection of several of the female personnel at Lenox Hill. They flashed playful smiles and when they spoke his name, they did so in an almost melodious fashion.

" 'Sup, Dr. Dix!"

Dr. LaRon Clayton was the exception. He was the one staff member Greg had gotten to know on more than just a professional level. He didn't remind Greg of himself as much as he exhibited what Greg wished he'd been like early in his career. Dr. Clayton was a smart, fun-loving twenty-six-year-old who did his job well, but didn't take everything in life too seriously. He was the perfect mixture of Greg and Derrick. At the same age, Greg remembered being smart and performing his job well, but because of his serious nature, most people thought he was older than his actual age.

Greg paused and greeted the intern with a slap to his hand and a quick embrace before moving on. LaRon Clayton was one of two black neurosurgeon interns at Lenox Hill. It was a sight to which Greg had to get accustomed. The entire time he'd been an intern at Robinson Memorial, he was the only African– American on staff. His residency had ended a year ago and he was still the only black neurosurgeon employed there.

Lenox Hill's other intern of color was a woman by the name of Nanya Bolton. Thanks to a warning given him by LaRon, Greg learned early on not to refer to her as black, or African– American. Her mother was a white woman from Shreveport, Connecticut, but her father was straight from Africa, a native of Kenya who had relocated to the States as a teenager seeking a better education. Her parents met on the campus of NYU and two years later, their daughter was born. Nanya hated the fact that she couldn't rid herself totally of her father's heritage or his native accent. To Greg, the whole façade was senseless. She couldn't deny her African lineage if she wanted to. The complexion of her skin was that of any fair-skinned black woman. She was about the same shade of honey brown as Jessica, but unlike Greg's wife, Dr. Bolton wanted desperately to be accepted by those of her white parent's race.

Finally reaching the door of his destination, Greg tapped lightly before pushing it and letting himself in. The room was dark and his patient was sleeping soundly. Greg turned on one lamp in the corner farthest from the bed to provide the lighting he needed in order to work. Checking the monitors that surrounded Sergeant Evan McDonald's bed, Greg was pleased that his patient's condition was on a steady uphill climb. Judging from the officer's progress, Greg would be able to release him from the ICU before he packed his bags for the final time on Friday.

"Dr. Dixon, is that you?"

Greg's back had been turned to his patient while he transferred the numbers from the monitor onto the chart in his hand. At the sound of Evan McDonald's voice, Greg faced the bed and returned a smile to the man who was smiling up at him.

"Well, now, who else would it be, Sergeant?"

"Well, yesterday it was somebody else in here poking and prodding," the man answered with a light chuckle. "I just wanted to be sure I had the right one in here with me today."

Sergeant McDonald was a handsome man, with a friendly smile and brown eyes that gave off an air of familiarity. Greg checked the stitches beneath his bandages and replaced them with care. He then pulled the rolling stool from the corner and sat on it to make more notations on the chart in his hand.

"How are you feeling today?"

"Like some blame fool bashed me in the head with a baseball bat. Oh, that's right," he said, laughing once more, "some blame fool *did* bash me in the head with a baseball bat."

Greg laughed with him. "You have a great

sense of humor, Sarge. If it's true what they say about laughter, you'll be going home in a few days."

"If it's true what they say about *you,* I probably will."

His patient's reply caught Greg off-guard. "What do they say about me?" he asked.

"They say I lucked up and got the best doctor in the world," Sergeant McDonald replied, adjusting himself to a more comfortable position against his pillows. "They say I got the same doctor that saved the life of Charlie Zimmerman a few years back."

Greg thought hard. He'd performed so many operations over the years that he'd stopped keeping up with names long ago. For some reason, this one sounded very familiar, but thumbing through the hundreds of files in his mind, he couldn't quite put his finger on a face to go with the name.

"Charlie Zimmerman," Sergeant McDonald repeated as though saying it twice would clear Greg's confusion. "*Chief* Charlie Zimmerman," the man clarified.

"Oh, yes!" Greg said. "How could I forget?"

Charlie Zimmerman was once the chief of police in Washington, D.C. When he suffered a gunshot wound to the head, he also became one of Greg's first surgical proce-

66

dures during his tenure as an intern. It was that lifesaving operation that quickly made Dr. Gregory Dixon a household name. He became the object of media attention when the President of the United States openly honored him for a job well done.

"Charlie never could return back to his post and carry out his duties after that shooting," Evan said. "Tell me the truth, Doc. Am I gonna to be able to do my job again?"

With the mediocre salary that policemen made, Greg never could understand why they so eagerly put their lives on the line on a daily basis. As senseless as it appeared though, Greg was thankful for the uniformed men and women who helped to keep the streets safe from the demons lurking in the corners waiting for the opportunity to wreak havoc on whoever was unprepared.

Whether his answer was to be grim or one that he knew the asker wanted to hear, Greg always made it a point to be honest with his patients. In doing so, though, it was never his practice to give a prognosis that erased all possibility of a full recovery. To do that would mean that he doubted God's ability to work a miracle and that was never the message that he wanted to convey.

Greg chose his words with care as he told the public servant that his years of full duty had possibly come to an end. But even if that were the case, there was no reason why, after successfully completing therapy, he would not be able to return to the force in an administrative position.

It was clear from Sergeant McDonald's face that, though disappointed in his doctor's answer, no surprises had been transmitted. Upon Greg's urging, the officer struggled to wiggle the fingers of his left hand. The instruction to try to lift his entire arm was met with facial grimaces and the sounds of effortful grunts, but no substantial movement to accompany them. Finally giving in, the patient allowed his tense body to relax and breathed a sigh laced with frustration. Movements in his leg were far better, but there were still some restrictions there as well.

"It's okay, Sarge." Greg smiled as he patted the gentleman's semiparalyzed arm. "It's still very early. You've got the determination that you need to make some incredible strides. I see it in your face. That alone will take you a long way."

"They train you all to say that, don't they?" The injured policeman appeared near tears. "Do you really know anybody to have had a head injury like mine and because they had determination, they recovered?"

A smile crept across Greg's face. He got up from the stool and guided it back into the corner where it had been earlier. Cradling the completed chart in his arm, he came to a stop directly beside the bed and looked down into the expectant face of Sergeant McDonald.

"With *prayer* and determination, yes, I know someone who had an even worse head injury than yours who pulled through just fine. You're not gonna die, Sergeant. And as long as you have life in your body, there's a chance of a complete recovery."

Greg hesitated to see if there was anything else in the man's heart that he wanted to say. After several silent moments, he promised to return later and headed for the door that would lead him back into the hospital's busy halls.

"Doc?"

The officer's voice delayed his exit. Greg turned to once again face the bed where his patient lay.

"This other man that recovered," Sergeant McDonald said. "Do you know how he's doing today? I mean, do you know for sure that he was able to get on with a full, independent life?"

"*She* is doing just fine, Sergeant," Greg corrected his assumption. "She went on to complete the hours needed for her to receive her college degree and to graduate with honors. She got hitched to an impressive gentleman several years ago and took on a job teaching music in the Fine Arts Department at Trinity College in D.C. Not terribly long ago, she gave birth to a son, so I'd say she's doing great, actually."

"You keep up with the lives of all your patients like that, Dr. Dixon?"

Greg laughed at the bewildered expression on the policeman's face.

"No, not all of them," he replied. "Just the ones I marry."

CHAPTER 6

For the last three years, excluding the months that Jessica was forced to take as an extended leave following her combined aneurysm surgery and cesarean, she and Sherry had made it a weekly ritual to meet together on Fridays for lunch. As an instructor at Trinity College, the distance between Jessica's job and her best friend's place of employment as a second grade teacher at Brightwood Elementary School was only about a three-and-a-half mile, ten-minute drive. With Greg in New York and Derrick and Sherry not being on the best of terms, their meetings had expanded to include Wednesdays as well.

About midway between Trinity and Brightwood was the Open Arms Day Care and Learning Center. Four days of each week, against their parents' wishes, Greg and Jessica insisted that Julian spend his days there. For his parents, it was important that Julian be exposed to a learning environment early in life to get a head start on his future education, so at six months old, they enrolled him. As with any child, Julian enjoyed spending days being coddled and pampered by his grandmothers, but Greg and Jessica knew that he needed a solid foundation to prepare him for the years ahead.

Because Sherry often scheduled clients for hair appointments after she finished her day of teaching, Denise, too, spent a few hours in the afternoon at Open Arms following her release from pre-K classes. Passing the brick structure on the way to meet Sherry, Jessica was tempted to stop in and check on her son, but she knew it was best that she didn't. Julian did well at the center as long as he didn't see either of his parents. With them in view and the perceived option of going home verses staying with Ms. Hamm, his provider, Julian was known to put on quite a show.

"Hey, girl," Jessica said, greeting her friend, who was waiting at the front entrance of Finemondo. Albeit, it was an Italian restaurant, Finemondo served one of the best salmon sandwiches that either one of the seafood lovers had ever had, thus making it one of their favorite places to spend their lunch hour.

Sherry returned her hug and they headed inside, but Jessica easily determined from Sherry's manner that things weren't back to normal in the Madison home.

"Normal?" Sherry grimaced when Jessica addressed her concerns. "What's normal, Jessie? I don't know what that is anymore. It's been so long since me and Ricky have been intimate that it ain't even funny. I'd settle for just a civilized conversation that did not reek of the subject that we'll never see eye to eye on."

Biting into her sandwich, Jessica tried to hide her disappointment in what she'd heard. When she and Greg had been engaged, she remembered praying that their future marriage would be as strong and filled with as much passion as that of Derrick's and Sherry's. The Madisons' union was the example she'd repeatedly used to dispute the claims of coworkers that marriages always lost their spark after a few short years.

Sherry had married the man who had taken her to her high school prom and had wooed her all the way through college. For eight years, they'd been inseparable, but now the Madison marriage seemed to be unraveling quickly from what weeks ago seemed to be just a harmless nick in the threads of their relationship.

"How's school today?" Jessica searched for a way to lighten the mood.

Sherry shrugged as though there was not much to talk about. It was another sign for dismay. Their lunch-hour meetings used to be filled with chatter about what some child had done that morning to either curl Sherry's lips into a smile or bring her teeth together in stifled anger.

"Maybe that's what I should do." Sherry suddenly spoke up as though picking up on a conversation that was already in progress. "I should suggest that Ricky take a day off from that cozy little office of his and spend some time in my classroom with twenty little tyrants. One full day in the environment that I work in and I guarantee you he'll change his tune about having two kids running around the house."

Jessica laughed, but somehow she doubted that Sherry's rhetorical plan would get the results that she presumed. Derrick's desire wasn't a shallow one. He wanted another child and, contrary to Sherry's words, being around other children only seemed to fuel his desire. She tried to push her worries aside, but Jessica couldn't pretend that she didn't feel that the road ahead of her friends was only going to get rockier.

The lunch hour ended far too soon and left far too many questions unanswered. Jessica could hardly believe that an argument that had once seemed so minute in her eyes had wedged a gap the size of Texas between the once passionate lovers.

It's been so long since me and Ricky have been intimate that it ain't even funny. The words that Sherry had earlier spoken had been accompanied by a dry chuckle that carried no hint of humor. Her words had been almost too foreign to comprehend. Jessica remembered the time when the two often seemed to make love with one another using only eye contact. Derrick never tried to hide his desire for his wife and Sherry, with eagerness, reciprocated her husband's not-so-subtle hints. Now, they seemed less than a shell of who they once had been.

Derrick and Sherry were two professionals with strong opinions that often clashed, so their having a spat was no rarity. Even so, Jessica would never have guessed that the subject of whether or not to have a second child would be the topic that would drive them so far apart. Sherry hadn't voiced it, but Jessica knew that marital happiness was fading from Sherry's heart.

As she drove back to Trinity College, Jessica took another glance at the preschool where Julian was. The children had gathered out on the grounds for their after-lunch playtime. She applied light pressure on her brake and took a quick scan of the small crowd in hopes of catching a glimpse of her son and felt disappointed when she saw no sign of him. Motherhood had definitely been a good experience for her. Julian may be the apple of his father's eye, but he was still her baby.

Inwardly, Jessica pondered her true feelings about having another child. Most days, she was sure that she didn't want to conceive again, and other days, she questioned herself. When she was planning for the arrival of Julian, there were several memorable things to which she had looked forward: the final push that would deliver him into the warmed hands of Dr. Debra Mathis, the sounds of his first cries, feeling him in her arms when they placed him against her chest and seeing the tears of elation in his father's eyes, despite the fact that Greg had hoped for a daughter. All of these things were moments that she had missed because she'd been unconscious and near death at the time of his birth.

Perhaps the greatest reason for her wavering was the latter. Although her husband seemed totally satisfied in the son that God had blessed them with, Jessica found it hard to erase those days of expectancy when he'd voiced repeatedly that he wanted, and had even prayed for, a baby girl. Not once, since Julian came into their lives, had Greg mentioned his former desire, but Jessica found it impossible to believe that it had totally dissolved. She had always wanted a son. But right now, even with the turmoil that she'd gone through during Julian's delivery, Jessica wasn't at all sure that she would never be willing try again for the daughter that both she and Greg would be delighted to welcome into their family.

As far as Derrick and Sherry's dilemma, Jessica had mixed emotions that she dared not voice to her best friend. As Lena and Mattie had said three days ago, Derrick was a faithful, loving, hardworking husband. Was having another child really too much to ask? Jessica had always viewed Sherry's adamant stance of never again going through the stages of childbirth a bit selfish. As hard as the last trimester of her own pregnancy had been and as recent as Julian had been born, Jessica wondered if she'd truly even give it a second thought if Greg asked her to do it once more.

Her husband had sacrificed so much for

her over the years that she couldn't imagine not granting him a wish as doable and as beautiful as possibly giving him a daughter. Though she'd not suggested to Sherry how to handle her own situation, Jessica did tell her what she would do if the tables were turned.

"Well, that's because Greg at least *tried* to pamper you the whole nine months of your pregnancy, Jessie," Sherry had responded as they stood in the parking lot preparing to leave the restaurant. "That's different. Ricky wasn't like that. Yeah, it's been years ago and yeah, maybe he has changed and would do differently, but I don't know that and once I'm pregnant, it would be too late to change my mind if he turned out to be the same Ricky he was the first time around."

Personally, Jessica believed that Derrick would be there for Sherry. Just in the five years she'd known him, he had grown both mentally and spiritually and there was little doubt in Jessica's mind that he would live up to his promises. She'd told Sherry that, too, but saying it didn't change her friend's thought process.

"Jessie, you live with Greg and that's why you see the world through rose-colored glasses. I know you'd have another baby for him if he asked. Heck, if I was married to

Greg, I'd have more babies if he asked too. But I'm not. Don't get me wrong. I love my man, but experience is the best teacher and I graduated magna cum laude with a bachelor's degree from the University of Having-a-Baby-with-Ricky. I remember the lessons I learned. I don't need a refresher course, and a sistah ain't even trying to go back for her master's."

Jessica sighed and mentally threw in the towel. The neck-rolling had begun and she knew that nothing could be said to convince Sherry to look at the situation from any other point of view except her own. Not only that, but there was something about hearing her friend compare Greg and Derrick that made Jessica want to end the conversation.

The day she had first met Sherry resurfaced in her mind. Jessica was in a hospital room at Robinson Memorial when Greg brought his best friend's wife into her room and introduced them. She had seen Sherry's interaction with Greg and immediately wondered if there was ever anything between them other than friendship. They'd both assured her that they had never been anything else and Jessica believed them. But hearing today's remarks made her wonder if there wasn't a part of Sherry that wished she could turn back the hands of time and rewrite the past that led to the present.

Parking her car and shutting off the engine, Jessica closed her eyes and scolded herself, shunning the idea that had made its way into her thoughts. Over the years, Sherry had been nothing but a genuine friend to both her and Greg and had given her no reason to believe that she secretly, on some level, desired to be with Greg. Even more importantly, Greg had given no reason for Jessica to doubt his love and devotion to her. Still, she couldn't deny that there was a twinge of selfishness attached to her desire for Sherry and Derrick to quickly find a way to settle their differences and mend their crumbling relationship.

CHAPTER 7

"I'm working with a pack of freakin' idiots!" The door slammed behind Dr. Simon Grant, causing those standing nearby to jolt at the noise.

It hadn't been a good day at Robinson Memorial Hospital. In fact, it hadn't been a good month. From the day that Dr. Grant's prize physician had walked out the sliding-glass exit doors to begin his vacation, life at the medical facility had begun losing its normalcy. Every day, there seemed to be something out of the ordinary happening. Car accident victims were certainly no rarity, but last Sunday, a six-car pileup that shut down a portion of Highway 95 landed sixteen members of a church group in the hospital; four of them with traumatic head injuries.

A few days prior to that accident, two eleven-year-old playmates both suffered severe damage to their skulls when they

81

decided to try to mimic their favorite professional wrestlers while jumping on a trampoline. The horseplay almost cost them their lives when they veered too far to the right while flipping in midair and landed on the pavement below. Before that, a domestic dispute reached a new level when a woman caught her husband in the act of adultery and sent him to the hospital with four bullets embedded in several areas of his body, including one to the head. He was brought into the operating room alive, but became one of the month's casualties halfway through his surgery.

The staff at Robinson Memorial was accustomed to being busy, but not to this magnitude. It seemed that in honor of his servant, God, too, had taken a vacation for the last twenty-six days and all the forces of evil were taking advantage of the time by sitting back and laughing at the chaos and faux pas that were taking place on a near daily basis.

On average, the head trauma staff lost only two patients per month. They'd already lost that many within the last twenty-four hours, bringing May's total to six with a little more than a week to go. Tempers were running high and blame was being tossed back and forth between the doctors on duty.

No one wanted to take responsibility for the lives that had slipped through his fingers on the operating table. The woman who had died just shy of an hour ago had been carrying around a one-inch sliver of glass in her right frontal lobe ever since she was twelve years old and her father had sent her through the front window of their home in a fit of drunken rage.

The day that it happened, the doctors had decided not to remove the glass, claiming that it posed no foreseeable threat. Dr. Grant had determined that the woman's family's lack of adequate insurance coverage had played a large part in that doctor's decision. For thirty years, the wife and mother of two had carried the glass in her head. But when loss of full movement and strength in her arms was blamed on the long-ago injury, the family turned to the hospital known for its neurological expertise.

A string of swear words poured from the Dr. Grant's lips as he cursed the day that he'd recommended Greg to his longtime acquaintance, Dr. Joseph Armstrong. He and Dr. Armstrong were making small talk over drinks several months ago when Dr. Grant lightheartedly suggested that Lenox Hill call on Greg if they ever got in a tight spot and were unable to find coverage in emergency situations. Dr. Armstrong never took a vacation of any length of time. Simon Grant had no idea that his suggestion would come back to haunt him. No doubt, if Greg had been there, Dr. Grant never would have had to deliver the grim news to the dead patient's husband and daughters.

"Can we come in?"

Dr. Grant turned to see his staff of neurologists standing in the doorway of his office. He had instructed them to report to his office, but he'd been so deep in thought that he hadn't even heard the door open. For a moment, silence was all that could be heard. Dr. Neal shifted his feet and dropped his eyes as the chief surgeon's stare burned into his flesh. Dr. Pridgen and Dr. Lowe stood back in childlike fashion as well. None of them seemed to know what to say or do.

"Close the door behind you."

Normally jovial and friendly, Simon Grant's alien demeanor appeared to put a strange level of fear in the members of his staff. The scuffle of chairs was followed by another eerie silence as each man sat and waited for the inevitable reprimand. Remaining in a standing position, Dr. Grant inhaled as much air as his lungs would hold and then exhaled with such vigor that the corners of the papers on his desk moved. For moments that felt like minutes, he said nothing in fear of what he might say.

"Dr. Grant . . ."

They were the only two words that managed to leak from Dr. Lowe's lips before he swallowed back the ones that were to follow. Dr. Grant still hadn't uttered a word, but there was lightning in his eyes when he cast them towards the man who had dared to be brave enough, yet foolish enough, to break the silence.

"What? You got more excuses?"

He'd finally spoken, but each of the doctors who sat before him knew that Dr. Grant's question was strictly rhetorical. Answering it would be professional suicide.

"That lady that just died in there has two kids who are barely in their teens. Daughters, no less," he added in a tone that suggested teenage boys would have been less devastated by the loss of their mother. "I've got daughters. You've got daughters." He pointed towards Dr. Lowe. "If we suddenly lose our wives, think of how those girls would feel. Mrs. Brookhaven never should have died. We've done operations that were ten . . . even twenty times as complicated as this one. None of us are green at this. We're all seasoned doctors. What happened in there?"

Even though they knew they were in hot water whose temperature was rising in two-degree increments, words like "we," "us" and "our" kept them from feeling the magnitude of the burn. The one thing the sitting doctors had to appreciate was Dr. Grant's ability not to place individual blame. He wasn't even in the operating room with Mrs. Brookhaven, but Dr. Grant placed himself in the middle of the crisis, softening the verbal blows that could have been far more devastating.

"Answer me!" he yelled, giving the doctors the permission they needed to speak.

"Her pressure plummeted." Unsure of how Dr. Grant would respond, Dr. Pridgen answered in low tones.

" 'Her pressure plummeted.' " Dr. Grant repeated the words, clearly not impressed by or satisfied with them. "You know, when Dr. Merrill finally retired last year, I thought that God had given us a piece of heaven. It was a day that couldn't have come a moment too soon. I'd never been so happy to shell out money for a farewell party in all of my life. With all that negative energy gone, I thought that together, my four remaining neurosurgeons and I would have the wherewithal to really show competitors like Providence and Georgetown how it's really done."

"And we have, Dr. Grant," Dr. Neal defended. "It's just been an off-month for us, that's all. Until now, we've had a stellar record since Dr. Merrill left. Believe me, this string of bad luck has nothing to do with us not having him around here. So, if you're concerned that people will think we can't function without the likes of Dr. Merrill —"

"Is that what you think I'm saying?" The frown lines in Dr. Grant's forehead deepened in spite of the short laugh that preceded his words. "Look around you, Neal." He waved his hands around the room, adding theatrics to the challenge. "Who else is missing from the equation? I know people won't be ignorant enough to think that the absence of Victor Merrill has anything to do with our recent failures. Nobody is *that* stupid. But who else hasn't been here for the last three and a half weeks?"

With the message behind Dr. Grant's words finally settling in, the doctors exchanged knowing glances.

"Exactly," Dr. Grant said, as though he'd heard their thoughts. "I'm not concerned that folks around here will think that we're incompetent without Merrill; I'm worried that they'll think that without Dixon, we're a bunch of worthless men with meaningless abbreviations that end in 'D' behind our names."

"Who's to say that Mrs. Brookhaven or any other of those who died in the past few weeks would have lived had Dr. Dixon been here?" Dr. Lowe offered.

The pounding of Dr. Grant's fist on the desk and another muttered oath abruptly planted all three of the doctors' backs squarely against the backs of their chairs.

"Did you see people dropping like flies before he left?" Dr. Grant's questions had once again become rhetorical. "Have you heard about any head trauma patients dying at Lenox Hill in the past month?"

Dr. Lowe hadn't been keeping up with what had been going on in New York, but he was smart enough to keep that bit of information to himself.

"I'm not trying to say that we can't run a successful head trauma unit without Dr. Dixon," Dr. Grant quickly added. "I'm just saying that we *aren't* running a successful head trauma unit without him. I can count on one hand the number of patients we've lost when Dixon was performing the operations. I need more than one hand to count the fatalities in our O.R. in this month alone."

"Well, only one of those happened on my shift."

Dr. Grant glared at Dr. Pridgen in disbelief and then burst forward with mock applause that resonated throughout the office.

"Well, whoop-de-*freakin'*-do!" he hissed through clenched teeth once his display subsided. "Guess what, Pridgen? *None* of them died at my hands, but that don't mean a hill of beans. We're all in this together. That one patient you lost was all of our patient and all of our responsibility. The other five that were lost, no matter whose knife they died under, were all of our responsibility. Remember that. Some of them couldn't be helped and I'm aware of that. But others like Mrs. Brookhaven could.

"If the same press that's been praising us for the past five or six years for our victories decides to turn on us for our failures, believe me when I say they aren't going to give the breakdown of which doctor lost how many patients. But you can bet your bottom dollar that they'll take note of the fact that Dr. Gregory Dixon was not on duty when things started falling apart. The media loves Dixon, and rightfully so. He's earned their affection and most of the medals they've pinned on us over recent years have been linked directly to him and what he's brought to this hospital. We are nothing if we can't prove to be just as proficient without him as we are with him."

The hush that blanketed the room upon the men's arrival had returned. This time it lasted for several minutes that seemed like hours. With Dr. Grant's back turned to them while he stared out the window behind his desk, the doctors didn't know whether or not they'd been indirectly dismissed.

"May I speak?"

Dr. Lowe's voice brought Dr. Grant's attention back to the center of the room. His first instinct was to ignore the request and send the men back to their stations. All things considered, he'd done a grand job of playing down the true magnitude of his disappointment and fury. If he heard one more excuse or had to endure one more attempt to shift blame, he might not be so successful in containing himself. Against his better judgment, Dr. Grant nodded.

"I'd never try and downplay how amazing Dr. Dixon is at his craft," Dr. Lowe said. "I've got way too much respect for him to do that. Other than Dr. Merrill, I think all of us who have ever worked with or around him know how brilliant Dr. Dixon is. But

I've been doing this job years before he ever stepped foot in Robinson Memorial.

Some of us were doing this when he was still in high school. All of us were here well before he started his internship. We ran the Department of Neurology before he got here and no disrespect intended, but I refuse to sit back and be made to feel like we can't do it or aren't doing it in his absence. Dixon doesn't have any more college degrees than I have and his pedestal is no higher than mine. He's just a part of the team like the rest of us and quite frankly, it makes me just a little bit angry that you, the press or anyone else thinks he's any better."

The air had become tense during Dr. Lowe's impromptu speech. His codefendants squirmed in their chairs as if the cushions had suddenly become hot or were sprinkled with invisible tacks. Silence reigned, but only for a moment before Dr. Grant broke into a faint smile and began clapping. This time, there was no revulsion in his applause. The unexpected reaction seemed to breathe fresh oxygen back into the room that had become smothering.

"Finally, somebody got it," Dr. Grant said. He gestured towards Drs. Neal and Pridgen, but continued to face Dr. Lowe. "Now, your mission, should you choose to accept it, is to take that anger that I have implanted, share it with your friends here and prove me and the rest of D.C. wrong by boosting the morale around this place and do the job that the Man upstairs put us on earth to do."

The doctors exchanged looks before bringing their focus back to Dr. Grant as though searching for further instructions.

"This message will self-destruct in ten seconds," Dr. Grant said, pausing briefly, wondering why they were still sitting. "I suggest you not be here when it does."

CHAPTER 8

Greg lay awake, watching the rise and fall of Jessica's head which had been using his chest for a pillow for the last five hours. It was good to be home.

He'd surprised his wife and son by catching the red-eye flight and getting home a full day before expected. When he made his appearance last night, Julian was drifting off to sleep, but was alert enough to comprehend that it was his hero who was standing by his crib, kissing his forehead. From the nursery, Greg could hear the shower running from the master bathroom. His timing was perfect.

After spreading the blanket, that was once his as an infant, over his son, Greg crept into the bedroom. First he lowered the lights and popped a CD he'd labeled "Mood Music" in the stereo and turned the volume down to a lovers' level. With the setting just right, Greg pulled out the long-stem white rose that he'd tucked carefully in his carry-on bag, clenched it between his teeth and stripped down to his boxers. He was glad he'd showered just before heading to the airport.

From the La-Z-Boy chair in the corner of the bedroom, Greg could hear his Grace singing as she stepped from her bath session. He could hear the sounds of bottles being retrieved from the closet where she kept her oils and lotions. The aromas of the fragrances he loved seeped underneath the closed door and teased him, causing him to unconsciously dig his teeth into the stem of the rose while he anxiously awaited his wife's emergence.

Wearing nothing at all, Jessica finally stepped out of the bathroom and into the room, where she gasped at the sight of him. For the first few moments, she covered herself with her hands as though he was an intruder or someone who'd never seen her nakedness before. Even after realizing it was him, her hands continued to shield parts of her body as she stared at him in silence.

"Greg?" Her voice quivered.

It was then that he became aware that she was unsure as to whether he was actually sitting there or if her desire to see him was casting a lifelike hologram. Jessica's reaction just added to his desires and Greg felt the stem of the flower break under the pressure that had become too much. He removed the broken stem from between his teeth and held what was left of the flower in one hand and reached for her with the other.

"Come here," he whispered.

Jessica obeyed, but it wasn't until he began exploring her lips that she became fully convinced that her eyes hadn't been playing tricks on her. That was seven hours ago and now hints of sunlight were beginning to show through the shades of their bedroom windows. Greg kissed the top of her head and then smoothed his hand over Jessica's hair, which was still in disarray from the couple's lovemaking that had reached an almost aggressive level. Most people viewed his wife as timid and subdued. In many ways she was, but there was a side of her to which only he'd been privileged to be exposed. Greg smiled. The stories he could tell!

Jessica stirred simultaneously with the rumbling of Greg's stomach. He hadn't eaten since he granted Sergeant McDonald's wish to eat dinner with him in his hospital room before leaving for the airport. One thing seemed to ring true, no matter what area of the country he was in. Hospital food was the worst. The recovering police-man had laughed at Greg's scowl at the first forkful of mashed potatoes that he placed in his mouth.

"They should make those cooks in the kitchen eat their own food, huh?" Evan Mc-Donald said.

"Well, one thing for sure," Greg said as he washed down the food with a large gulp of water, "my mom and mother-in-law could teach them a thing or two."

"I could teach them a thing or two, and I don't even know how to cook."

Greg laughed at the officer's remark and then watched him use his right hand to massage his still semiparalyzed left arm. Greg's last order of official business at Lenox Hill was to set in place the physical therapy that would help McDonald get back some usage in the weak limb.

"Administrative duty, huh?"

Greg nodded. "At the very least," he said, making another effort to give the man back some of his lost hope. "Where you go from here is up to you and the Lord, Sarge. Work hard in your therapy sessions and keep a positive outlook and that great sense of humor. And pray," Greg added.

"You know, I used to pray a whole lot as a kid," Sergeant McDonald said.

Greg looked at him and nodded, like he'd known the man as a child. The police officer had to be near twice Greg's age.

"I stopped praying when my father got killed trying to stop a man from stealing our car. We found out later that he was a crackhead that just needed the car for what its parts were worth. My daddy was an honest man and he worked hard for everything he got. To have some punk come in and take it all away changed me. It changed all of us. I was the oldest of three kids. . . . I think I was about fourteen when all of this happened. I grew up in the Baptist church and my whole family went to church every Sunday morning without fail. But after Pop died, none of us ever went back again."

Greg had placed his fork on his plate and had shifted all of his attention to Evan, who removed his hand from his arm and used it to smooth the bandages that were still wrapped around his head. Greg wanted to urge him to continue, but feared that the story would come to an abrupt end if he spoke.

After an almost pitiful sigh, Evan resumed. "I used to say that I was going to be two things when I grew up . . . a butcher and a deacon. That's what Pop was and I wanted to be just like him. After he got gunned down, I knew then that I was going to be a policeman."

He stopped talking long enough to notice the empathetic smile on Greg's face. The smile faded when Greg saw him shake his head and listened to his next words.

"I didn't choose this job for the honor that the uniform brings, Dr. Dixon. I chose it because I wanted to take down every man who even looked like he could be involved in street activities. For years, I thought all black men were murderers or at least criminals on one level or another. Our unit would stake out areas where drug and gang activities were prevalent. The dealers and users were so smart that most times we couldn't find the stuff on them, although we knew they were guilty of selling and possessing it at one time or another. If we couldn't catch them in the act, we had to leave them alone.

"I started carrying drugs with me into these places and planting them on the people so I could have the evidence I needed to put them behind bars. I didn't feel like I was doing anything wrong, because they really were criminals. We just didn't have the timing to catch them red-handed. By this time, I was a husband and father of two. I had to make the streets safe for my family — that's what I kept telling myself. Catching them and removing them from the free world became an obsession."

Greg remained silent. He never would have known this about the man who had in some ways become his favorite patient at Lenox Hill.

"It was a fixation that started destroying the very thing I thought I was protecting . . . my family. My wife eventually left and she took my son and daughter with her. I picked up on a drinking habit and I found some sort of sick comfort in streetwalkers."

"Prostitutes?"

Sergeant McDonald nodded in answer to Greg's question. "Black ones," he added. "For some reason, they had to be black. I think at first it started out as another avenue for me to get back at black people. I knew that most prostitutes were owned by drug dealers, so I felt like if I screwed their women, I'd be hurting the men who made their money through them. That turned out to be a bad idea."

"What happened?" Greg couldn't hide his fascination with the story.

"Let's just say it didn't work out like I planned," he said. "A couple of years later, my wife wanted to reconcile, but I'd done so much stuff that I couldn't even give her the love she deserved anymore. I'd changed in those two years and so had she. There was no real love left between us."

"Your marriage ended?"

"Yeah, but it may have been a good thing in the long run. I went through some counseling and got my life back together and became an honest cop. Nancy, my ex-wife, died a couple of years ago after a four-year battle with breast cancer. While she was sick, I made my peace with her and my children. My son's name is Richard. He works for WSB-FM Radio in Atlanta, Georgia. His best friend's name is James. James is a black architect. I'd already softened my stance on black men while I was in counseling, but James was one of the people who really taught me how to see them as individuals and not lump them all up in one mold of clay."

"How'd he do that?"

"He married my daughter," Evan said with a burst of laughter. "He married Alyssa and he's a great husband. I wasn't thrilled last year when he decided to take a job in Paris, but it was what both of them really wanted, so I didn't try too hard to stop them. Last time I saw my daughter and him was eight months ago, when he arranged for me to fly there right after the birth of my granddaughter, Jamie. She's a beautiful combination of both of them, but I'd say she has her mother's eyes."

From the drawer beside his bed, Sergeant McDonald fished out a recent photo of his daughter's family. Greg agreed. Jamie was beautiful and she did have her mother's eyes, which also happened to be the brown eyes of her grandfather.

"Do you still want to have a daughter?"

Jessica's question snapped his ceiling stare and his mind's stroll back to his last hours in New York. Greg looked down and briefly thought that the words had never been voiced. Jessica's position was the same. The side of her face rested against his chest. When he didn't immediately reply, she shifted and looked up at him in anticipation.

"What did you say?" Greg still needed to be reassured.

Jessica pulled herself into a seated position, placed her bed pillow in front of her and leaned forward. "Remember how much you wanted Julian to be a little girl? Did that just go away when he was born?"

Greg sat up, too, resting his back against the headboard of the bed. "Were you dreaming about this or something? Where is this coming from?"

"Right here," she said, pointing to the left side of her chest. "I know we both went through some unwanted drama during the time I was pregnant, and even with my last operation, but I just want to know how you really feel. Sherry and Rick are going through some heavy stuff right now because Rick didn't tell her how he really felt from the beginning. I don't want us to go through anything like that."

Greg smiled and reached forward to rake his fingers through hair that was still muddled. Even with signs of sleep lingering on her face, she was still beautiful.

"We're not going to go through that, sweetie," he said with confidence.

"It's bad, Greg. I know it's worse than you think and it's probably worse than I think too. I'm really worried about them."

The concern that could be seen on Jessica's face disturbed Greg. He'd only had one chance to talk to Derrick in detail, and although Sherry had mentioned confiding in him about it, their talk had never materialized. He had assumed that over the past week, they'd reached a common ground.

"They're sleeping in two different rooms now, Greg. When we met for lunch on Friday, Sherry said they've been sleeping in separate bedrooms for the past three or four days."

Greg's earlier plans to skip Sunday morning services and sleep in with his wife were erased. He'd had no idea that the disagreement between his best friends had reached such an intense level. Most likely, they'd be at church whether they were on good terms or not. He needed to be there in case either one of them wanted to talk.

"Do you still want a daughter?" Jessica reverted back to her original question.

"Grace, we could have a daughter and I'd be elated. We could *not* have a daughter and I'd still be happy. We could have ten Dixon kids running all over the place and I'd be content, or we could have just the one that we have now, and I would feel just as fulfilled. I admit that I wanted a baby girl, but not having one didn't disappoint me. If we decide later to have more children, we'll decide it together. But until then . . ."

Greg reached out and tugged at the pillow that had been impeding his view since his wife sat up. She loosened her grip and allowed him to admire her body without obstruction. Greg tightened his lips and shook his head, releasing a low-toned grunt. Had it not been for the faint scar at her bikini line, one would never know that she'd given birth. Jessica stopped his hand when he reached towards her.

"We have to be at church in a couple of hours, Greg. We can't be late. I promised Pastor Baldwin that I'd sing today."

"Fine," Greg whispered. "But you need to warm up your vocal chords first. Let's test your octaves."

"Greg . . ." Jessica warned as she began inching away from him.

"Come on, baby. I know you can go higher than that."

Jessica giggled as she scooted back another inch as Greg began to crawl towards her. "Greg . . ."

"Higher," he said, just before grabbing her around the waist and using the full strength of his arm to pull her into him.

Jessica let out a squeal. "Greg!" she screamed through more laughter.

"There you go," he said, looking down into her eyes before covering her lips briefly with his. "That's more like it."

CHAPTER 9

"Because He Lives" had always been one of Greg's least favorite songs. Occasionally, he'd hear it played on the local Christian radio stations and as soon as he heard the musical introduction, he'd turn it off. When people sang it in church, he would use that time for a bathroom break. When as a child he'd hear his mother humming it around the house, he'd close his room's door or grab his basketball and head to Derrick's house to shoot a few hoops.

The last time Greg could remember hearing the song in its entirety was as a three-year-old boy, sitting in the front pew, staring at a black casket that held his father's body. The choir members were dressed in black robes that were ordered especially for somber occasions such as this one. In his young mind, it seemed that the song would never end. Greg couldn't fully understand what was going on back then, but he remembered that somewhere during the singing of this song a loud, curdling scream, like none he'd every heard before, escaped from his mother's mouth just before she collapsed on Julia Madison's shoulder. A domino effect followed. Before long, funeral attendants were scampering with hand fans and boxes of Kleenex, tending to grief-stricken family members and friends. Their mission had been accomplished and the choir ended their sad serenade. Greg had reached for his mother, but the attending ushers stopped him with white gloved hands. Moments later, he remembered placing his own head in Derrick's little lap and crying until his friend's brand-new black suit pants were saturated with moisture. Greg wasn't really crying because his father was dead. The comprehension that Phillip Gregory Dixon wouldn't be coming back home still hadn't quite registered with his son. Greg cried only because his mother cried and in his mind, the song was responsible. He grew to learn the true cause of her tears, but still, it had remained a song he refused to listen to . . . until now.

From the seat where he sat, water clouded Greg's vision — not because the song brought back remembrance of his father's funeral, but because his heart felt as though it would burst with joy while he listened to his wife belt out chords that brought the crowd to its feet. Pastor Baldwin stood behind her, swatting her with a handkerchief, with his face crinkled as though there was a stench in the air. That was an unmistakable sign to any Sunday morning songster that the pastor was pleased with her performance. Today was one of those days. Today, the song wasn't about death, but about life. Today, Greg heard his mother squeal again, but this time Lena Dixon was overcome with happiness and not grief. Today, "Because He Lives" was his favorite song and no voice other than the incomparable one of the woman he loved could have given it such new meaning.

This was God's doing. Even in jest, Greg couldn't take credit for the warming of Jessica's vocal chords. Just before what would have been a delightful Sunday morning rendezvous, Julian's calls to be rescued from his crib altered his parents' plans. Greg wanted to tune him out just for a few more minutes, but the father in him wouldn't allow it. He was home for good now. No Monday morning flight would be waiting to take him back to New York. There would be plenty of time for intimacy, but now Julian needed him. Greg spent the next hour nestled in the bed with both his wife and son, enjoying their last few moments of solitude before preparing for church.

"Baby, you sung that song!"

Greg whispered the words in Jessica's ear when he embraced her upon her return to the pew where they sat. She'd had to weave her way through a mass of worshippers who had "caught the Spirit" during her song, including both their mothers. It took a few minutes for Pastor Baldwin to begin his sermon, but not because of the congregation only. He, too, was having trouble composing himself. Every few seconds, the seventy-year-old preacher would kick up his left leg with the ease of a teenager and become the vision of a still photo while he steadied himself perfectly on his right before slowly bringing his left foot back down to the carpeted pulpit. In secret, Greg and Derrick referred to this move as "the hup," named after the sound Pastor Baldwin made at the time of his famous leg lift. As teenagers, they would mimic the move and get scolded by their mothers for "poking fun at the man of God." The hup was an endearing sight that, just a few months ago, Fellowship Worship Center thought they'd never witness again.

With all of the excitement that had followed Jessica's musical introduction to the message of the day, Greg had forgotten about the plight of his friends. Now that they were all settled back in their seats, Derrick and Sherry's troubles silently screamed in a volume that nearly drowned out Pastor Baldwin's message. Their body language said what they never voiced. Even nearing five years old, Denise generally sat on her mother's lap during services. Today, her parents had conveniently placed her between the two of them. Greg glanced to his left. Sherry sat directly beside him. She turned, allowing her eyes to briefly meet his before returning her attention to the pastor.

For a fleeting moment, Greg looked at his own right hand, which was linked with Jessica's left and felt a twinge of guilt. His marriage couldn't be stronger and if the flame in his love life burned any higher, his bedroom would be a fire hazard. Yet, he could almost feel a chill from the coldness that radiated from the touch of Sherry's arm against the fabric of his suit coat. The service-ending dismissal had barely been given before Greg, ignoring Derrick's stares, pulled Sherry into the room where the teenagers convened each Sunday morning for Sunday School.

"Okay, Sherry. What is *really* going on?"

The final word to Greg's question hadn't fully left his lips before Sherry grabbed him around his waist and pressed her face into his chest. He had seen her get emotional before, but not like this. Sherry was known to be a strong woman. In their middle school years, the full-figured, softball all-star was almost notorious for being the one *not* to mess with. She'd only fought a few times, but when she did, it was always one for the win column. Seeing her cry like this was a first for Greg, and he hadn't prepared himself for the possibility of her doing so.

"It's okay, sweetie," he said, wrapping his arms around her in hopes of providing the comfort he sensed that she needed. "It's okay."

"No, it's not, Greg." Her voice was muffled, but he understood her well. "Ricky is being a big, stupid jerk and I can't take it anymore."

Derrick's stubbornness was no secret to anyone. He'd always been that way, making him a frequent candidate for the leather strap that his mother kept in her closet when they were growing up. His pigheaded nature had been as much of a blessing as it had been a curse in Derrick's life. His unwillingness to back down or give up was one of the strong points that gave him a winning record in the courtroom. But it was also the characteristic that nearly cost him his friendship with Greg a few years ago when he blamed Jessica for his mother's death. Greg was accustomed to hearing the words "stubborn" and "Derrick" in the same sentence, but it was the last five words Sherry spoke that concerned him most.

"Okay, come here."

Greg pulled her away from him and led Sherry to a nearby table, where they both sat facing one another. Sherry tried to dry her face on the handkerchief that Greg had fished from his pocket, but the continuing flow of fresh tears made it impossible.

"Is this just about the baby, Sherry? I mean, is that all there is to it? Rick wants another kid and you don't? Is that all there is?"

His skepticism that the disagreement could cause such a sizable disturbance in his friends' marriage could clearly be detected in Greg's voice. He hoped that she would reveal some new information that Derrick hadn't shared with him, but Sherry's answer erased his doubts.

"Yes, and that's what makes me even madder, Greg. You were there with us on the swings in Ms. Julia's backyard when both me and Ricky agreed to only having one

111

child. He looked me right in my face and told me that one was enough. Don't you remember?"

Greg remembered it well, but he had hoped that neither Derrick nor Sherry could recall that summer afternoon. The last thing he wanted was to somehow be dragged into the middle of the brewing controversy.

He purposely avoided a direct answer and instead said, "Sweetie, listen to me. Both of us know how adamant Rick can be about stuff, whether it's personal or professional. But, we also know that when he changes his mind, it's usually based on something that has taken place in his life."

"Like you having a son?" Sherry jumped in. "His best friend has a son and now all of a sudden, he wants one too. Well, why should I be expected to change just because he wants to change? I don't want to have another baby, Greg. I don't want to go through that again. You think I'm being unfair to him?"

Sherry's eyes were wide and expectant, reminiscent of those of a child who awaited an answer from the one person whose opinion mattered to her. What Greg really wanted to tell her was how Derrick's change of heart had far more to do with Travis Scott than Julian. Travis's unexpected death and the bond that Derrick had established with him before it was the happening that fueled this change.

"No, I'm not saying that you're being unfair to him." Greg decided not to disclose the information that his best friend had shared in confidence. "I'm just saying that like with the whole situation he had with Grace a few years back, he's going to need some time. He'll be okay, Sherry. I'm not telling you to give in to him. I'm telling you not to give up on him. I'm sure that the issue with having a baby will pass, but it might take a little time and patience. You understand what I'm saying?"

"I don't want to give up on my marriage, Greg, but right now, I don't feel like me and Ricky even have a marriage. We don't talk to each other anymore. We don't eat dinner together anymore. We don't even sleep together anymore. It's like I don't have a husband . . . I have a housemate. If I didn't want to have another baby when we were acting like a married couple, I sure don't want to have one now. I can't believe Ricky is acting like this, Greg. He's just so darn stubborn until it makes me sick. Why can't he be more mature about stuff like this? Why can't he be more like you?"

Greg reached across the table and placed

his hands on top of Sherry's and then got up, pulling her into a standing position with him. Her tears had subsided, but she welcomed his embrace as he pulled her back into his chest in a firm hold.

"Our differences are what make us closer than most brothers, Sherry. Most times his stubbornness isn't a bad trait. It's his tenacity and determination that make him the man that he is. He's always been that way, sweetie, and it's probably not going to change. That's what he was when you fell in love with him, so it can't be all bad. Just give him some time to get over this hurdle. When the smoke clears, Rick will be fine. He always is."

Sherry pulled away just far enough to look up into Greg's face. "You'll talk to him?" She pressed her cheek back into his chest and resumed her grip.

Greg saw the door to the room open slightly and Jessica peeked in. She stared for a moment and then displayed a slight tug at the corners of her lips. Greg returned her smile and then watched her close the door, once again leaving him alone with Sherry.

"Yeah, sweetheart," he promised. "I'll talk to him."

Chapter 10

"So let me get this straight. Your son shot and critically wounded the woman at the pawnshop over the worth of a gold watch and you want me to defend him in court?"

Derrick sat behind his desk and looked into the face of two parents who sat with their teenage son beside them. He knew that aggravation could be heard in his voice, but the parents were only a part of the heaviness on his mind. Three hours ago, he'd called a nearby florist and had ordered a dozen roses to be delivered to Sherry's classroom. She had to have gotten them a long time ago, but no matter how much Derrick sat and stared at his phone, it wouldn't ring.

Two hours ago, his secretary had made the appointment for him to meet with George and Barbara Wilson, who had just posted the bail to get their son released from jail pending his trial date. Generally, work kept him from dwelling on personal affairs, but this meeting added to Derrick's frustrations. Seventeen-year-old Perry Wilson wriggled in his chair, popped chewing gum, folded his arms and looked defiant as he locked his eyes on the outside world as seen through the window Derrick's office provided.

"We need a good lawyer for our son, Mr. Madison," George Wilson said. "We understand that the defense of young black men whom society wants to cripple and keep locked behind the white man's bars is your specialty. You are the right man for this job, Mr. Madison and I promise you, you will be paid handsomely for your time and efforts. Money is no object, if that's your concern."

George Wilson was the proprietor of a chain of successful dry-cleaning operations in and around the D.C. area. He'd been born with a silver spoon in his mouth and had never wanted for anything. The stores he now owned had been in operation for three generations and were applauded for their prompt, professional and courteous service. Two years ago, the man moved his family from Austin, Texas, to collect his inheritance, which included the family business, after his father died. Recent news of

Perry's arrest had shocked the area and Mr. Wilson's televised blatant denial of his son's guilt had temporarily won his family the sympathy and support of the community's elite. He knew, though, that as soon as the truth was discovered, a lot was at stake for him, both personally and professionally.

"I am indeed the best your money can get you, Mr. Wilson, but money is never my motivation or my concern," Derrick assured him. "I'm a defense lawyer. My concern would be a defense of your son's actions. I have at least three newspapers in my possession that give your statement of Perry's innocence. But what you're telling me is that he, in fact, carried out this shooting. I can only guess that your change of tune means that there were witnesses to this crime that contradict your initial story. So, if I'm going to defend him, I need more. Was the shooting in self-defense? Was it accidental? I need something to work with here, Mr. Wilson. Enlighten me."

The man looked towards his son, who showed a twinge of concern before turning his face back to the window. Mrs. Wilson stared into the fabric of her silk pants and had remained quiet throughout the meeting. They were all silent for several moments before Mr. Wilson leaned in close to the desk and spoke again.

"What would I be paying you for, Mr. Madison? Is it not your job to create a defense for the accused?"

Derrick leaned back in his chair and returned his stare, without intimidation. "You want me to lie?"

A single tear dropped from Mrs. Wilson's eye and fell into her lap without ever touching her face. The sight of the mother's dejection prompted Derrick to soften his tone.

"Mr. Wilson, your belief that I will defend young black men to the extent of lying to draw a picture of innocence is incorrect. Admittedly, my clientele is probably ninety-eight percent black, but I don't run a racially biased firm here. If an innocent boy of any other race was unjustly accused and needed my legal skills, I'd render my services to him just as I would a black boy. But I don't knowingly go into a courtroom and lie to get a guilty person out of taking responsibility for his actions."

"What kind of lawyer are you?"

"An honest one, Mr. Wilson. When I worked for my previous employer, I was obligated to represent clients whether they were innocent or not. If they weren't innocent, I had to say something to make the jury think that they were. Here, I'm the one who tells me what to do and I can't and won't tell myself to lie for any amount of money. If you want me to defend your son and go to bat for him for a lesser sentence, I'll see what I can do. But I won't go into a court of law and lie for him. He got hot-headed and shot a woman who is on life support as we speak. That's a serious crime, Mr. Wilson, and his fate will ultimately be at the mercy of the court."

"So, you'll defend him?" The man reached into the inside pocket of his suit coat and pulled out his checkbook. Placing it on Derrick's desk, he flipped to his first blank check and pulled a pen out of the pencil holder beside him. "What do you need from me in order to get started?"

In a mixture of disgust and anger, Derrick reached across this desk and swatted the pen and checkbook from Mr. Wilson's grasp. Both objects sailed across the room and landed on the floor beneath the window. The sudden, unexpected movement got the full attention of all three of the people who sat on the other side of his desk.

"Did you even hear a word I said?" Derrick demanded. "You want to know what I need from you? Instead of trying to use your resources to get someone to cover up the truth, I need for you to teach this boy to take responsibility for his actions. Show him how to have remorse when he's done something heinous to someone that will, *if* she survives, alter her life forever. Tell him that he's been blessed with only one mother and he's callously breaking her heart. Teach him how to pull his pants up to his waist, tighten his belt and sit up straight in his chair. Tell him that nobody truly likes a man who goes around committing crimes because he knows his daddy is gonna bail him out. Tell him *that,* Mr. Wilson. That's what I need you to do. What's nine times twelve?"

Derrick looked directly at the teenager as he demanded an answer to his question. Perry looked at Derrick and then at his parents as if expecting them to answer on his behalf.

"Look at him," Derrick resumed, turning back to Mr. Wilson. "He's about as intelligent as molded cheese. You're raising a sorry, two-bit rapper wannabe who's on the verge of having his whole future taken away from him and all you can offer is money? You think that's gonna answer his problems? This is your son, Mr. Wilson. He should be worth more to you than that."

An expression of total outrage had begun to creep onto George Wilson's face from the moment that Derrick had sent his engraved, sheepskin-covered checkbook flying onto the carpeted floor. By the time Derrick had finished his lecture, Mr. Wilson was on his feet and motioning for his wife and son to join him.

"Do you have a son, Mr. Madison?"

The question felt like a personal retaliation on what Derrick had been going through in his life for the past several weeks, but his professional defense mechanism kicked in and he held his face steady, not showing a hint of the mixture of hurt and anger that he felt inside.

"I am a father, if that's what you're trying to find out," he responded. Derrick was satisfied that his answer appeared to cripple whatever speech the man was prepared to spill.

"Well . . . fine!" he barked while retrieving his checkbook, opting to leave Derrick's pen on the floor. "I hope you know what an opportunity you just passed up. You can turn up your nose at my money if you want, but I was willing to pay you enough to put your kid through college just to take on this case. What do you say to that?"

"I say give it to charity, Mr. Wilson," Derrick said, while jotting down notes in the open file that lay on his desk. "My kid is going to earn a full scholarship. And you certainly won't be needing it for your son. The campus he'll be living on for the next four years and beyond doesn't have tuition and his roommate, no doubt, will be delighted to tutor him free of charge."

Derrick didn't look up again until he heard the slamming of his office door. When he was sure that his guests were gone, he dropped his pen on the desk and ran his hands over the top of his head. His low fade needed trimming, but his wife was his barber and he'd been too proud to ask her to groom it for him. The telephone that had held much of his early morning attention caught his eyes again. Derrick picked it up and put it to his ear. Though he knew that it was working properly, he needed to be assured.

"Bad day at the office?"

Derrick winced and turned to see Sherry standing in his doorway. Embarrassed, he returned the phone to its cradle and jumped to his feet.

" 'Bad day?' " He even sounded foolish to himself as he repeated her words. "What makes you think I'm having a bad day?"

Sherry closed the door behind her before she continued. "Well, I've been sitting in your waiting area for over half an hour and

I just saw three people bolt from your office as if they all caught a sudden case of diarrhea."

"Oh, them." Derrick motioned for her to sit in the chair that Mrs. Wilson had vacated. "They weren't determining factors to how my day turned out."

Sherry bypassed the chair he'd directed her to and instead came to a stop in front of the window. Derrick watched her in silence. Her long thick curls fell just beyond her shoulders and came to a rest against her back. He liked it when she wore her hair down. She had on an outfit he'd not seen before. It was a leopard-print top and black silk slacks and they hugged her steep curves well. Derrick swallowed to control his watering mouth.

"Thanks for the flowers," Sherry said, not turning from the window.

"You're welcome."

"The note card said you wanted to see me. Unfortunately, my lunch break is just about over now, so I can't stay long."

Derrick walked from behind his desk and joined her at the window, standing so close behind her that he could smell the scent of her hairspray. Not sure of how she would respond, he was cautious when he reached out with both his hands and touched her arms. When he felt the immediate appearance of fine bumps beneath his fingertips, Derrick pulled Sherry closer to him, wrapping his arms around her and planting a gentle kiss on the side of her neck. It had been too long.

"Then, let's not waste time," he whispered

Sherry wrestled from his grip and turned to face him. She stared into his eyes briefly before pulling his face downward and parting his lips with hers. Derrick's entire body felt as though it was on fire. He pulled away and rushed to his phone and pressed one of the buttons.

"Robin, take the rest of the day off," he said to his secretary. "And lock the door on your way out. I won't be taking any more clients today."

Immense appreciation could be heard in the lady's voice, but Robin barely had time to thank him before Derrick released the button and cleared the top of his desk with one sweep of his arm, sending all of his things, including the phone, onto the floor. When he turned around, Sherry had already saved him the trouble of removing her outerwear. Releasing a deep moan, Derrick picked her up and sat her on the edge of the varnished wood grain.

"Wait," Sherry whispered. "Robin might

not be gone yet."

"The walls are too thick," Derrick said between kisses. "Besides, Robin is forty-four-years old, been married twenty-three years and has six children. She won't hear nothing she ain't heard before."

CHAPTER 11

"Is it feeling like home again, yet?"

Greg snapped from his daydream to find Dr. Grant standing in his doorway, leaning against the wooden frame.

"It never stopped feeling like home," Greg responded with a laugh, before making a notation in the file he'd been mindlessly staring into.

It had been three days since Greg had returned to the halls of Robinson Memorial, and although he had begun noting some changes, it really did feel good to be back in more familiar surroundings. He dared not tell Dr. Grant that his mind had been firmly planted in the New York hospital just before he walked in.

Dr. Grant invited himself to the chair across from Greg's desk and smiled. "Good to know, Dixon. For some reason, New York has a way of growing on the minds of progressive people."

Greg's only response was a silent smile. He had visited New York on several occasions, but he'd never remained there for more than two days and, until the past month, he'd never even visited Lenox Hill Hospital. The Big Apple did have a way of growing on a person and so did Dr. Armstrong's big office. Greg had missed Robinson Memorial while he was away, but not enough to not savor his moments at Lenox. It was his longing to spend more time with his family that made him wish for these familiar halls.

"We had some pretty bad luck while you were away," Dr. Grant said.

"Yeah, a copy of the memo you sent to the neurological staff was sitting on my desk when I got here on Monday morning. I've been hoping for a moment to talk to you about it. We lost seven patients?"

Dr. Grant removed his glasses and rubbed his forehead, appearing almost regretful that he'd brought up the subject. He replaced his glasses, released a heavy sigh and then allowed his fingers to run through his graying hair.

"We lost five on the table," he said. "The last two were members of that church group pileup. They made it through surgery, but died later."

"Wow."

"Yeah. Like I said, we had some bad luck. Amazing how we just seemed to have head injuries flying in this place left and right when you weren't here and now that you're back, we haven't had one in the past few days." The sound of laughter came from Dr. Grant's mouth, but there was no sign of amusement on his face.

"Well, after what I dealt with at Lenox, I can appreciate a few days of stillness," Greg said.

"Have you heard from Joseph since you left?"

Greg nodded while taking a sip of water from his cup. "Dr. Armstrong left a message on my voice mail on Monday, telling me how much he appreciated my assistance in his absence. The policeman that I was called in to operate on is recovering well from the surgery and he was set to begin physical therapy yesterday. Aside from him, I performed three other surgeries and all were successful. So, I feel that God was with me and now, I guess my work there is done."

"Well, good." Dr. Grant stood and smoothed out his white coat. "Now it's back to the patients at Robinson, huh? I know you have quite a list of them to check on today, so I'm going to skedaddle and let you get started. Good to have you back, Dixon."

"Thank you, Dr. Grant. Good to be back."

Greg took a few more moments to look over the revisions on his list. Some of the patients that he was treating at the time of his vacation had been released. He felt a bit of sadness that he hadn't been there to see them through to the end of their recovery, but their being dismissed was a good sign that wouldn't allow for regrets. One name on the board in front of him caught his eye and momentarily held him captive.

"It couldn't be," he whispered. Setting the clipboard aside, he searched through the folders that sat on top of his desk until he came to the one marked "E. Cobb."

The only E. Cobb that Greg had ever known was Evelyn Cobb. Evelyn had been the star of a nightmare that had lasted nearly ten years. Her one and only purpose in life seemed to be to capture Greg's heart. He never gave her the title of a stalker as others did, but she definitely had an obsession. Even his marriage to Jessica didn't stop her. Nothing seemed stronger than her desire to marry the husband "God had ordained" until nearly two years ago when she finally crossed the ultimate line and ran head-on into the wrath of Lena Dixon and Mattie Charles. The encounter involving the women was something that Greg never got the full story on, but the result was Evelyn's abrupt disappearance from his life. To Greg's relief, she and her mother had removed their names from the membership roll at Fellowship Worship Center and chose to attend church elsewhere. The last time Greg had heard anything about her, the Lord was now telling her that the organist at her new place of worship was her chosen husband.

As Greg skimmed the information sheet on the patient that had been admitted two weeks ago, his heart pounded and anger began to brew inside of him. E. Cobb was a black female, five-feet-ten, one-hundred-thirty pounds and she was a part of the interstate pileup involving the church group. Until today, she'd been Dr. Neal's patient. Slipping into his physician's coat, Greg headed into the hallway with his clipboard and Ms. Cobb's file tucked under his arm.

"Neal!"

His voice level was louder than normal and gained the attention of several bystanders. Dr. Neal turned from the nurses' station and looked at his approaching colleague.

"My hearing aid works well, Dixon. You don't have to yell."

"You had Ms. Cobb for a patient, right?"

Dr. Neal took a closer look at the file in Greg's hand and then said, "Oh, yeah. I had to give her some stitches for two gashes that resulted from her head going into the windshield of her vehicle. She's recovering really well and should be able to go home in a day or two."

"If she's expected to be released in a couple of days, why would you transfer her to me? You performed the operation. Why couldn't you just keep her on your list?"

"She *asked* for you, Dr. Dixon," Dr. Neal said, obviously irritated by both Greg's tone and his line of questioning. "I didn't think it would be a problem. Unless, of course, your time in New York somehow elevated you above the consideration of a patient's request."

Greg locked his jaws to hold back the response that begged to be released. Since his return to Robinson Memorial, he'd noticed a transformation in the attitude of his fellow surgeons. He'd never been close friends with any of them other than Dr. Grant, but they'd always gotten along well. Having helped Greg carry out Jessica's most recent surgery, Dr. Lowe had taken a special place in Greg's heart. The forty-something doctor still greeted Greg warmly on a daily

131

basis, but the afternoons that they used to spend chatting by the coffeemaker had ended. Dr. Pridgen and Dr. Neal both appeared to go out of their way to avoid him and Greg was beginning to feel more like a stranger at Robinson Memorial than he did in his first few days at Lenox Hill Hospital.

Without addressing Dr. Neal's response, Greg took two steps backward before turning around and walking towards the room marked 460. He'd vowed a long time ago that one more stunt by Evelyn to get close to him would cause him to lose all professionalism. She'd gone too far when she left the sympathy card in his mailbox when Jessica was awaiting surgery. The only reason he hadn't already clawed into her was because his mother and mother-in-law had beaten him to the punch and he'd not seen her since. But today was her unlucky day. The knowledge that she was nearly well enough to send home only encouraged Greg. He didn't have to worry about her having any medical setbacks. As far as her personal feelings were concerned, he couldn't care less. Protecting her emotions was the last thing on his mind.

The door to room 460 swung open behind the force of Greg's arm, and when his newly assigned patient turned from the television screen and tried to focus on him, he felt the blood flush from his face. Her eyes were wide. His dramatic entrance had startled her.

"Ms. Cobb?" he asked.

The woman was much younger than he'd expected. Her hair was pulled back into a short ponytail and the threads that Dr. Neal had sewn into her forehead were in plain view. The physical description on the paper fit Evelyn Cobb almost to perfection, but the woman in the semiprivate room wasn't her.

"Yes," she responded. Retrieving her eyeglasses from the table beside her, she put them on and then broke into a wide grin. "Oh, my God, it's you! You Dr. Gregory Dixon, ain't you? Ooh, you even cuter up close than you were on stage. My mama 'nem ain't even gonna believe this right here. I told them I was gonna get seen by you before I left here. Hold on a minute. Don't go nowhere."

On stage? Greg decided not to ask the question on his mind. Instead, he took a few cautious steps towards the bed and watched the young woman punch numbers on the telephone pad and then listened as she reported to her mother that "he" had arrived. She spoke with the enthusiasm of a starstruck child as she urged her mother to return to her room. She'd barely placed the phone back on the table before turning to Greg.

"I ain't glad I'm in the hospital, Dr. Dixon, but I'm shole glad I'll be able to tell all my friends that you were my doctor. Please don't leave before my mama gets here, okay? I just called her on her cell phone. She was using the toilet, but she'll be here in a minute or two."

"Uh, okay." Greg couldn't prevent himself from chuckling at the all-too-detailed report. "Why don't you answer a few questions for me while we wait for your mother, okay?"

"Okay."

"What's your first name?"

"Errka."

"What is it?"

"Errka."

"Could you spell that for me?"

"E-r-i-k-a."

"Oh, *Erika.*"

"Yeah, that's what I said: Errka."

"Okay, then, Erika. How old are you?"

"Eighteen and I'll be getting out of here just in time for graduation. Please tell me I can march with my class."

"Well, I don't see why not, but we'll give

you a definite answer upon your release. Congratulations on your graduation. How are you feeling?" Greg leaned in closer and inspected Dr. Neal's handiwork.

"Good."

The door swung open again and a heavy-set woman and two smaller children burst into the room.

"Ooh, Mama, where's the camera?" Erika asked. "Get the camera and take a picture. I want a picture of him touching my stitches. Touch my stitches again, Dr. Dixon. Get the camera, Mama."

Erika's mother fished through her large purse, all the while looking at Greg as though she were experiencing a celebrity sighting. "Lord have mercy, that shole is him. We saw you on television and in the newspaper. Plus, you spoke at Erika's school last year for career day. Lord have mercy, if I was single and ten years younger . . ."

"Mama, take the picture!"

"Girl, wait a minute. He ain't made of ice. It ain't like he gonna melt before I can get the camera ready."

Greg had never seen a display quite like this one. This one wasn't an everyday response from his patients, but as undignified as it was, Greg was flattered. Uninterested in the commotion around them, the younger boys found chairs and focused on the television screen that was mounted on the wall in front of them while their mother snapped pictures.

"I'm gonna put these pictures in my senior memory book," Erika announced.

After the eighth flash, Greg had had enough fun for one morning. Motioning for Mrs. Cobb to have a seat, they spent the next several minutes going over Erika's chart and discussing future appointments to follow up on her progress. One of the two church members who hadn't survived the accident was Erika's best friend. According to her mother, Erika hadn't smiled since finding out her friend had died. She thanked Greg for giving her daughter a reason to be happy. When Greg left the room, he headed towards his next stop and spotted Dr. Neal coming out of a room just down the hall.

"Neal!" Greg called out, breaking into a trot to catch up with him.

Dr. Neal looked at him without response. The message behind his cold eyes dared Greg to interrogate him about anything else that he may have done in his absence or upon his return. Greg understood his demeanor.

"Look. Man to man, I just want to apologize for what happened back there," Greg said. "I never should have stepped to you like that and it won't happen again."

Dr. Neal stared at Greg's outstretched hand for a moment and then took it and shook with firmness. It was clear from his expression that the apology was not expected. He didn't verbalize a response, but the quarter of a smile that he displayed was enough for Greg.

CHAPTER 12

The smell of homemade peach cobbler wasn't a peculiar one at the modest brick home that sat on the corner of Apple Road. On any given Sunday, the common by-stander could smell it if he or she happened to walk by when the breeze outside was blowing just right. What made the smell an odd one today was that it wasn't Sunday, but Thursday.

From the kitchen where she was boiling the potatoes that would be used to make her very own cheddar mashed potato recipe, Lena could hear her housemate coming in the front door mumbling about how peach cobbler wasn't really fresh if it was three days old by the time it was served.

"What you doing?" Mattie stood in the doorway that separated the combination kitchen and dining area from the hallway where a never-used piano sat.

"Building a tree house," Lena responded

138

in sarcasm. "What it look like I'm doing?"

"Why you making cobbler today? By Sunday, it'll have to be reheated and the crust won't be nearly as crisp."

"I didn't make it for Sunday. I made it for today."

"We don't make no peach cobbler on Thursday. It ain't nobody here but me and you and it'll just go to waste. What you? Pregnant? Since when have you ever wanted to eat dessert in the middle of the week? Naw, you ain't pregnant, you just dumb, that's all. Ain't even got the sense you were born with. I tell you the truth! I leave for a couple of hours to go and get my hair done and just that fast, you done lost your mind."

Before Lena could respond, Mattie stormed into her bedroom, where she closed the door behind her. Lena chuckled. She had to admit that she'd done quite a nice job on grooming Mattie Charles over the past few years. When she first moved in with her, Mattie's reflexes were slow and she could barely keep up with Lena's quick wit and sharp tongue. Now, she could represent herself well . . . sometimes, too well. A few moments later, Mattie had returned. Lena said nothing while Mattie opened the pots to see what else was being prepared.

"What's all this, Lena?" Mattie asked. "I

thought we had decided that we were eating meatloaf, rice and collards for dinner. This ain't no meatloaf," she added as she peeked in the oven at the turkey that was baking inside.

"I changed my mind," Lena said.

Mattie looked at Lena in disbelief and crinkled her face as she spoke. "*You* changed your mind? Since when you get to make that decision all by yourself? The deed on this house got more than one name on it and dinner is one of them things we decide together. This here what you're cooking is stuff that we need to save for when the children come over or on Sundays when we invite the pastor. This ain't no dinner for just the two of us."

"That's 'cause it ain't just for the two of us," Lena said, adjusting the heat that burned under the green beans.

As an immediate reaction, Mattie's hands went towards the top of her head, smoothing out-of-place hairs that didn't exist.

"Who's coming over? We having company? Why you ain't tell nobody? How you gonna just invite people over and don't tell me? Who's coming over?" she repeated her first question and continued grooming while looking at her reflection in the glass of the oven door.

"Didn't you just get your hair done?" Lena asked. "What you pay Sherry for if you got to come home and redo what she done already did?"

"Are you gonna tell me who's coming for dinner or not?"

"Pastor Baldwin," Lena said over the sound of the flow of water from the kitchen sink where she stood, rinsing her hands.

Mattie stepped away from the oven and looked at Lena in disbelief. Then, as though thinking she'd heard incorrectly, she inched closer and waited for the faucet to be turned off.

"What you say?"

"I said, Pastor Baldwin is coming to dinner."

"On a Thursday?"

"You got a problem with the man of God coming over for dinner?" Lena challenged. "The Lord said that when we feed the least of his little ones, we're feeding him too. You got a problem with feeding the Lord on a Thursday?"

"Well, you could have at least told me about it."

"I didn't know 'bout it before you left. He called because he was at the church and found your Bible . . . the one you been turning the house and car over looking for. You left it in the bathroom at the church and he was calling to say that he'd found it and was placing it in the seating area where we sit on Sunday."

"Thank you, Jesus!" Mattie said with raised hands. "My mama bought me that Bible twenty years ago."

Lena turned off the burner of the stove where the potatoes had been boiling and proceeded to pour the contents into a strainer that she'd placed in the sink. Thick steam poured towards the ceiling, followed by the thudding sounds of the vegetables falling onto the surface below. As she set the hot pot on the countertop, Mattie walked to the sink and opened the window just above it.

"So, how did his finding my Bible lead to him coming over for dinner?"

"That's the only trait that Julian got from you, you know that?" Lena began the task of gathering the potatoes for mashing. "That's why he always looking in every-body's mouth when they talk, 'cause his grandma Mattie is so devilish nosey."

Lena resumed her dinner preparations, but from her side view, she could see that Mattie hadn't moved at all. When she turned and looked at her, she found her standing with her hands planted on her hips, still awaiting the answer to her question. Persistence was another thing that she'd taught Mattie too well.

"While he was on the phone, he mentioned that he was going to wrap it up at the church around dinnertime," Lena said. "I asked him what he was going to eat for dinner and he said he hadn't decided yet. I told him he was welcome to eat over here. At first he declined, but he called back about ten minutes later and said he'd be delighted to join us. Is that enough information for you? You want to know how many times the phone rang before I answered it? What was playing on television at the time? What color drawers I had on? What else you want to know, Mattie?"

Standing with her arms folded and her lips pursed, Mattie looked at Lena from head to toe. An amateur would think that she was trying to intimidate her, but Lena knew better. It was the look of Mattie trying to think of what to say next: the look that resulted from the frantic search for a comeback for the humiliation she'd just endured. Lena knew the look well. It was the look of defeat. She almost wanted to raise her arms above her head and give Mattie the standing eight-count. It was a TKO and Lena was still the undisputed champion. She may have taught Mattie a lot about the art of cynicism. But any artist knew that you never revealed to your students *all* of your tricks.

"What else needs to be done?" Mattie asked.

How sweet it is! Lena smiled at her own thoughts. She'd definitely give Mattie an "A" for effort, but she'd have to get up pretty early in the morning to outwit her.

"The macaroni and cheese I prepared is in the refrigerator. It can go in the oven with the turkey now," Lena told her. "By the time the turkey and macaroni get done, everything else will be ready too."

"You heard from the children today?" Mattie asked as she tied her apron around her and got ready for duty.

Another war had come to an end without bloodshed.

For most of his adult life, Luther Baldwin had played out the same routine. He would wake up every morning at seven and spend about an hour in his home office with God. This time of meditation included the reading of several passages of scripture, followed by a quiet moment of prayer. Next to his office was a smaller bedroom that he had converted into a personal gym. A ten-year-old treadmill that sat in the corner was the most used piece of equipment that the room housed. There was a bicycle and some free weights, but the most use they got was when one of his three sons would come to town for a visit. For Pastor Baldwin, it was all about strengthening the heart, so he walked religiously for thirty minutes every morning. When he really felt energized, he'd double that time and even throw in a little jogging.

The workout was always followed by a nice long shower that did more than clean his body: It also helped to clear his mind for the day ahead. Pastor Baldwin's doctor said that his fifty-year exercise regimen was what gave his seventy-year-old body the heart of a man twenty years younger. But Luther couldn't take all the credit for his health consciousness. Much of his daily routine was a carbon copy of what he'd been exposed to as a child. Pastor Baldwin remembered his early years of living in an oppressed black neighborhood in South Carolina. Every child of every Negro was as poor as the next, so most of the children had no idea that they were poverty-stricken.

Roscoe Baldwin was Luther's father's name. He worked from sun up to sun down, repairing and shining shoes. But before he went to work in the mornings and before his children were sent to school, he'd gather the family together to pray and read scriptures. Then, before Luther and his siblings would leave for the mile-long walk to the school for colored children, he'd hear his father lifting the homemade weights he'd built out of iron rods and sand bags. Roscoe Baldwin taught his boys that a man was supposed to be strong so that he could provide for his family.

"A weak Negro is a dead Negro."

Luther couldn't begin to count the number of times he'd heard his father say those words. In other words, if you were born black, nobody was going to give you anything. If you were going to survive, you were going to have to be strong enough to work for a living. By the time he was fourteen, he and his brothers were delivering newspapers and grocery shopping for the elderly, doing anything to help bring money into the home. It wasn't optional. Roscoe needed his boys to understand that life as a black man trying to make it in a white man's world wasn't going to be easy.

From the time he was sixteen, the neighbors began calling Luther "preacher boy." They'd say things like, "Roscoe, that's a lil' preacher boy you got there. You know that, don't you?" Luther would smile, but he knew that preaching wasn't the future that his daddy was grooming any of his sons for.

"Preaching is good for saving souls, but it ain't gonna put food in my future grandchildren's mouths," Roscoe would say. He needed Luther to understand that knowing how to build the church was what would earn him a good living, not standing on the inside of it.

Pastor Baldwin listened to his father back then, but in his heart he already knew that he was destined to preach. On every job he ever took, Luther was a hard worker just like his father had taught him to be. But delivering the Good News of Jesus Christ was his true calling and when his daddy heard him preach his first sermon at the age of twenty-two, even Roscoe had to agree. And through the years, God had never let Luther down. His children never went hungry and his wife . . .

Pastor Baldwin stopped in mid thought. Every morning since Clara had died, he'd awakened with her on his mind. The empty bed reminded him of how much he missed her sleeping beside him. When he sat down to eat breakfast, he was reminded of how much he missed her cooking. When he ironed his clothes, he was reminded of how much he missed her humming as she pressed his garments as well as any dry cleaners could.

The day was almost gone and until now, he'd not thought of Clara. Errands and the business at the church had kept him occupied for most of the day. He'd thought to call Lena Dixon about her friend's Bible. He thought to call Lena again to accept her dinner invitation. He even considered calling Lena for a third time to ask if there was something she wanted him to bring. But not once today had he thought of Clara. Not once.

CHAPTER 13

"So, what are you saying, Sherry? Are you saying that things are better with you and Rick or not?"

Saturday had brought with it cloudy skies, but Jessica and Sherry took advantage of the offer from Lena and Mattie to keep the children for the afternoon while they went shopping. Jessica fiddled with the diamond tennis bracelet that Greg had presented to her on her twenty-seventh birthday a few days ago. He'd surprised her with the beautiful piece of jewelry as they sat for dinner at the same restaurant where he'd taken her every year for her birthday since they'd met. Their first date was to celebrate her twenty-second birthday and Jessica remembered being captivated, not only by the attention of her debonair date for the evening, but also by The Sax, an upscale restaurant on Virginia Avenue that was already gaining popularity in the six months since the doors had opened for business. Over the past few years, the delicious cuisine and the red carpet service had made it a definite hot spot for those fortunate enough to be able to handle the pricey menu. Jessica loved the intimate atmosphere and looked forward to spending her special day there with Greg each year.

Sherry broke Jessica's brief stroll down memory lane as she parked her car in the lot of PG Plaza in Hyattsville, Maryland. "Honestly, Jess, I don't know if things are really better or not. What Ricky and I are doing, basically, is avoiding the issue totally now."

"But I thought you said the two of you had recaptured the magic. I thought you said you've been having some steamy nights."

"We have. But all that means is that we've resumed the physical intimacy in our relationship."

Jessica shrugged. "That's good, though, right? I mean, it's a start."

"If we were two high school or college kids in an uncommitted, sexually-based relationship, maybe it would be a start. That's not us. Our relationship has never been based on sex. I mean, don't get me wrong. That's always been a great part of our relationship, but Ricky and I have a very serious issue that we still haven't settled, Jessie. So, when you think of it in that manner, I'd have to say that our lovemaking isn't a start at all. Frankly, we're going about this in a very backward manner. We should have started the mending process in the dining room. Maybe talked this out over dinner, come to some kind of mutual agreement and *then* took it to the bedroom. Instead, we started in the bedroom . . . well, technically in his office on the desk. . . ."

Jessica held up her hand. "TMI!" she announced.

"The point is that the problem isn't just going to disappear."

"Why not?" Jessica tried to control the annoyance in her voice, but couldn't. "If you pray and ask God to solve a problem in your life, who's to say that He doesn't do so by just dissolving it completely with no residue to sort through? Why can't it just disappear? Maybe it can if you'll just let it go, Sherry. Just let it go and stop rebuilding something that God has torn down. It's like you're just not going to be satisfied until you and Rick are fighting again."

Sherry shut off the car's engine and then turned to face her friend. Jessica could feel the anger from Sherry's eyes burning into the side of her face as she kept her eyes fixed on the car parked directly in front of them.

"You think I *want* to be right about this? You think I *like* having strife in my marriage? How could you even shape your mouth to say something like that? If I thought it was truly all resolved, I would be the first one kicking my heels up and shouting for joy. I'm the one who lives in my house, Jessie, not you. All you see is that the tension has eased between me and Ricky. That's all you see. You don't see us when we're behind closed doors. You don't see the struggle in his face as he tries not to once again bring up the subject of another kid. You don't see the look in his eyes when the simplest commercial comes on that shows images of fathers with their kids.

"Don't try and make it seem like this is something I'm just conjuring up in my mind, because it's not. If I say the problem hasn't disappeared, it's not because I don't want it to; it's because I live it every day and I know it hasn't. Being married to someone like Greg, I can understand how you might not be able to fathom that most men aren't as open as yours. I can rejoice with you that you're blessed with a husband that likes to talk about everything with you. Can you at least *pretend* to sympathize with me that I don't?"

Sherry snatched her purse from the floor beside her feet and got out of the car, slamming the door behind her. Jessica watched her take quick steps, with hips swaying, towards the mall entrance. She reached for the door handle to let herself out of the car and released a sigh that was filled with regret. Jessica wished she could withdraw her last remarks, but she'd let her own anxieties get the best of her. The week-ago image of Greg's arms wrapped around Sherry, comforting her following services last Sunday were still imbedded in Jessica's mind and hearing Sherry compare their husbands once again reminded her of how close her husband and best friend were.

After Greg and Derrick had spoken at length on Monday, all seemed to return to normal. Derrick and Sherry were talking again, even laughing together when they came over for dinner two nights later. To hear Sherry still speaking words that proved that all wasn't well wasn't the flow of conversation that Jessica had prepared for. The sounds of her heels clicking against the paved parking lot resonated as Jessica ran to catch up with Sherry, who had already walked through the mall doors and headed towards their favorite bookstore.

Karibu was a store that the women frequented when they needed a good read. Whether they had a thirst for the work of African–American bestsellers or the desire to give new authors a try, the store never disappointed. With little or no visible effort, Sherry moved at a speed that gave validity to the truth that "full-figured" didn't necessarily mean "out-of-shape." She had already made it inside the bookstore and was reading the back cover of Pearl Cleage's latest novel when Jessica finally caught up to her.

Stopping momentarily in the entranceway of Karibu to catch her breath, Jessica returned the greeting of the store manager and then found Sherry nestled between two rows of bookshelves. Jessica searched for words that would bring relief to the sore spot she'd created just minutes earlier. There seemed to be no acceptable excuse for her actions, so instead of trying to fabricate one, Jessica tried to apologize it away.

"I'm sorry," she whispered.

"As well you should be." Sherry tucked the book under her arm and without making eye contact with Jessica, walked to the opposite side of the shelf.

Jessica followed. "Sherry," she called after her.

Though she was a few inches taller than her friend, Jessica winced and took a step backward when Sherry, without warning, spun around and faced her. Jessica had seen that look on Sherry's face before, but had never experienced it directed at her. The last time she'd witnessed that look was when Lena and Sherry had it out at the kitchen table during the baby discussion. Unlike her mother-in-law, Jessica wasn't about to challenge Sherry. As an alternative, she sealed her lips and awaited the verbal punishment that she knew was coming.

"You know what, Jessie. I thought you were the one woman who I might be able to talk to who wouldn't get judgmental on me. I thought that if there was any one female that would just allow me to vent and even possibly feel where I was coming from, it would be you. Guess I called that one wrong, huh?"

"Sherry . . ."

"When your pregnancy got hard, who was the one that listened to you, Jess? I listened to you because I knew what it was like. I'd been there. I even listened to you vent when you were pissed off at Greg for not understanding the changes in your body and your hormones."

"Sherry . . ."

"When the physical intimacy in you and Greg's relationship resumed after your patient, little Travis died, did that solve everything? Did that make the root of your problems go away? No, it didn't. So why are you trying to make me believe that I'm making a mountain out of a molehill when I say it hasn't made my problems disappear? I stood up to Greg for you. Greg and I had been close friends forever, but I had to be able to see beyond that and not be partial because you were my friend, too, and you needed me to be unbiased. Do you know how difficult it was for me? The only man who knows more about me than Greg is Ricky. That's how close we are, Jessie. So why can't you be that kind of friend to me? Why can't you see my predicament through my eyes?"

"For that very reason, Sherry!" The truth was finally setting itself free. Jessica's voice was in a whisper, but in the fairly small bookstore, the women had already begun attracting the attention of nearby shoppers.

"What reason?"

"Because Rick is the *only* man who knows you better than my husband does. Do you know how hard that is for me to hear? Sherry, you and Greg are very close. Sometimes, too close."

"What?"

"I'm sorry, but you wanted to know why I feel like I do and this is it. Besides Rick, my husband is the closest male friend that you have. Sometimes I feel like he's the closest male friend you have *including* Rick. I mean, I know that Rick is your husband and you love him, but sometimes I think that when it boils right down to it, Greg is the one who you consider to be closer when it comes to friends. You seem to be able to talk to him easier than you can your own husband and something about that doesn't always sit well with me. I'm sorry, but that's the way I feel."

Tears welled in Jessica's eyes as she spoke and the momentary silence that followed her discharge of emotional words was ghost-like. The handful of patrons that was in the store continued moving about, purposefully avoiding the aisle where the two women had failed in their attempt to keep their conversation private. The loud laughter that broke their silence brought Jessica's eyes from the floor where they'd been fixed since the end of her monologue. She didn't speak a word, but her eyes said, "What's so funny?"

"You're jealous?" Sherry's question was more of a statement, but she stood back in wait of an answer.

"No, I'm not."

"Yes, you are. I can't even believe this, Jessie. After all these years that you've known me and my relationship with Greg and I'm just finding out that you're jealous?"

"I'm not jealous. I'm just . . ." Jessica dropped her eyes back to the floor. "Well, maybe I am a little, I don't know."

Sherry placed the book she'd been holding in a spot on the shelf where it didn't belong and pulled Jessica's arm, leading her back into the traffic of mall shoppers. Sherry sat on a bench not far from the store's entrance and Jessica followed her lead with hesitation. It was Sherry's turn to search for the right words to say and Jessica could see her mental struggle. There were no remnants left of the laughter she'd earlier released.

"Do you honestly think I want Greg?"

"I . . ."

"Be real with me, Jessie. Is that what this is about? You think I want my marriage to fall apart so that I can get with Greg?"

"No. I don't think that, Sherry. I don't think you want your marriage to end. It's just that sometimes I think . . ."

"Go on," Sherry urged as she noted Jessica's voice drifting.

"Sometimes I think that you wish you'd chosen Greg instead of Rick. I mean, sometimes I wonder if you had it to do all over again, if you'd still choose Rick over Greg."

Sherry was rendered speechless. Her mouth opened, but no sound came out to accompany the movement.

"It's not just you, Sherry," Jessica quickly added. "Sometimes when I see you and Greg together, I wonder what's going through his mind too. I fully trust my husband, but the two of you are so tight-knit and sometimes I just wonder."

"I can't even believe I'm hearing this from you." Sherry had finally found her voice. "Girl, where is this coming from? Everybody who has ever come in contact with Greg knows how he feels about you. All he talks about is his Grace. How could you think he could even remotely wish to be with me? He married you because he loves you. I married Ricky because I love him. I admit that sometimes I don't like him, but there's never a time that I don't love him."

"I know, Sherry, and I know I may sound melodramatic right now, but put yourself in my place for a second. Lately, you're always harping on how great Greg is and complaining about how unreasonable Rick is. And

159

you keep comparing the two and saying that you wish your husband was more like my husband. Couple that with the fact that you guys are so devoted in your friendship and that you've been confiding a lot more in him lately and I guess it all added up to me letting it get the best of me. You're so tight, it almost seems unnatural. And look at you. It would be understandable if Greg were attracted. You're confident, you never wear anything twice, your hair is always flawless and your face belongs on the cover of a magazine."

Jessica's words brought the smile that tugged at Sherry's lips into fullness. The irritation and disbelief that previously engulfed her face had now been replaced. Now, she seemed not only astounded by the confession, but even a bit pleased. Placing one arm around Jessica's shoulders, Sherry delivered a brief, tight squeeze.

"Girl, you're a hot mess," she said through a halfhearted laugh. "As much as I probably should be, I can't even be mad at you after hearing you describe me like that." Sherry's face turned serious. "Jessie, I'll admit any day of the week that I love Greg. I always have and I always will, but not like that. I mean, yeah, sometimes I wish Ricky would look at his best friend and take a lesson, but very little about my husband has changed since I met him in middle school. He's always been hotheaded and strong willed. But he's also always been funny and loving. I guess when it comes right down to it, that crazy combination is what I fell in love with. I grew up in a home where, for as long as I can remember, all we ever did was church. I knew God was gonna net him one day, but even before Ricky established a personal relationship with God, he always brought excitement to my routine life. Maybe it was his rough edges that attracted me to him to begin with."

"See, that's what I mean. That's the kind of stuff I never hear you say; at least, not lately. Why is that?"

"Because he makes me sick, that's why. This whole baby thing that's still looming is getting on my nerves." Sherry repositioned herself on the bench so that she almost faced Jessica. "Doesn't Greg make you sick sometimes? Aren't there moments when you just want to strangle him?"

Noting Jessica's clueless, almost apologetic expression, Sherry turned her eyes up to the ceiling and shook her head.

"Of course, he doesn't. What was I thinking?" she said with a short laugh. "Greg is perfect. I'll bet all the things you used to hope your husband would be like when you were a teenager, Greg embodies."

"Actually, believe it or not, he doesn't."

"Really?"

Jessica nodded. "I'm a fairly tall girl, Sherry. I had always said that I would never marry a man under six-three. I always wanted to have to look up to him, even when I wore heels. Well, Greg is six-one. I wear three-inch heels on most days and that puts me right at six feet, almost eye-to-eye with him."

Sherry sat in silence and waited for the next item on the list. When nothing more was offered, she looked towards Jessica with a grimace. "That's it? That's all you got? Girl, please!" Smacking her lips, she gave her hand a dramatic wave. "I thought you were really gonna lay a bomb on me and all you got is that Greg is height challenged by two measly inches? If that's his biggest flaw, then you need to be shouting every Sunday, girl. No wonder you think everybody wants your man."

"I don't think that everybody wants Greg."

"No, not everybody," Sherry said. "Just me, right? Jessie, if you have a problem with me confiding in Greg, just say so."

Jessica used her right hand to smooth the short hairs behind her ear. She knew that her silence wasn't sending the best message, but Sherry's challenge had caused her to think. Did she have a problem with it? Sherry was her best friend and in her heart of hearts, she knew that she wouldn't try and move in on her husband. Greg and Sherry's closeness had never affected her as much as it did right now. All those years that Evelyn had chased Greg never even remotely bothered Jessica. She knew the unrelenting, devious woman posed no genuine threat. Even though she was physically attractive, her spiritual disorder and her aggressive personality were enough to repel Greg. Sherry was different. The basis for a relationship had been established years ago. She and Greg were friends. Good friends. Still, Jessica felt stupid for ever having considered the possibility.

"No, I don't have a problem with it."

"You sure?"

"Yeah." Jessica smiled, but simultaneously searched her soul, hoping she was being totally truthful. "Yeah, I'm sure."

CHAPTER 14

Greg stood over the sink, washing away the residue of his latest successful surgery. It had taken all of four and a half hours to do the work necessary to mend the fractured skull of an eighty-year-old slip-and-fall victim of a local nursing home. Days like this made him think of his mother. Lena was still in good health and got around better than most women her age, but the aging process was inevitable. Sooner or later, she would possibly need the assistance of others. But Greg had long ago made a promise to himself and to God that he'd never allow her to be placed in the typical nursing facility. He'd seen too many "accidents" and had doctored too many victimized patients to trust the overcrowded facilities staffed with underpaid workers with the care of the woman who had sacrificed so much for him.

"Great job, Dr. Dixon."

Greg barely heard the accolade that his

favorite O.R. assistant, Kelly, gave as she walked past him towards the exit door. He nodded in her direction, but his previous thought process was never fully broken.

When Greg's father passed away nearly thirty years ago, Lena was still in her early thirties. In her younger years, she was very eye-catching and had aged quite gracefully, still showing clear signs of attractiveness. Greg had often wondered why his mother had never remarried. He'd asked once, but never got a clear answer that day as he sat at the kitchen table completing the last of his tenth-grade homework assignments.

"It would take a woman to understand," Lena had said back then. "Men don't understand this kind of thing, but women like me and Coretta Scott King, now, we understand."

It was a reply that didn't answer his question, but it was all the explanation that Lena offered and Greg didn't press for more. Over the years, he'd drawn his own conclusion. His mother was still in love with his father. Phillip Gregory Dixon had made an impact on her heart that even the grave wasn't strong enough to rob her of. In hindsight, Greg was glad that she'd never married again. Her singleness had given him the opportunity to try to repay Lena for all of the sacrifices that she'd made as a single parent raising a son. Greg remembered her struggles and the days she went without so that he could have the things he needed. For the rest of her life, he'd do whatever it took to make sure she never went lacking again.

"I hear you and the Man upstairs saved another one." Dr. Grant patted Greg on the shoulder as he exited the operating room and started down the hall.

The Man upstairs. Greg chuckled at the reference to God that he hadn't heard in quite some time. "Yeah, we make a pretty good team."

Their conversation was brief and the two men parted ways when Dr. Grant stepped into an open elevator. For Greg, walking into the waiting room and giving good news to disconcerted family members was one of the best parts of being a surgeon. It came second to the instant a successful operation ended. Each of these moments gave him immeasurable relief and a new reason to rejoice. For his latest patient, however, the moment was bittersweet. The only person waiting in the room was one of the male nurses from the home where the elderly woman was a resident. She'd outlived two husbands and two of her six children. The surviving children were either too busy or didn't care enough to come to the hospital to see about their mother.

When Greg delivered the good news to the nurse, he flamboyantly flung his arms up in the air and said, "Good! Glad that's over. Now, I can get on back to the home in time to see my show. Honey, if that old lady had a made me miss *Oprah,* it was gonna be on up in here!"

Back in his office, Greg attempted to drop the envelopes he'd taken from his mail slot onto the corner of his desk. Missing the target, the papers fell to the floor and scattered. Greg sighed in frustration before bending to pick them up. Then he removed his white jacket and slung it over the back of the couch that sat in the corner. His frustrations had nothing to do with the letters or the fact that he dropped them. His disturbance was with the man in the blue uniform that had just left the waiting room and all the others like him who halfheartedly cared for those who couldn't care for themselves.

There was no way he'd hand his mother over to strangers. Greg knew that all nursing home staff members weren't as incompetent as the one whom he'd had the dishonor of speaking with, but it wasn't a chance he'd be willing to take. Not with Lena Dixon. If the time ever came that his mother needed around-the-clock attention, he'd quit his job if he had to, to be sure that she got the care that she deserved. When he thought of how she'd just danced in church on yesterday morning and how happy and lively she was in the afternoon as their family and Pastor Baldwin shared dinner at the dining room table, the day when Lena would need home care seemed light-years away. But Greg had always been a planner. Things that happened in the normal cycle of life didn't often sneak up on him.

He had started saving money for his high school class ring in the tenth grade when he and Derrick began a paper route in their neighborhood. Five years before he planned to marry, he started saving for his honeymoon. That day came three years earlier than he'd expected, but he'd still saved enough to give his Grace the retreat of a lifetime. Julian wasn't even two years old, but Greg had already begun making financial plans for his college education. The bracelet that he'd given Jessica on her twenty-seventh birthday had been paid in full and tucked away six months earlier. If the time came and his mother grew too old and feeble to maintain her independence, Greg would be prepared for that as well. As the closest male relative in her life, it was his duty and he would count it an honor to carry it out.

Forcing himself to think more pleasant thoughts, Greg pulled his chart in front of him and began reviewing the list of patients that he'd already seen today and those that were yet to be checked on. Over the past few days, he'd had the pleasure of being able to delete names from the list that had been given to him when he returned to Robinson Memorial. Several of the members of the church pileup had been released, including Erika. She'd been so excited about meeting him that her mother had gotten one of the photos Erika and Greg had taken together blown up to poster size and Greg had autographed it upon the teenager's release. Fortunately for Erika, she'd also been given clearance to attend her high school graduation.

Thinking about recovering patients took Greg's mind back to New York. On many occasions, he'd been tempted to pick up the phone and call to check on Sergeant McDonald. Upon ending his short tenure at Lenox Hill Hospital, he'd asked LaRon to give him a call if there were any major setbacks with the policeman or any of the other patients that had been placed under his care. Greg had heard nothing and in this case, no news was good news. Realizing his thought process, Greg almost laughed out loud. For the weeks he'd worked at Lenox Hill, he wanted nothing more than to be back at Robinson Memorial. Now that he was back on home court, he fought to keep his thoughts away from the hospital where he'd once felt held hostage.

Perhaps it was the still strained relationship that he felt with Doctors Neal, Lowe and Pridgen that made him have a strange longing for the halls of Lenox Hill. Greg wasn't sure, but the New York hospital and its warmth and hospitality seemed to beckon to him. Perhaps, he'd take a trip next weekend just to check on the friends he'd made while there.

Dr. Grant yawned as he entered his private office and sat in the chair behind his desk. Over the past couple of weeks, he'd felt more relaxed than he had in the month that his star physician was away. For some reason, just to have Greg's presence in the hospital lifted a weight from his shoulders. As much as Dr. Grant respected Greg on both a personal and professional level, he knew it was much more than those qualities that set him apart from the others. It was his strong faith and belief system. Admittedly, when Greg first began his residency at Robinson Memorial, Dr. Grant had been wary of his insistence to pray before entering the operating room. One prayer per day seemed like enough, but Greg would pray before every single surgical procedure. Not aloud or to make a scene, but in the privacy of his car, his office, en route to the O.R., or sometimes just within his heart.

There had been a couple of times when Dr. Grant had walked in on him in prayer in his office. Respectfully, he'd backed out without disturbing him. It had seemed fanatical back then, but Greg's phenomenal success rate in the operating room had even prompted Dr. Grant to pray a time or two when the heat was on him when he was the one whom someone's life depended on.

Simon Grant wasn't ignorant of the fact that the others on his team of neurological specialists took issue with Greg's success. They respected the younger doctor for his skillful work, but there were still some jealousies that they couldn't seem to shake. Dr. Grant hadn't had to address the issue yet. Greg was pretty good at handling himself and the other doctors were experts at keeping it professional, despite their personal issues. Simon tried to be mindful of the insecurities of the others. Since his last talk with them, he'd been careful not to say things that might make them feel inferior to the doctor who was far less experienced yet far more gifted and qualified than they.

Dr. Grant's eyes fell on the large calendar that lay flat across the top of his desk. "Glad to have you back home, Dixon," he said, tapping his pencil eraser on a date two weeks in the future.

He never would have felt comfortable taking his scheduled weeklong vacation to Cozumel if Greg hadn't been back on staff. Now, he could take his wife and daughters and feel confident that business would be well taken care of at Robinson Memorial. The ringing of his telephone snatched Simon's thoughts away from the sandy beaches of Mexico.

"Dr. Grant speaking."

"Hey, Simon. How are you, old buddy?"

The familiar friendly voice on the other end didn't bring the smile to Dr. Grant's face that it normally would. As cheerful as his caller's tone sounded, Dr. Grant immediately knew that something was going to be said that he didn't want to hear.

"Listen," the voice continued. "I don't

have much time to talk, but I just wanted to tell you this. I didn't want you to hear about it from anybody else but me."

CHAPTER 15

"Have you given me the whole story? I can become your worst enemy if I'm embarrassed in the courtroom because the prosecutor uncovers something that you didn't tell me yourself."

Derrick was never concerned with losing clients. He was the best at what he did. He knew it, and sooner or later those people who thought they could hire better representation knew it too. Seventeen-year-old Perry Wilson no longer displayed his previous rude behavior. There was no chewing gum in his mouth and his shirt was tucked in pants that had been professionally pressed, most likely by the cleaners that his father owned. The teenager's eyes stared at his own knees as he nodded.

"Perry, look at me."

At the sound of Derrick's commanding order, George Wilson sat forward in his seat. But before he could speak, he looked into the unquestionable silent dare that Derrick's eyes delivered. George Wilson wasn't accustomed to being ordered around and biding his tongue, nor was he familiar with needing the help of others. But today, his worldly wealth meant nothing. Swallowing what would have been defensive words he would have regretted, George settled back in his seat and watched his son continue to stare into his lap. Derrick's eyes returned to their original target.

"Perry," he repeated, this time slower and with more authority. "Look at me."

Little by little, the boy's eyes lifted until they looked into Derrick's burning stare.

"Have you told me everything?"

He nodded again.

With the absence of Perry's fragile-hearted mother, Derrick felt little need to withhold his thoughts. "You've committed the crime of a grown man, Perry, so act like one. Grown men don't mumble and they don't answer questions like a ten-year-old kid. Talk to me. Have you told me everything?"

"Yes."

"Tell me again."

"For the love of God, man!" Mr. Wilson jumped from his chair and delivered a single pound of his fist on Derrick's desk. "No disrespect intended, but it took him half an hour to tell you the story the first time. Weren't you taking notes? Why do we have to go through this again? I thought you were good at what you do. If you were good at what you do, why does he have to tell this story again?"

Derrick stood too. Only he was about five inches taller than the well-to-do business man and the look on his face was even more intimidating than the one George exhibited.

"He's not having to tell this story because I, as his lawyer, am not good at what I do, Mr. Wilson. He's having to tell this story because *you,* as his father, weren't good at what *you* were supposed to do. Now sit down."

The pronounced Adam's apple that bobbed in his neck signified that George Wilson had once again experienced the displeasure of swallowing his own bitter pride. Following Mr. Wilson's lead, Derrick also returned to his chair.

"Now, Perry. Start from the beginning."

The teenager's eyes pleaded with his father. George looked at his son, but remained silent. With no hope for another attempt to help him, Perry's eyes returned to their downward stare before he finally spoke.

"It's like I said before. I went to the store

to cash in a watch I found and that lady . . . she didn't want to give me the money it was worth. She was trying to cheat me out of my money . . . like she was trying to steal the watch from me by not giving me nearly what it was worth. I pulled out the gun just to scare her. I didn't mean to shoot her for real. She reached and tried to snatch the gun out of my hand and that's when it went off. I ain't even know it was loaded or nothing, man. I was just trying to scare her. She's the one who made it go off like that."

"Where did you find the watch?"

Perry shrugged.

"Where did you find the watch, Perry?" Derrick insisted.

"At the dry cleaners one day when I was there chillin'. I think it might have fallen out of somebody's clothes . . . like they forgot to clean out their pockets before they brought the clothes in to be cleaned."

"What made you think the watch was worth any more than what Ms. Owens told you?"

Perry shrugged again.

"Perry . . ."

"I told him." Mr. Wilson jumped in. "I guess I should say I made the mistake of telling him."

Derrick looked towards him with inquisitive eyes, prompting Mr. Wilson to continue.

"It was a women's Movado watch, Mr. Madison. Those watches sell upwards of eight hundred dollars. I buy expensive jewelry. I know the quality and cost of Movado."

"So, you were aware that he was going to pawn the watch that didn't belong to him?"

"Of course not!" Mr. Wilson sounded insulted.

"You told him the value of the watch. That means you knew he had the watch. I'll ask again, Mr. Wilson. Did you know he was taking it to the shop to sell?"

In an instant, George was back on his feet. He uttered an expletive and delivered another fierce pound to Derrick's desk.

"What are you doing, Mr. Madison? You are supposed to be defending my boy and you're acting like the prosecutor. Why are you questioning me? I'm not paying you to question me! We've been sitting in this office for over an hour and haven't done anything except be questioned over and over again by you. Now, either you defend him or you don't!"

"Fine," Derrick said as he closed the file in front of him and stood. "You can both leave now."

"What?"

"Get out of my office." Derrick stood and pointed towards the door as he gave the order.

As though a sudden drop in temperature had frozen him solid, Mr. Wilson stood motionless, staring in disbelief at the man he'd paid a retainer fee just an hour earlier. For the first time, Perry appeared to be near tears. He covered his face with his hands and then quickly removed them and released a puff of air from his mouth. Derrick looked down at the boy and then back at his father.

"Look." Mr. Wilson's tone was softer now. "When Perry brought the watch to my attention, I looked at it and told him then that it was a costly timepiece. I tucked it away in a drawer behind the counter and intended to come up with a way to find out who it belonged to. He apparently went in the drawer and removed it later after I left. I didn't know he'd took it and I didn't know he'd tried to pawn it until it was too late."

Without inviting George to do the same, Derrick sat back in the seat he'd just risen from and stared across the desk at Perry. This time, George followed Derrick's lead, seeming relieved that he'd gotten another chance.

"So, you retrieved the watch from the

drawer and took it to the store to pawn. Is that what happened?"

Perry nodded.

"Perry?"

"Yes. That's what happened."

"Why were you trying to pawn it?"

"For cash."

"Why did you need the cash?"

Perry shrugged and then said, "Just to have some money."

Derrick brought his palms together and then placed his hands in front of his face, almost as if he were preparing to grace an invisible plate of food. For several moments silence encircled them. It was Derrick who spoke first.

"Your father is a successful proprietor, Perry. Why would you need to pawn a watch in order to have money? I'm asking Perry," Derrick added when George opened his mouth to answer.

Perry's only response was the shrug of his shoulders that Derrick still hadn't completely broken him of.

"Are you on drugs, Perry?" Derrick asked.

George fidgeted in his chair and then crossed his arms in silent protest, but he held his tongue.

"No," Perry answered.

"Are you telling me the truth?"

"Yes."

"Have you ever used illegal drugs?"

"I smoked a joint once, but that's it. That was when I was in the ninth grade."

"Have you ever been in any trouble in school? I don't see any references in your records to any suspensions or major infractions."

"I've never been suspended, but I've been in trouble a time or two."

"For?"

"Being late for class, mostly," Perry said. "I cheated on a test once and got sent to the principal's office and once, I got in trouble for fighting this other dude for talking about my mama."

Derrick kept flipping through more pages of the file in front of him. He wanted to reprimand the boy for fighting for such a foolish reason, but he remembered doing the same thing as a teenager. His mother was where he drew the line too. "You make decent grades," he observed.

"I do aiight." Another shrug accompanied Perry's response. "B's mostly. But I get some C's too."

Derrick made a thoughtful-sounding grunt and scanned a few more of the pages in front of him before closing the folder and reaching for a pen to scribble a note on the back of a business card he retrieved from the holder in front of him. It only took a split second for him to finish the short note and as soon as he placed the pen on the desk, Derrick deliberately covered the note as he rested his arms on the desk in front of him.

"I think I've taken up enough of your time today," he said, directing his words at Mr. Wilson. "I will need a few days to look over this information and come up with a creditable defense to take into court."

"So, it's official?" George Wilson's face brightened just a bit at his inquiry. "You are definitely taking this case?"

"Yes."

"What are the chances that you'll be able to get him out of serving actual jail time? At least if we can avoid him being locked up, that will work in my favor and I still have a chance of salvaging some of the dignity of my family name."

Derrick glared at George. The man may have had more money than him, but he was older, shorter and weighed less. Derrick knew he could take him on and win easily. At the moment, he wanted nothing more than to grab him by his silk tie and tighten the flawless knot until it made his eyes bulge. Listening to him was sickening. After a moment to reevaluate his initial temptation, Derrick chose his words with caution while he stood to walk his clients to the door.

"Even with the magnitude of this crime, I think avoiding jail time is an attainable possibility for Perry. However, much of that depends upon him and his testimony. As I indicated earlier, if I have the whole truth, I can find ways to make this work in *his* favor."

Derrick's intentional emphasis on the word "his" seemed to escape George. Derrick's thoughts raced as he watched the man prepare to leave at a speed that suggested he thought his son's new attorney would change his mind if they didn't depart soon. At the door, Derrick extended his hand to shake that of Mr. Wilson's and then waited for him to step through the doorway. Then, turning his back to him and facing Perry, Derrick took his hand as well. He shook it a bit longer and forced eye contact.

"We have to trust each other if there is any possibility of us winning this case, Perry. Do you understand that? You'll have to trust that I will have nothing but your best interest in mind and I'll have to be able to trust that you will do the right thing leading up to your case. Don't defy any of the stipulations surrounding your bond and follow *whatever* instructions that I give you. Understand?"

Perry looked at his hand and then balled it into a fist as Derrick released his hold. He paused, not immediately knowing how to respond to Derrick's words and actions. Understanding the boy's hesitation, his attorney gave him a slight nod.

"Do you hear Mr. Madison talking to you, Perry?" George Wilson asked, stepping from behind Derrick, where his view had been obstructed.

Perry shoved his hands in his pockets and nodded, never taking his eyes off Derrick. "Yeah," he said. "Yeah, I understand."

CHAPTER 16

Though they often enjoyed flirting with one another over the telephone, actual phone sex was one of the few things that Greg and Jessica hadn't experimented with as a part of their intimate relationship. Because they strove to keep an open and honest marriage in which they shared just about every detail of each other's life, the topic was one that they'd talked about, thought about and laughed about, but it was one they hadn't carried out. Today's telephone tease fest, however, had come dangerously close.

It wasn't uncommon for Jessica to give Greg a call after she'd gotten off from work, picked up Julian and made it home safely. Generally, their conversation ended with her finding out if he wanted anything in particular for dinner and today's telephone conversation had started out no differently. It was when she mentioned dessert that Greg's mind took a turn and headed down a path that his wife had unknowingly carved.

"I was talking about the kind of dessert that has to be purchased." Jessica blushed and giggled in response to the naughty insinuation Greg had just made.

Over the past fifteen minutes, the temperature in his office had seemed to increase in five-minute intervals. The warmth had earlier prompted him to remove his white medical jacket. Now, he was tugging at his collar, which felt as if it were tightening around his neck.

"Oh, it's like that now? I got to pay for it?"

Jessica decided that it would be more fun to join in than to fight it. "Well, if it makes it any easier, I could deliver. And if I'm not there in thirty minutes or less, it's free."

Greg grunted as he wiped away moisture that had begun surfacing on the top of his shaved head. He stared at the lock on the door that separated his office from the business of the sick and the sicker. When Jessica played along, the telephone game was almost agonizing.

"Grace, there's no way you could get here in thirty minutes during rush hour."

"I know."

Greg had begun viewing a mental picture of his wife . . . all five-feet-nine inches of her. Her legs were two of her best features. The other brothers at church complimented them often, congratulating Greg as if he'd personally designed them. Phrases like, "Nice legs your wife's got there" and "Now that's what I call some pretty legs" were commonly heard, followed by a pat on his shoulder that silently said, "Good job." Fortunately, Greg was not a jealous man. The admiration Jessica got from his friends made him proud.

Two Sundays ago, Jessica fished the car keys from her husband's suit pocket as he spoke with some of the church brothers. As she walked away, one of the brothers remarked, "She should get a trophy." Greg was almost sure that the man wasn't quite looking down far enough to be watching his wife's legs, but he still didn't mind. As a matter of fact, he couldn't have agreed more. She wore the tangerine-colored dress well.

"You want to place an order?" Jessica's voice brought Greg's mind back into his office.

"Huh?"

"An order," she reiterated, "for delivery."

"How about you just talk to me," he suggested. "What's the going rate now? Three ninety-nine a minute?"

There was silence on the other end of the phone. Greg knew that she was slowly processing his proposal.

"Greg, you're at work." Her words spoke caution, but Greg could tell that she was as intrigued as he.

"I can lock the door."

"Are you sure?"

"Yes."

"Hold on. Let me make sure that Julian has enough toys in his crib to keep him busy."

While she placed the phone on hold, Greg tapped his desk impatiently. Placing the phone on the desk, he slid his chair back in preparation of making sure that he wouldn't be disturbed. Just as he stood to lock the door, he noted a white envelope that was lying on the carpet under the desk where his feet had been resting. It must have been among the mail that had fallen from his desk earlier today. He'd failed to see this one when he was gathering the scattered envelopes.

Picking it up, he noted the sender's address and proceeded to tear away the seal. His eyes scanned the wording on the enclosed letter. Greg rubbed his eyes, thinking that perhaps he had read the words wrong and then started back at the top and began to read the letter more slowly. The sensations that his Grace had set into motion just a few seconds earlier were replaced by feelings he couldn't quite distinguish. As soon as he'd completed reading the letter for the third time, Greg's office door opened and Simon Grant stood there, looking about as troubled as Greg had ever seen him. At the same time, he could hear Jessica's voice calling him over and over again from the phone that still lay on his desk. Dr. Grant didn't move. Greg reached for the telephone.

"Grace."

"Hey. Where'd you go?"

"Uh . . . I'm sorry, baby. We'll have to rain check those plans."

He could hear the disappointment in her voice. "Is everything all right?"

"Dr. Grant is here. We need to discuss something. I'll see you at home later, okay? I'll be home by six."

"If you're more than thirty minutes late, do I get it free?"

Greg closed his eyes. The timing couldn't have been worse for the letter, or for Dr. Grant's visit. There was so much more that he wanted to say to Jessica, but couldn't with his mentor making no attempt to give him any privacy.

"The company is running a special," he

said into the telephone. "Whether the delivery is late or not, just because they messed up on carrying out the initial request, when they deliver this evening, you get two for the price of one. So, you go ahead and pick out the areas of the house where you want it . . . delivered."

Jessica giggled. "Is Dr. Grant still standing there?"

She was having too much fun at his expense. "Yes." Greg struggled to keep his professionalism.

"You're *real* good, Dr. Dixon," she said.

"Thanks. I'll call you later." Greg could still hear his wife's laughter as he ended the call and returned the phone to his desk. He understood her amusement at the unexpected turn of events, but the sight of the downcast eyes of Simon Grant wouldn't allow him to share in Jessica's fun.

Greg didn't know whether or not to offer Dr. Grant a seat. More often than not, when he was preparing to lecture one of his staff members, Simon chose to stand and pace, causing the eyes of his listeners to travel back and forth as if they were watching a tennis match. Both men remained quiet. Greg looked back at the one-page letter that he held in his hand. The initial fleeting thought that it was some kind of inside joke was partially erased when his thumb brushed over the stationery's raised seal that proved the letter to be official. Any remnants of doubt were shattered by Dr. Grant's bizarre behavior. He still hadn't moved from his place at the door.

Finally extending the invitation, Greg said, "Please, sit."

It was only then that Simon's eyes shifted from the carpeted floor to Greg. Seconds after their eyes met, Dr. Grant moved his attention to the letter that now rested on Greg's desk. Removing his glasses, he used his thumb and index finger to rub his eyes and then replaced his frames before honoring his finest surgeon's request.

In all the years he'd known Dr. Grant, Greg couldn't remember a time when the two of them hadn't been able to express themselves. Even two years ago, when Simon was completely outraged at Greg for defying his orders not to perform Jessica's surgery, he didn't bite his tongue. Dr. Grant had yelled at him, cursed him and even threatened to relieve him of his duties. The thick cloud of silence that the business of this letter had delivered was a first.

"Would you like something to drink?" Greg gestured towards his personal water cooler, which sat against the wall.

Dr. Grant shook his head. The silence was almost unbearable. Greg would trade this quiet for a good cursing out any day. At least, then, he would know what his mentor was thinking. Not knowing what else to do, Greg pulled his chair away from the desk and sat. Any other time, his phone would ring, his pager would alarm or someone would come knocking on his door. But not today. Today, the only sound that could be heard was the faint ticking of the clock on his wall. It was too much to handle.

"Dr. Grant —"

"Yes or no?" Simon interrupted.

"Pardon me?"

"Your answer to Lenox Hill's offer," Dr. Grant clarified as if there was any real possibility that Greg hadn't understood him the first time. "Yes or no?"

Rubbing his hand over his head, Greg sighed. In a million years, he hadn't expected the letter that held the key to change his whole life. In it, Lenox Hill Hospital was offering him the job that he'd temporarily taken on in the absence of Dr. Armstrong. The perks they'd outlined were more than generous for a man who had less than ten years of surgical experience under his belt.

"You got a copy of the letter?"

Simon shook his head. "Joseph called me," he said, referring to Dr. Armstrong. "He told me that he had turned in his resignation. He's decided to take an enormous pay cut and trade in the hospital for mission work overseas somewhere. Whatever he was exposed to on his extended vacation seemed to change his outlook on life. He wants to 'make a difference in the world' as he put it. Are you going to accept? Be frank with me, Dixon."

A multitude of memories flashed in Greg's head all at once. He remembered the first day he walked through the doors of Robinson Memorial. His mother was so proud of him that she'd sat in her car in the parking lot for hours, waiting for his shift to end so that she could hear the details of his first day as a surgeon on staff at the popular medical facility.

For Greg, Robinson Memorial took some getting used to. He'd received a full academic scholarship that paid his way through college and medical school, but his mother had always taught him the importance of working. She said that college was no reason not to have a job.

"The Bible says that a man who won't work, ain't fit to eat," Lena told him.

For years, as a teenager, Greg believed his

mother had made up the saying and tacked the Bible's authority on it just so he'd see it as the gospel. He was surprised when he challenged her at the age of seventeen. Lena wasn't one to take any talking back from anybody's child, let alone her own, so Greg posed the entrapment in as innocent a package as he could.

"I was trying to tell Rick that the other day," Greg lied, "but I couldn't tell him where in the Bible it was. Where is that in the Bible, Mama?"

"The Apostle Paul said it in Second Thessalonians 3:10," Lena had answered him without a moment of hesitation. And then as if to drive her point in with the force of a broken-bat home run, she went on to quote the entire verse. " 'For even when we were with you, this we commanded you, that if any would not work, neither should he eat.' " Then she smiled, knowing she'd foiled another one of her son's pitifully planned schemes. "Now take that back to *Derrick,* and tell him to read it for himself."

In Greg's opinion, whoever it was that said that single women couldn't successfully raise sons was sorely mistaken. He had two degrees, great memories, strong faith, a loving family life and a promising career that proved differently. True, the years he'd spent serving the patients of Robinson Memorial had been good to him, but with what Lenox Hill Hospital was offering him, Greg could, finally, not only give his Grace and their son the life they deserved, but he could also afford to do some extra-special things for the woman who sacrificed so much of her life so that he could be the man he was today. Lena had earned the right to be taken care of.

Dr. Grant had been waiting patiently for Greg's answer, but now shifted in his seat at the lingering silence. His exaggerated movement regained Greg's attention. He looked across his desk at the man who had treated him with nothing other than respect, even when they were at odds with one another.

"In all honesty, Grant, I can't give you a definite answer right now. I'm sorry. I know that can't be easy for you to hear, any more than it's easy for me to admit. I love Robinson and you know that, but this . . ." Greg paused and looked again at the letter that now lay open on his desk.

Dr. Grant spoke. "I wish I could say that this hospital could offer you the same kind of incentives to stay here as Lenox Hill is offering you to join them, but I already know that's not going to happen. We don't have the same kind of revenue that they have and, quite frankly, if Robinson handed you a package to match what Joseph has offered, I'd be pretty peeved. That would basically match my salary.

"I wouldn't blame you one bit if you went for it, Dixon. Who would? But I will say this: Money isn't everything. Weigh all the issues. You mean something here, Dixon. Robinson Memorial values you. That's why we try to meet as many of your needs as we can. We know how invaluable you are. At Lenox Hill, that may or may not be the case. I mean, it's obvious that they know you're a jewel or else they wouldn't have started the auction off with such a high bid. But that's just math and geography, Dixon."

Dr. Grant stopped long enough to tap his chest several times with the tip of his index finger. He continued, "It's here that I know they can't touch what we have for you . . . what *I* have for you. And sometimes that's where it counts."

Greg watched in silence as Dr. Grant got up from his seat and headed towards the door. His body language spoke words that his mouth never uttered. Downcast eyes and drooped shoulders resulted in an awkward posture that made him appear slightly shorter than his normal six-foot-two stature. Greg knew that his mentor was torn inside and he knew that Dr. Grant meant every word that he had spoken. Still, he had too many things to consider to flatly turn down what might be a once-in-a-lifetime offer.

"I know how close you are to your family, Dixon." Dr. Grant stopped at the door and turned. Pausing, he removed the frames from his face and, from across the room, his eyes met Greg's. "But please let me be second only to your wife to know your final decision. Can you at least promise me that?"

CHAPTER 17

From the kitchen, Jessica listened to nine soft, melodious chimes from the grandfather clock in the living room as she turned off the oven after reheating the food for the third time. Greg loved grilled salmon, but he was running late and she feared that tonight's meal had already lost the flaky freshness that made it so appealing. Since there had been no phone call from him, Jessica assumed that nothing was wrong, but at more than an hour past his normal arrival, she began to worry.

The table had been set for three, with Julian's high chair put right next to the place where Greg would be sitting. But the toddler didn't appreciate the wait and his mounting irritation prompted Jessica to move forward with his feeding. Still, had Greg arrived a half hour ago, he would have had some time with his son. But by eight o'clock, Julian lost the battle to stay awake and Jessica put him to bed for the night. Afterwards, she showered and prepared for Greg's arrival, wearing nothing but a knee-length satin robe. He would be disappointed that the boy had tuckered out before he got a chance to play with him, but Jessica knew of ways to get her husband's mind elsewhere. Generally, Greg's tardiness was a sign that some unfortunate critically injured person had been brought in with little hope of survival and Greg had been assigned to the case. Events like that were out of his control and Jessica had grown accustomed to them. What concerned her was the absence of his normal phone call.

Despite the dismal possibilities of what may have caused his delay, a smile broke through on Jessica's face. She was proud of her husband and the respect his success had earned him. Among the media, former patients and just ordinary people in surrounding communities, he'd built up quite a fan base, though he never admitted it. As Jessica walked back into the living room to peek through the curtains once more, her eyes fell to the hardcover leather-bound book that sat on the coffee table. She flipped through the early pages of the glossy-page, full-color book and stopped on page thirty-eight. With her index finger, she stroked a picture of Greg, dressed in his surgical garb, with a stethoscope hanging around his neck and his surgeon's hat in his hands. Flashing a sexy smile that Lena said his father had given him, Greg looked more like a male model than a neurosurgeon. Last year, he'd been honored with being named one of the most influential black men in Washington, D.C. At the start of this year, the book immortalizing all of the honorees not only hit bookstores all across D.C., but became a hot commodity for the city's females of all ethnic backgrounds. Several of Jessica's students at Trinity College had copies and by special request, Greg had made a visit to the campus the week before Valentine's Day for an autograph session.

Most days, Greg chose to park in the driveway of their home, but Jessica closed the book and stood upon hearing the automated lifting of the garage door. Oddly enough, as she walked towards the side of the house to unlock the door in preparation for her husband's entrance, the doorbell rang. Jessica stood for a moment in silence as she tightened the belt of her robe. She was confused by the echo of Greg's feet approaching the stairs that would bring him to the side door and the simultaneous and continuous ringing radiating from the front door.

Opting to wait for Greg, rather than open the door to the unknown, she accepted a brief kiss and a vase of red roses from her husband. Bringing home flowers of some type wasn't unusual for Greg, but even after almost five years, Jessica never tired of being presented with them.

"Thank you." She flashed him a smile after a quick sniff of the fresh flowers. Before she could tell him that they had unexpected company, he winked, brushed past her and headed towards the front of the house.

"You didn't hear the doorbell?" Greg's tone was somber. He lacked the usual enthusiasm he had when coming home from work — especially after they'd had a conversation like the one they'd shared earlier today.

Jessica nodded and tried not to show her disappointment that he barely noticed her outfit. "I didn't know who it was," she remarked as he reached for the doorknob without even looking through the peephole.

"Come on in, Sherry." Greg stepped aside and Jessica watch in mounting confusion as Sherry entered the house, holding Denise's hand on one side and a small suitcase on the other. Something was definitely wrong.

Jessica looked from her husband to her best friend. "What's going on? What happened?"

Sherry glanced at her daughter and then said, "Let me put Dee-Dee to bed, okay? We'll talk about this later."

"You know where the guest bedroom and bathroom is," Greg said, gesturing towards the upstairs area. "Make yourself at home."

"Thanks."

With mixed emotions, Jessica watched Sherry walk up the stairs with Denise in tow. Neither she nor Greg spoke for several moments. Even after hearing the upstairs bedroom door close, Jessica couldn't seem to take her eyes off the top of the staircase. A variety of scenarios waltzed into her imagination as to the purpose of Sherry's stay at their home, and none of them were pleasant. She pulled her focus away from the shadows that the lighting cast on the upstairs wall only when she felt Greg tug softly at her arm.

"What's going on, Greg?"

"Come with me."

With a sinking feeling that her husband's behavior was doing little to relieve, Jessica held on to Greg's hand and followed his lead into their bedroom, where he closed the door behind them. This strange turn of events caused her nerves to jitter. She placed the vase of flowers on the dresser for fear she'd drop it. Greg sank onto the bed and rubbed his hands across his dome. Jessica stood by the door, not quite knowing what to say. Instead, she waited for him to reopen the conversation.

"Rick and Sherry had a big argument this evening. It wasn't made clear to me how it all got started, but I got a call right when I was getting off from work, so I went by to try and play referee. As you probably already figured out, it didn't work. So, I got Rick to agree to let Sherry come and stay over here for the night. It didn't take much convincing."

"Is this about the baby issue? I thought they had gotten past that."

Greg sighed heavily as if whatever it was that had taken place at the Madison house had left him physically exhausted. "Yeah, it's the same issue," he answered while removing his shoes. "As best I can figure, Rick thinks George Wilson, from the case he's working on right now, is a poor excuse for a dad and he's pretty angry that a man like Mr. Wilson gets to have a son and a man like him, who wants to be a good father to a son can't because he has a wife who is taking that option away from him. Well, let's just say Sherry loathes being compared to somebody else's wife, so she was pretty upset that Rick compared her to Mrs. Wilson."

"Why?" Jessica blurted. "She does it to him all the time."

Her reaction startled Greg. He looked at her for a split second as though he'd only imagined the words his wife has just spoken. "Grace, what on earth are you talking about?"

"I'm talking about Sherry. She compares Rick to . . . other people's husbands all the time. How can she get angry when he does the same?"

Greg could sense a deeper issue. He patted the mattress beside him. "Come here, baby. Come sit down."

Jessica ignored his request. "Who called for you?" Her question had more of a demanding tone than that of an inquiry.

"What?"

"Between Rick and Sherry, who called for you to come over during their argument?"

"Sherry did. Why?"

"That was so inappropriate, Greg. You had just finished an extended shift at the hospital. She knows how tired you are when you get off and she knows how much it means to you to be able to leave that chaotic environment and come to one that's peaceful. So, what does she do? She lures you from one stressful scene right into another one. That's just not fair."

"I think she was just at wit's end, Grace. Rick was being totally unreasonable at the time and —"

"Was he, really? I happen to think that Sherry is the one being unreasonable. I agree with our mothers on this one. Sherry's unwillingness to even consider giving her husband a second child is selfish and disrespectful. Rick deserves a little bit more than that."

"She shouldn't have to feel pressured into having a baby."

"He shouldn't have to feel denied the chance of having one."

"A baby is something that they should both agree upon having, Grace. I mean, put yourself in her shoes. How would you feel if you knew for certain that you didn't want another child and I just kept badgering you about giving me a son, which would be no guarantee anyway?"

"Put *yourself* in Rick's shoes, Greg. How would you feel if you wanted more than anything to have a second child and I was totally unwilling to even consider it based on whatever shortcomings you may have had in the past? It's been *five* years ago, Greg. How would you feel if I held a five-year-old mistake over your head, even when you had proven yourself to be more mature now and had assured me that things would be different?"

"All I'm saying is that this is something that had to be dealt with tonight. They need to talk this out and come to an agreement if they're ever going to get the peace back in their home."

"I agree," Jessica said. "But how are they going to do that when she's here and he's there? She should be at home, not here. Running away isn't going to solve anything."

"Sweetheart, you weren't around back then when Sherry was pregnant. Rick didn't leave her a lot of fond memories to relate to. He didn't mean any harm, of course, but he was all but absent when she needed him the most. I was there. I saw her loneliness. I saw her tears."

"And I'll bet every last one of them fell on your shoulder."

The root of Jessica's indignation gradually became clear to Greg. It wasn't really about Derrick and Sherry at all. It was about him and Sherry. Once again, Greg patted the mattress beside where he sat. "Come sit with me."

Jessica blinked away tears of frustration and fidgeted in the place where she stood before taking slow steps and easing onto the bed. Greg looked at her in silence. She didn't return his gaze, but instead chose to stare at the vibrant roses on the dresser in front of her. She felt the tenderness of Greg's hand when he placed it on top of hers before lifting her hand to touch his lips. A sigh from him followed and then, once again, complete silence.

"I'm sorry," Jessica whispered.

"I don't want you to tell me that you're sorry, Grace. I want you to tell me what's really bothering you."

In her mind, Jessica considered at least a dozen ways that she could perhaps state her case without ruffling Greg's generally calm feathers. His bond with Sherry had always been strong and neither he nor Sherry had ever tried to hide that fact. The last thing Jessica wanted was for him to see her as one turning into a nagging, jealous and petty wife. She had to be mindful of her words.

"Be honest with me, Grace." It was as though he could see her mental struggles and was reminding her of the promise they'd made to one another as they lay wrapped in each other's arms on the first night of their honeymoon in the unparalleled beauty that winter in Anchorage, Alaska, offered.

Jessica's voice trembled and it was barely above a whisper, but it was loud enough for Greg to hear. "I don't like it that she runs to you with her marital problems."

"Okay." There was an urging in Greg's voice, encouraging her to say more.

A lone tear rolled down Jessica's cheek, but she continued. "I don't like that she runs to you when she's mad at Rick or that she expects you to be available to her whenever she's in need of an ear. I don't like that she constantly compares her husband to you and I don't like that she's here tonight, Greg. I mean, I love Sherry, but you have to draw the line somewhere. Besides, you promised me."

"Promised you what?"

"Delivery," Jessica said. "The guest room was one of the places that I wanted *it* delivered."

"I'm so sorry, sweetheart. I just saw a couple of friends in need and wanted to try and help. I didn't know that you had a problem with Sherry's confiding in me and I didn't consider that you had other plans for the guest room. It's probably a good thing that I had no advance notice of that, because I probably would have put them on indefinite hold. Although I know you're not happy about this right now, she really did need my help. *They* needed my help."

"No, Greg. I'll agree that they needed somebody's help, but it didn't have to be yours. Sherry has family in New Jersey. She could have called her parents, or one of her siblings or me, even. Why didn't she call me?"

Jessica felt a chill as Greg ran his fingers through her short hair. "Sherry and I have always shared, Grace. We've just kind of always been there when we needed each other."

"But I'm your wife." A new tear escaped Jessica's pool and trickled down. "I had plans for tonight including a family dinner, time for you and Julian to play before he fell asleep and then time just for me and you. But because you were so busy being there for *her,* the salmon is dry, our son had to fall asleep without seeing you and I'm not even close to being in the mood any-more."

Her words stung. Deep inside, Jessica found a degree of satisfaction in knowing that Greg felt at least a smidgen of the hurt that she did. She wanted him to know how disappointed she was. He seemed to have no words to explain away what she'd just said. Sounds coming from above their head signified Sherry's descent from the bedroom into the living room. The touch of Greg's hand to her cheek caused Jessica to look directly at him.

His voice was at a whisper. "Maybe I made a bad judgment call. I should have let them work it out, but in my fatigued state of mind, bringing the ladies over here seemed like the right thing to do at the time. I'm sorry about ruining dinner and about missing my time with you and Julian. I promise to make it up tomorrow. Grace, let's not let Rick and Sherry's problems spill over into our household, okay?"

"Greg?" Sherry's call stopped Jessica's initial response, prompting both of them to look towards the door that separated their bedroom from the living room.

"Too late, Greg. You already did," Jessica said. Then she sighed, stood and disrobed, knowingly adding to Greg's suffering. She could see the longing in his eyes just before she pulled back the bedcovers and slipped underneath them, turning her back to him. Jessica lay still, not moving from the position of nonverbal protest until she was sure that her husband had left the room.

CHAPTER 18

Derrick stared across the table as he ate lunch at Georgetowne Station Restaurant & Bar. It was one of his favorite places for casual dining, but he couldn't remember the last time he'd come without Greg. The calamari was delicious, as always, but he barely touched it while watching Perry Wilson devour a signature Station Burger with all the fixings. Although it wasn't a pretty sight to witness, Derrick was glad that the boy had a good appetite. Predicaments like the one he was in Could easily rob him of his desire for food. Their orders had only been served a short while ago, but Derrick needed to get down to business as quickly as possible before it could be determined that Perry wasn't at the cleaners on the northwest side of town where he was to go after his tutoring session.

"Thanks for meeting me here," Derrick said, noting Perry's less-than-perfect table manners.

"You're welcome," he responded after maneuvering the food in his mouth into one side of his jaw.

"You know I didn't ask you here just to treat you to lunch, right?"

Perry took a moment to gulp down several strawsful of Coca-Cola and then nodded. "Uh-huh. That note you handed me that day said to call you on the down low, so I knew something was up." The end of Perry's statement was muffled from the napkin he used to wipe condiment residue from his mouth.

"Why else do you think I brought you here?" Derrick challenged.

Perry's mood seemed to degenerate at the speed of light. He placed his napkin on the table and never took his eyes away from the crumpled cloth while he shrugged his shoulders in silence. Derrick wasn't sure if the boy knew what he suspected, but Perry's reaction gave him all the convincing he needed to pursue answers.

"Perry, I need for you to talk to me. We're both men here. So, let's talk. Can we do that? No mumbling, no shrugging, no bottling up and please, no lying. I'm your attorney and the only way I can help you is to know everything so I can know what I'm

212

dealing with. Can we talk?"

Derrick watched Perry's chest swell as he took in a deep breath. It seemed like forever before he saw indication of an exhale. Perry's eyes still rested on the ketchup-stained napkin and Derrick noted a hint of fear. Perhaps it was the realization that he was now forced to face his straightforward attorney without the protection of his father. Whatever the reason, it was a facial expression that Derrick had not noticed during either of their prior meetings.

"Perry?"

"What you want to talk about?" he asked, raising his eyes, but not looking directly at Derrick.

"I'm a very smart man, Perry. See, I don't need you to tell me every little detail. I'm pretty darn good at figuring things out. You can give me a sketch drawing on a sheet of typing paper and I can look at it and see it as a full-color oil painting on high quality canvas. You get what I'm saying here?"

For the first time since Derrick brought up the subject of business, Perry looked at him eye-to-eye. He shook his head, but quickly remembered the agreement he'd just made with Derrick.

"No," he said, verbalizing his answer.

Derrick slid the plate of cold calamari to

the center of the table to make room for his elbows. Clasping his hands together in a fashion that reminded him of Pastor Baldwin, he leaned in closer.

"What I'm saying is this, Perry. If you're totally honest with me, I can ask you one question and this meeting will be over. *One* question," Derrick stressed. "But you'll have to be honest. You see, because I'm such a smart man, I've all but figured out this case. One question, answered honestly will give me all I need to really get your defense together. So it's really all up to you as to how long we'll be here and how much talking we'll have to do. You get me?"

Perry licked his drying lips and then swallowed. "Yeah."

"Cool. So we have a deal?" Derrick reached his right hand across the table as he spoke.

"Yeah." After a moment's hesitation, Perry accepted his hand.

Derrick took a drink of water and then settled back in his seat. He could see beads of perspiration breaking through Perry's skin. It wasn't necessarily his intention to frighten the teenager, but he needed him to know how important his honesty was to the process of building his defense. It would be a crime in itself for a child, however misguided he was, with such good grades and a possible promising future ahead of him to suffer any more than he should for what had happened.

"One question," Derrick reiterated, leaning forward once more. "Did you act alone in this shooting? In other words, was there anyone . . . anyone else at all involved in what transpired that day?"

Immediately, Perry began shaking his head, but then his eyes met the unyielding, but trustworthy, eyes of his attorney. In his head, the teenager replayed the conversation he'd had with his partner in crime, over and over again. He'd promised, swore on a stack of Bibles, even, that he'd stand strong and not become dishonorable or ungrateful by becoming a snitch. Telling the whole truth would land him in a world of trouble that he knew he'd never be able to get out of. He couldn't tell. He just couldn't.

"We just made a deal, Perry," Derrick reminded him. "I can't help you if you don't help me."

"But my daddy said that you already agreed. He already paid you and everything. You have to do this."

Derrick reached into his pocket and pulled out a folded slip of paper. Opening it, he laid it flat on the table in front of the boy and watched his startled reaction. It was the original check that George Wilson had signed, paying the retainer fee.

"I don't have to do anything I don't want to do, Perry. I can't be bought out, nor will I be a sellout. People don't buy me — they pay me. I'm a man first, and then I'm a lawyer. I don't need your daddy's money and I promise you: If you don't tell me the truth, I'll give it back to him in a heartbeat and there will be no third chance for you to have the best defense lawyer in D.C. to handle your case."

Perry's lips trembled and tears threatened his eyes. The smidgen of the tough image from the first meeting that could be detected in their second meeting was indiscernible in their third. Perry looked as though he wanted to get up from the table and run for cover, but there was nowhere and no one to run to.

"I can't . . ." he stammered. "I can't tell you nothing. I can't tell you no names."

"I didn't ask for names. I'm a smart man, remember? I can figure out the names all by myself. That's what your daddy paid me to do. But I need something to go on, Perry. It's just you and me, dog. Man to man . . . I just need a 'yes' or a 'no.' All the rest is up to me. You wouldn't have ratted anybody out and no one other than the two of us will ever even know that this conversation took place. That, I can promise you. All I need from you is an answer."

The few silent seconds that passed felt like minutes — hours even — as Derrick waited for an answer, almost hoping that it wouldn't be the one that he knew it would be. When Perry began nodding slowly, Derrick closed his eyes and sighed.

"I need you to talk to me, Perry. *Tell* me."

Perry's voice was barely audible. "Yes."

Instinctively, Derrick almost asked a followup question. How many other people had been involved? But he'd promised only one. This wasn't going to be pretty at all. A woman's life hung in the balance and Perry had pulled the trigger that got her there. This case was unlike any that Derrick had taken on, but he knew what he had to do.

"Come on," he said, standing from the table and tucking the check Mr. Wilson had given him back into his pocket. "Let's get you to work before we get into trouble."

Jessica was surprised when Greg walked into her music class as she and her students were sharing cake and ice cream to mark the final day of the regular school year. It had been three days since Sherry had spent the night with them at Greg's invitation and uncharacteristic tension had remained in their home, even after he had apologized for his decision.

Her back had been turned to the door when he entered, but the hush that suddenly came over her giggling, chatting class of eighteen girls led to her turning and noting his appearance. It was the middle of the afternoon and a time when he was definitely scheduled to be on duty at Robinson Memorial. At first, Jessica thought that something was wrong, but when he kissed her to the delight of her students, she knew it wasn't a visit to be concerned about.

One of her favorite colors to see her dark-skinned husband wear was blue. Certain tones of the color seemed to accentuate the smoothness of his skin. The shirt he wore today, a cross between navy blue and royal blue, was the perfect shade to accomplish that. Jessica wasn't angry with him, so accepting Greg's kiss took no effort on her part. In fact, she'd been trying to figure out a way to apologize to him for her reaction to his decision to help their friends. Jessica had already decided that the strain between them had gone on long enough. Today was the day that she would make amends. But Greg had beaten her to the punch.

"Hello, ladies."

"Hi, Dr. Dixon." Delivering the response in perfect harmony, the girls sounded like a fine-tuned chorus.

Greg smiled at the blending of their voices. Then turning his attention to his wife, he whispered, "Can I steal you for a minute?"

The look in his eyes was one that Jessica loved and had seen hundreds of times since the moment he had expressed his love for her. She'd seen the look even before they got married, but it was one that he'd not once acted on until after he made her his wife. It was a look that said more than "I love you." It said, "I love you. I adore you. I want you." Jessica wasn't sure how to respond to "the look" when she was standing before the watchful eyes of her students.

"Can it wait?"

"Only if I have no other options."

Jessica felt herself flush. Greg was the only man she'd ever known intimately. She remembered her grandmother being an advocate of abstinence and preaching it to her often from the time she became a teenager. Grandma Agnes told her that sex was worth waiting for and if a man really loved her, he'd be willing to wait for that level of intimacy.

"It ain't always easy, honey," Grandma Agnes had said once when her grand-daughter was a tenth-grader, "but it's always right and when you do it God's way, He'll reward you like Christmas in July."

Romance had always been Jessica favorite genre to read as a high school and college student. She'd read and took pleasure in the fictional tales of men whose mere presence had the ability to weaken the knees of the women they loved, but she'd never thought that a love and desire so powerful existed in the real world. She was wrong. Perhaps it was a command that few men possessed, but Greg was definitely one of them, and for nearly five years he'd proved her grandmother's words true. Jessica couldn't imagine being married to a man who could fulfill her more.

She turned to her students, who were watching her and Greg's every move. "I'll be right back. Don't eat all the cake."

No words were spoken between them as Greg followed her out of her classroom and into a vacant break room just down the hall. No sooner had Jessica closed the door then he pulled her into a tight embrace.

"I'm sorry," he said, still holding her as though fearful of letting her go. "I don't know what else to say, Grace. If I knew more words that would make you realize how regretful I am for messing up the night you had planned for us, I would. But all I can say is I'm sorry."

Jessica struggled not to burst into tears. Greg had already apologized numerous times over the past few days and she'd been determined to hold on to her disappointment and make him bear the consequences of choosing to bring Sherry home. She still believed that he should have at least consulted with her before making the decision, but her stubbornness was rooted in a jealousy that she hadn't even known existed until recently.

"No, I'm sorry," she whispered while pulling away and walking towards the open blinds, hoping to hide her tears.

"You don't have anything to be sorry about, Grace. You were right. I should have let them work it out between themselves. Bringing Sherry to our house wasn't really solving anything. It was just a quick fix for the moment."

"But both she and Derrick would have done the same for me," Jessica said, turning away from the window and facing him from across the room. "They would have done it for either one of us. I was just . . ." Just the thought of admitting her pettiness was a struggle.

Greg walked over to her and pulled her into his chest. Jessica knew that he understood. Despite the fact that she'd forced him to endure the punishment of her barely speaking to him for the past three days, she knew he wouldn't ask her to complete her sentence. Instead, he took her hand and led her to one of the round tables where instructors at the college generally sat when taking a temporary leave from their classrooms.

Jessica felt ashamed of how she'd acted and could only imagine what her husband was thinking as he quietly held her hands in his. She struggled hard not to give way to the tears that begged to be released from her eyes.

"Grace, I love you, sweetheart. I know you know that."

Without a tearful outburst, the best she could offer was a nod.

"You know my history with both Sherry and Rick. I've known Rick my whole life and Sherry's been my friend since middle school. We grew up closer than the Three Musketeers. Sherry and I have been through a lot of things together, but only as friends. There's never been anything at all between us except friendship. If I wanted more, I could have gone after her years ago. Not saying that I would have succeeded, but I could have tried had I been interested in more than a platonic friendship. I dated in high school. I dated in college. I was never afraid to ask a girl out if I was interested, so had I wanted to cross the line with Sherry, I would have had no problem telling her so. Yes, I love her and I would never deny that. But what you and I have is a whole different kind of love, baby, and I hope to God that I haven't given you any reason to question that."

His words were more than reassuring, but in the process, they also made Jessica feel even more foolish for the reason he had to say them.

"Aside from all of that, Sherry is Rick's wife. Rick is my best friend in the whole world. I would *never* even think of stepping to his wife and if I thought for one minute that Sherry thought of me as anything other than her friend and confidant, I'd cut her loose like a brain tumor. And yes, I could be wrong, Grace, but I honestly don't believe that Sherry wants me to be anything other than the friend that I've been to her for nearly twenty years. But if it will make you feel better and if it will get us, you and me, back on track, I'll talk to her."

"No." Jessica vigorously shook her head at

his compromise. "I don't need you to talk to her. I know there's nothing there other than what you've said and what she's said."

"You've spoken with her?"

Another layer of embarrassment surrounded her as she looked at the table and nodded her reply. "Just briefly. I told her that her closeness to you wasn't a concern for me, but I guess I lied because apparently it was. I'm so sorry, Greg. I just feel so stupid right now."

"You want to know a secret?"

Jessica looked up at his surprising query. "What?"

"I am so flattered right now that it ain't even funny."

"Flattered?"

"Grace, since we've known one another, I've been hit on by doctors, nurses, patients, church missionaries, church ushers, even some of your own students and you've never shown any concern. Call us shallow, but most men, whether they admit it or not, like when their woman feels a little bit jealous when they think other women want him. I mean, I've always been happy that you had such a high level of security and confidence in the solidity of our marriage, but to know that you felt vulnerable about this makes me feel just a little bit pleased."

Jessica watched the dimple in Greg's left cheek deepen as he lost his battle to hold back a satisfied smile.

"So you're not disappointed to know that your wife can be trivial sometimes?"

Greg broke into a laugh and then kissed the back of her hand before responding. "Listen, you've survived two major surgeries that could have and by all accounts, *should* have taken your life. My mother thinks you're actually an angel in human form and Pastor Baldwin, of all people, agrees. Sometimes I even think you're too good to be true. So, to know that you have a flaw is almost refreshing."

Jessica laughed with him. She'd always thought he was the one that was too good to be true and most of the women she knew agreed. Even Sherry agreed. To hear him express the same about her was beyond appealing. In her opinion, Greg deserved a woman that was uncommonly good, so she had to be doing something right.

"There's something else that I've been meaning to tell you, but haven't because of the tension for the past few days."

"What?"

"Not now. Not here. I'm already off from work for the day. So when you get home, we'll plan to go out to dinner. Okay?"

Jessica searched his eyes. The laughter was gone and had been replaced with a calm seriousness. She wanted to probe him for more information, but he'd already made his stance clear. Before leaving, Greg walked her back to her classroom and gave her a lingering kiss at the door. Jessica watched her husband walk down the hallway, relieved that they'd finally cleared the air between them, but curious as to what it was he wanted to discuss that had to wait until tonight.

CHAPTER 19

"Moving to New York?!" Lena's voice was at least two octaves higher than its normal pitch.

Greg had tried unsuccessfully for two days to get his whole family together to discuss the opportunity that Lenox Hill had presented him with. On Friday, Derrick, with a highly publicized trial approaching, had been out of his office making visits, doing some investigating of his own of the haunting suspicions he had about Perry's case. Saturday, when Greg called for his mother, Mattie had informed him that Pastor Baldwin had come to pick her up to assist him and several of the other board members with tying up loose ends for the upcoming Men's Day service that would be held next Sunday on Father's Day. Today, a rare Sunday off from Robinson Memorial, was the first opportunity he'd had and the very mention of it seemed to cause chaos around the dinner table.

"Mama, I didn't say for sure that we were moving to New York. I have to fly out that way for a couple of days this week to meet with some people, but we're not moving, at least not yet. But if I decide to take this job, that's what would have to happen."

"You ain't taking my baby to no New York," Mattie said emphatically.

"Mama!" Jessica said, shocked at her mother's tone of voice.

"Girl, New York ain't no place to raise no family. It's too fast and too crime infested."

"New York is not crime infested, Ms. Mattie," Greg explained. "There are areas in New York where the crime rate is high, just like there are places here in D.C. where it's high. We don't live in that type of environment here and we won't live in it there."

"So, you *have* decided that you're moving," Lena said. Her voice was stern, but her disposition was one of sadness.

"No, Mama, I haven't. I'm just speaking hypothetically."

Greg felt trapped. He'd expected everyone to be surprised by the possibility of his moving his family to New York, but he hadn't expected to start a small riot. He looked across the table at Derrick and Sherry, who had been quiet for most of the dinner and hadn't offered any words since his announcement. Sherry stared back at him as if she was waiting for the punch line or some indication that it had all been a joke. Derrick looked at him as well, realizing now why Greg had insisted that he and Sherry join their family for dinner, despite Derrick's protests following morning worship.

"Man, you know me and Sherry aren't on the best of terms right now. I don't want to bring everybody down. We'll just go to a restaurant or something."

When Derrick said those words, Greg had been adamant about not taking no for an answer. It wasn't an easy victory, but after several minutes of what had nearly turned into a filibuster, Derrick gave up and agreed to accept the invitation that was being forced on him. Now, after placing his fork on the table beside his plate, he looked in disbelief.

"Man, you love Robinson Memorial. In a million years, I never would have guessed you'd give a moment's thought to leaving that place. What is Lenox offering you?"

"A more comfortable life for my family, for starters," Greg answered. "We're talking about a dream promotion, a more fixed schedule, more weekends off, a major pay raise, a larger office, moving expenses, temporary housing . . . man, this is an opportunity of a lifetime."

"Have you prayed about this, son?" Pastor Baldwin had been sitting quietly while the others had been throwing out questions and demands. Now, his elbows rested on the table in front of him and his hands were clasped together.

Silence rested among them for the first time since the conversation began. Not only did Pastor Baldwin's James Earl Jones– type bass voice command that sort of attention, but he'd tossed out a question that forced Greg to mentally replay the past few days. He remembered thanking God for being deemed worthy of the offer that Lenox Hill Hospital had put on the table, but he'd never specifically prayed for guidance on what decision to make. For him, as bittersweet as leaving Robinson would be, it would almost be idiotic not to accept.

"It would be erroneous of any of us to downplay what a wonderfully lucrative opportunity this would be, should you decide to accept. But sometimes things that feed our natural beings aren't what are best for our spiritual selves and it's important that the total you is nourished by the decision you make. Now, by no means am I saying that you should not take this job or that it's not a blessing sent directly to you from heaven. I'm just imploring you to seek God's guidance because ultimately, His approval is the one that counts the most. You understand me, don't you, Greg?"

Greg's eyes were fixed on his pastor as the older, wiser man spoke. Since he was in his early teens, Pastor Baldwin had been the man he'd gone to for words of wisdom and prayer. The preacher was to him what Greg liked to believe his father would have been had he still been living. There was no measuring the respect he had for his pastor and when he called him "Greg," instead of "Brother Greg," the words Pastor Baldwin spoke seemed to carry a more personal meaning. Lately, he'd been referring to Greg without the church title attached, more often than customary.

"Yes, sir," Greg said. "I understand what you're saying and I can't honestly say that I've prayed about the specifics of this offer, but —"

"But, nothing," Lena said. "If you ain't prayed about it, then there ain't much more to say. If I didn't teach you nothing else, I know I taught you 'bout the importance and the power of prayer. Now, here you go talking 'bout the possibility of uprooting from the only city you ever lived in and moving my daughter-in-law and my grandson way over to New York and you ain't even talked to the Lord about it? How much sense does that make, Greg?"

Greg rubbed his forehead. There was so much more he could say, mainly on how she was presently talking to him as though he were still a child, but he'd learned at a very young age that trying to get in the last word where his mother was concerned was a battle not worth taking on. While she had taught him about the significance of prayer, Greg had a feeling that this subject was more of a sore spot to his mother because if he took on this position, for the first time in their lives they wouldn't be living in close proximity. Perhaps letting the subject rest was a better choice.

"Jessie, have you had your say?" Mattie suddenly asked. "You ain't never lived in a city the size of New York City. This will affect your life just like it will his. You got a good job up there at the college and them girls you teach love you to death. You don't have no problems with changing your life around like that?"

"Mama, I could get another job at another school."

Greg broke in. "With the money I'd be making, Grace could be a stay-at-home mom. She could do that now if she wanted to and she could certainly do it then if she decided she didn't like the school system or just didn't want to work."

Jessica jumped back in. "The point is, the girls at Trinity have had instructors that they loved before me and they will have more that they will love after me, if we decide to make this move. My job is just a job to me. I love what I do, but it's just a career choice. Greg's job is a ministry. God uses his hands in a way that's out of the ordinary and if God says this move is in His will, then so be it. I'll have no problems at all about moving. Maybe God has used Greg as much as He destined to at Robinson. Who knows how many more Sergeants whatever-his-name-is, there will be that will need —"

"Sergeant Evan McDonald," Greg said with a laugh.

"Who?" Mattie's face wore a look of marked surprise and confusion.

"Sergeant Evan McDonald," Greg repeated.

Jessica further explained. "That's the name of the officer who Greg initially went to New York to perform surgery on. My point is that I've never lived in New York before, so I can't say that I'd be thrilled about the move either, but it has to be his choice. I'm not worried about New York. I'll adjust there, just like I adjusted to living here with you after Grandma Agnes died. Julian and I will be fine. I know that Greg wouldn't intentionally put us in danger and he wouldn't make a decision like this one without being one hundred percent sure it was the right one. I'm with him on this, Mama. So, now I guess you can say that I have had my say. I totally agree with Pastor Baldwin that it's something that he . . . that we need to pray about, but in the end, I'm going to support whatever decision that Greg makes."

By the time Jessica had finished her speech, Greg almost felt emotional. Looking at her, he smiled and then gave her hand an appreciative squeeze. The tender moment came to an immediate end when Derrick made a strange noise that sounded like a combination of a grunt and a mumble. Sherry immediately took offense to his reaction to Jessica's words. She knew it was directed at her.

"What's that supposed to mean?"

All eyes at the table shifted from Greg and Jessica to Derrick and Sherry.

"What's what supposed to mean?" Derrick asked, looking at her as though he had no idea what she was referring to.

Sherry grumbled, trying to mirror the sound that her husband had made just moments earlier. *"That,"* she stressed. "That's what."

"Come on, guys," Greg said, trying to calm the situation before the argument escalated to the point of no return.

"It can mean whatever you want it to mean, Sherry, since what you want is all that matters to you anyway."

"Oh, don't even start with all the insinuations, Derrick Jerome Madison. If you got something to say, then be a man and say it."

Two things were a sure sign that Sherry was angry. One was when she rolled her neck when she spoke and the other was when she referred to her husband by his full given name, and she had done both during the course of her last statement.

"Oh, so I'm not a man now?" Derrick became quickly offended by his wife's words.

"Did I say that?"

"Sounds like it to me."

"Well, it *sounded* like you said something to me eight years ago that you don't want to own up to and honor, so I guess that makes us even, doesn't it?"

"I'll tell y'all what," Lena said, raising her

voice and her body from her chair simultaneously. "Y'all better start to showing some respect in my house. Not only that, but don't y'all see the man of God sitting here? Do both your tails need scaling with a switch?"

The scene had taken Pastor Baldwin by surprise. His eyes were glued on the couple, who each were making no attempts to hide their present displeasure with the other. Their blatant disregard for one another was cause for concern and in his opinion, totally unacceptable, especially in the house belonging to women that they both viewed as mother-figures. It was a typical behavior for the well-loved preacher, but he forcefully pushed his chair back from the table, causing a commotion that stopped Derrick in the middle of his rebuttal to Sherry's last statement. Pastor Baldwin didn't noticeably raise his voice level, but the austerity of his tone was unmistakable.

"Both of you, come with me *now.*"

"What?" Derrick's appearance was one of surprise. He'd been reprimanded by his pastor on more than one occasion in the past, but never in that tone of voice.

"Lena, may we use one of your rooms?"

All eyes were on the pastor as he spoke, but Greg's eyes were on him for a far different reason than anyone else's.

"You most certainly can, Pastor," Lena answered, her voice laced with the same disgust as his. "Since the babies are in the playroom, you're welcome to use Mattie's room. Just step over all her junk."

Mattie had been sitting quietly for a while, but no one had noticed in the middle of the drama that had unfolded. She didn't even lash out at Lena for her remark. Instead, she nodded in agreement and watched along with the others as Pastor Baldwin physically led Derrick by the arm, with Sherry following close behind.

With calm returned and everyone either finished with their meal or no longer interested in eating, Lena began gathering plates from the table and emptying the contents in the garbage disposal. Greg turned his attention back to Jessica.

"Thanks, baby," he said after planting a kiss on her cheek. "I appreciate everything you said."

"I meant every word of it."

"I know," Greg said, smiling in admiration. "That's what makes it mean so much." Releasing her after a second kiss, Greg noted his mother-in-law's disposition. "Ms. Mattie, are you okay?"

"Yeah, Mama. It's not like you to be this

quiet." Jessica reached across the table and gently touched her mother's hand.

"Yeah, I'm fine, but I would like to make one more plea for the two of you to stay put here in D.C. I don't want y'all to move there." She turned her eyes to Greg and delivered a earnest look. "Please, don't leave and move there. Don't take my baby away from me."

"Mama . . ." Jessica started, but Greg held up his hands to silence her.

"Ms. Mattie, even if we do move to New York, I won't be taking Grace from you. We'll still come here often, at least twice a month to attend church on Sundays. That's a part of the contract they are offering. I can get two weekends off each month and I promise we'll spend them right here in D.C. We'll still have so much of our lives here, with you, Mama, Rick and Sherry. It's not like you won't get to see us anymore."

Greg tried to sound as convincing as he possibly could, but the whole while he was speaking Mattie was shaking her head, still voicing her objection and fighting back tears. Her voice had taken on a frightful tone that got Lena's attention as well, bringing her away from the kitchen sink and back to the table.

"Now, I know how you feel, Mattie. I ain't

never been separated from my son, either, but like Pastor said, they need to pray about it. Until they get an answer from God, they don't need to start packing no luggage. But we don't need to be unpacking either. Jessie made a good point earlier when she said that God might have a plan for Greg there. I mean, the good Lord shole did put him at Robinson Memorial. He done saved so many lives there, including his own wife's. Maybe there are more lives for his hands to touch that won't ever come in to Robinson. Maybe there are more people like that policeman who need Greg to be placed in their lives too."

Mattie still sat in disagreement. Her head never stopped shaking from the time Greg spoke until Lena had finished her input. "I don't like it," Mattie said, getting up from the table and backing away from it. "I ain't never asked y'all for much," she said, with tears beginning to stream down her face. "But I'm asking y'all not to move there. Can you do that one thing for your mama?" She looked tearfully at her daughter.

Jessica stood slowly and began walking towards Mattie, but her mother turned and disappeared behind the closed door of Lena's bedroom. Greg and Lena exchanged confused glances before he rushed to catch up with Jessica, who stood knocking on the locked door. Pulling her away, Greg held his wife and allowed her to release her bewildered tears on his shoulder.

CHAPTER 20

"Dr. Dix! My man, my man!"

Knowing who it was before he even turned around to face the man approaching behind him, Greg smiled. Dr. LaRon Clayton was the only staff member he even knew well enough to miss after his extended tenure ended at Lenox Hill Hospital.

"Dr. Clayton," Greg said, accepting the intern's hand and welcoming his embrace. "Have you been staying out of trouble?"

"I been trying, man, but these folks ain't making it easy for a brotha, you know?" LaRon laughed and Greg laughed with him. He was such a free spirit with no overwhelming concerns, unlike most of the other doctors whose collars seemed stiffer than plywood.

"But on the real, though, Doc. What did we do to get you to leave that gorgeous wife that you never stopped talking about and come back to visit us here?"

Leaving Jessica had been difficult for more than one reason. Greg always missed her welcoming arms after a hard day's work, but it was the disarray that had suddenly seemed to take over the lives of their entire family circle that made the timing of this trip an increased inconvenience for Greg. He'd tried to get Jessica to come along with him, but she didn't want to leave with her mother still so upset over the possibility of their moving to New York on a permanent basis.

"I have a meeting with Montgomery Price, Joseph Armstrong and Miles Tanner."

"Dang, man, what you did?" LaRon said, twisting his face as he spoke. "You got to meet with the hospital's director, the chief neurologist and the director of the Division of Neurosurgery? Do you need me to come up out of this uniform and just be LaRon for a couple of hours? 'Cause you know I don't mind taking one for another brotha."

Greg burst into a hearty laugh. LaRon's sudden breakout into his best rendition of the fancy footwork that Muhammad Ali made famous temporarily relieved him of the burden that thoughts of Jessica's worries had brought on.

"Thanks, LaRon, but it's not a bad meeting."

"No?"

"No. If I tell you something, can you keep it to yourself for now?"

"Yeah. What's up?"

Greg did a quick scan of their area to be sure no uninvited listeners were within range. "Dr. Armstrong is leaving Lenox to do some overseas charity-type medical work. I've been offered his position."

LaRon placed his hand over his mouth in an exaggerated attempt to stifle a jovial scream. He spun around one time and then grabbed Greg around his waist and squeezed as tight as he could. Releasing him, LaRon swore and then covered his mouth again, this time apologetically.

"My bad, Doc, but that's tight, man. I can't believe they offered that position to a brotha. Aw, man, that's gonna be great! Congratulations, Dr. Dix."

Greg held both his hands out in front of him. "Whoa, Dr. Clayton, slow down. I said they offered the position. I didn't say I accepted it."

"You're kidding, right?"

"I'm very serious. It's a great opportunity, but it would change my whole life as I know it, so I have to consider some things."

"You're kidding, right?" LaRon repeated.

"I'm not like you, man," Greg said. "I

have other responsibilities and other important people in my life to consider. There are issues to weigh to see whether or not the balance tilts in this direction or not."

"I guess." LaRon shrugged. "But I'll bet they're offering you some mad money, aren't they?"

Greg nodded. It was a truth that he didn't dare deny. "Yeah, it would be a substantial raise from what I'm presently hauling. But in all honesty, I don't need the money. I'm living well right now and there's nothing my family needs that I can't provide. If I make this move, it won't be based on the pay raise. I'd have to feel that I'm needed here."

"Well, I can answer that for you. Yes, you're needed here. If nobody else don't need you, I do. The Division of Neurosurgery definitely could use you, if for no reason but to add some color to the roster. I look like a token, man."

"Why? Has Dr. Bolton left?"

"Come on, Doc. You know Nanya don't claim us. And if she doesn't want to be black then, get gone," he said, waving his hand in a shooing motion. "But if we suddenly have a racial setback, I guarantee you she'll be a cotton-picking cotton picker picking cotton just like the rest of us."

Both Greg and LaRon shared a brief laugh, but the intern quickly sobered.

"Listen, man, I know I never told you this while you were working here, but I enjoyed serving under your leadership. In just those few short weeks, I think I learned more from you in the O.R. than I'd learned in all the time I've been here with Dr. Armstrong. He's an okay dude — don't get me wrong. I'm just saying that if you took on this job and I had the opportunity to see you here every day, occupying such a respected position, it would give me so much more to strive for. You'd help me prove so many people wrong who said black men like me could only get so far in this hospital. Man, you'd be my hero."

In silence, Greg looked down at a man he considered to be a younger, more happy-go-lucky version of himself and suddenly felt pulled in different directions. Dr. Clayton's words did nothing to make whatever his final decision would be any easier.

"I appreciate that," Greg said as he shook his hand once more. "I can't say what I'm going to do right now, but either way, you can mark my words: *You*, Dr. Clayton, will prove those people wrong whether I'm here to help you do so or not. I know when I see a promising successful neurosurgeon in the making and it's written all over the script of your life."

"Thank you, Doc," LaRon said, while wearing a wide grin. "But keep what I said in mind. I'd love the chance to be groomed by you."

"I gotta run now," Greg told him. "When I make a decision, you'll be one of the first to know."

Within seconds, Greg was exiting the elevator on the third floor. He glanced at his watch and took long quick strides so that he wouldn't be late for his three o'clock meeting. Dr. Armstrong was approaching the meeting room door from the opposite direction just as Greg arrived.

"Dr. Dixon," he said, nodding his head.

He didn't offer his hand, so neither did Greg. "Dr. Armstrong. Good to see you again."

"The pleasure's mine."

As the men walked into the room, they were greeted individually by Mr. Price and Dr. Tanner. Greg had met Miles Tanner during the time he served in the hospital, but it was his first time making the acquaintance of Montgomery Price, the director of Lenox Hill Hospital. After declining the offer for coffee, Greg sat in the seat to which Mr. Price had directed him.

Just as Greg had expected, a lot of small talk preceded the business at hand. The men chatted about everything from the difference in the weather in D.C. versus New York to the record of the Washington Wizards versus the New York Knicks. Fortunately for Greg, he was both patient and deeply into the goings-on of professional basketball. Had he not been, he would have been on the verge of insanity by the time the hour-long conversation on statistics, injured players, trade options and draft predictions finally came to a close.

"So," Mr. Price said, directing his full attention to Greg, "what are the chances that we can make you a Knicks fan?"

"The chance that you'll get me to be a Knicks fan is next to impossible, Mr. Price," Greg said with a chuckle. "But if the chance of my accepting your offer of employment here at Lenox Hill is what you're inquiring about, that one has potential."

"Well, in the end, that's the one that really matters," Mr. Price said, laughing a systematic laugh that the others joined in on. When he sobered, he added, "And we firmly believe that if we can get you here, the Knicks will grow on you eventually."

"They'd have to," Dr. Tanner put in. "You'd never survive the punishment of being here and not being a Knicks fan. These guys can be brutal."

Greg's silent prayer for them to get on with business so that he could get checked into his hotel room to catch a nap was answered when Mr. Price spoke again.

"Dr. Armstrong, here, has been with Lenox Hill for most of his career and while it saddens us that he's decided to take a different route with the future of his profession, we applaud the good that we know his decision will do for the people abroad. He has just over two more weeks before he'll bid us farewell and your name was the first and only name he submitted to us as his successor."

Mr. Price looked at Dr. Armstrong, granting him silent permission to pick up where he'd just left off.

"You did an immaculate job of covering for me during the time when I thought my leave was temporary. As you know, your reasons for being the one chosen to be called in for the emergency surgery of one of New York's finest was because of high recommendations you received from Dr. Simon Grant and for your unparalleled work at Robinson Memorial. Sure, there are other doctors who would be glad to fill my space here at Lenox, but you are the one that I advocate and the one who is best suited."

As though they'd rehearsed who would talk first and at what point the other was to jump in, Dr. Tanner, without pardon, chimed in.

"I had the pleasure of working very closely with you, Dr. Dixon," he said. "You are a perfect match for our staff of doctors. This job offer isn't based on age or experience. We know a lot of older doctors and those who have been practicing longer. Still, you are our choice because what we want is proven performance. On the performance scale, the others can't touch you. You are wise beyond your years and like Dr. Armstrong, you work admirably with others and are well-liked. Although your time here was brief, there was not one unkind word said about you while you were here or after you left. As a matter of fact, I think a couple of our student doctors went through a period of mourning."

Dr. Tanner stopped long enough to chuckle and then he continued. "The bottom line is that Lenox Hill Hospital is one of the highest respected hospitals in the country and Dr. Armstrong is a part of why we wear that badge of honor. You, Dr. Dixon, with your youth, ability and charisma can only make us better. Coming in, you wouldn't be an unknown who has to prove himself. Your record and your reputation speak for themselves. Robinson Memorial may be a great place to work, but Lenox Hill is greater. We can take you places that Robinson can't. The possibilities are endless, Dr. Dixon. You have the wherewithal to fly and unlike Robinson, Lenox has the space for you to spread your wings."

CHAPTER 21

Even with school being in recess and neither of them on staff to teach courses during the summer months, Jessica and Sherry allowed their children to attend Open Arms Day Care and Learning Center. The facility offered a summer program that allowed children to be in a less structured atmosphere than it offered during the school year, but still kept them in the educational environment that they needed to keep them on track for the coming year. Over the past month, the preschool had gone through a major management overhaul, but the women were still comfortable with their children remaining there.

The center had been the brainchild of Deloris Miller, but both she and her husband shared ownership of the flourishing fifteen-year-old business. Neither Jessica nor Sherry had any firsthand details, but Ms. Hamm, Julian's caregiver, had told them that Mrs.

Miller discovered that Mr. Miller was skimming funds from the business to pay hush money to a woman he'd had a three-year affair with eight years ago. The affair eventually fizzled, but their intimacy resulted in a child that Mr. Miller didn't ever want his wife to find out about.

To his detriment, Mr. Miller missed three consecutive payments due to the fact that in recent months his wife had begun watching the books more closely for monies she felt were unaccounted for. The former mistress, unsympathetic to his predicament, sent copies of pictures, letters and canceled checks to Mrs. Miller that told her the story she had no idea even existed. The final straw, Ms. Hamm had told them, was when Mrs. Miller found out that her center had cared for the child for two years while the affair was going on and her husband had voluntarily paid the fees. The reconciliation that she'd given consideration to after realizing how much time had passed was totally forgotten when she replayed memories of changing the child's diaper and feeding him on days when they were short staffed.

In the divorce settlement, Mrs. Miller, who now preferred Ms. Tucker, her maiden name, was awarded the business and the home that she and her husband had shared. According to Ms. Hamm, Mr. Miller had been forced back into the workforce to try to find new employment at the age of fifty. So far, all he could find were odd jobs here and there, including some grounds-keeping chores. If his former wife was affected by the liquidation of her thirty-year marriage, she didn't show it and she seemed even less concerned that her ex-husband was now struggling just to keep a roof over his head.

The matter of the Millers had been the initial topic of discussion for Jessica and Sherry as they ate salmon sandwiches at Finemondo, but Jessica refused to use it to avoid what was really on her heart. Instead, she used it as a launch pad to take her there.

"Sherry, please don't let that happen to you and Rick. You guys are so perfect together. Don't let it all fall apart over a baby. I try not to worry about whether this will lead to divorce or not, but I can't help but be concerned."

"Yeah, well, I'm concerned, too, Jessie. I don't know how much more of this I can take."

The response wasn't the one that Jessica had hoped or even expected to hear. "Sherry, don't say that."

"Jessie, Father's Day is four days away and

the closer it gets, the more unbearable Ricky gets. He acts like I've robbed him of the opportunity to be a father. You would think Dee-Dee doesn't even exist anymore. You know what she told me yesterday when we were out shopping for Father's Day gifts? My baby looked at me and said, 'Daddy said if you ask me what to get him for Father's Day to tell you to make him a father.' Can you believe that? I was so mad I left the store without even buying him anything."

Jessica gasped. This was one of the first instances where she didn't feel that Sherry had overreacted. She was sure that Derrick didn't mean to disrespect his daughter by what he'd said, but Jessica couldn't even make herself come to his defense. For him to think something like that to himself would have been bad enough. But for him to plant that seed into Denise, intentionally or not, was inexcusable.

"We started our counseling sessions with Pastor Baldwin last night. Ms. Lena was at the church when we first got there, but she left shortly thereafter. The session was supposed to be only an hour, but we ended up there for two."

"Why so long?"

"Because both Ricky and I are stubborn,

that's why. It took just about the whole hour for Pastor Baldwin to get us to talk. The meeting actually went well. I found out some of his issues lie in the fact that his father walked out on him and Ms. Julia. We used to talk about it a little as friends in school and he opened up a bit more during the time we were dating. But since we've been married, Ricky has never really referred to his dad. At the meeting, he talked about how he didn't even know where his dad was or even if he was still alive."

"You didn't already know that?"

Sherry nodded with a sad countenance. "We've been married seven years and not once did he ever tell me that. I just assumed his father was dead. The few times that I heard Ms. Julia refer to him, she always did so in the past tense, so I just concluded that at some point after he walked away from his family, he died."

"So Rick's desire to have a son is really because he's longing for his own dad?"

"No, I don't think so. He made it very clear in the meeting that although he'd forgiven his father for abandoning him and Ms. Julia, he never wanted to see him again ever in life. But he did want the chance to give to a son what his father never even tried to give him."

Jessica sighed. If Greg had laid a heart-breaking story on her such as that one, she would have taken him straight home to get started on making the baby he wanted. She and Sherry were so different. Both of them were independent in their own ways, but Sherry was far more self-reliant. Jessica remembered when Sherry told her that her mother had raised her and her sisters to support their husbands, but to always have money saved in a separate bank account that their men had no knowledge of. That way, if anything ever happened and their marriages fell apart, their survival wouldn't depend upon what kind of alimony the courts awarded them. Over the years, Sherry had accumulated quite a savings in her advised private account.

For years, Jessica's grandmother had endured an emotionally and physically abusive marriage that she'd literally fought her way through until the day that she found the courage to separate from her abuser. Yet, she still believed in the power of love and instilled values of trust in her grand-daughter. Grandma Agnes taught Jessica to support her husband as well. But she also instructed her to always honor him, trust him, allow him to head the household and to love him so much that all he would know to do in return was love her back and do everything within his power to make sure that she was happy. Grandma Agnes told her granddaughter that if she waited for God to send her the right man, and if she loved him the right way, even in those times when they were apart, he'd crave her like a junkie craved drugs. Jessica didn't have a private stash, but she'd opt for the passion, adoration and security that Greg gave her any day over the precautionary nest egg of her friend.

"What are you going to do, Sherry?" she finally asked.

"I don't know. I'm praying that something positive comes of these sessions with Pastor Baldwin because I get the feeling that it's our last hope. I'm not blaming all of this on Ricky. I know I have issues and phobias where pregnancy is concerned. I have memories from my first experience that were etched in my mind with a dull knife laced in alcohol. But now he's starting to discount our daughter and I won't even consider ignoring my fears before he re-kindles his love for the child he already has."

As much love that Jessica knew she and Greg had, moments like this automatically made her search for the little things that she could do to ensure her marriage's happiness. At the five-year mark, no doubt, Sherry never imagined her marriage would be going through such a rough patch. At the seven-year mark, where Sherry and Derrick now stood, Jessica was certain that Mr. and Mrs. Miller never thought they'd go through such a bitter divorce. The lesson that she'd learned from all of this was to never take a day of her marriage for granted. Love was too fragile to leave dangling on the edge, unattended.

"How's your mom?" Sherry asked the question just as Jessica had finished making her mental note.

"She's okay, I guess. I'm just so surprised at how hard she's taking the possibility of us moving. You'd think we were moving to Canada or Mexico or something. It's just an hour or so flight from there to here and I'd definitely make the time to come see her."

"Maybe she's scared of losing you again," Sherry offered, glad to shift the conversation away from her own life. "Back when we first met you all, she told us about how her mom had raised you and the two of you didn't really bond until after your grandmother passed. Maybe she's just afraid of losing that bond."

Jessica considered the possibility of Sherry's theory as she sipped sweetened tea through her straw. She'd not thought of that, but it didn't seem to fit the script that her mother's life had religiously followed.

"Mama and I started spending time together before Grandma Agnes passed away. Our bonding really began years earlier, when she started going to church with us. I'll admit that Grandma's death pulled us towards each other for comfort and then our moving in together made that bond stronger. But I would think that my mother knows that a few hundred miles wouldn't change that. Not after all we've been through together."

"Well, something is terrifying her," Sherry said, regaining her appetite and biting into her lukewarm sandwich. "Are you really okay with moving to New York?"

Jessica nodded. "I really am. I mean, I'd miss just being able to hang out with you guys on any given day and I'd miss witnessing fights between Ms. Lena and my mom, but yes, I'm okay with it. I don't want to leave with Mama being upset like she's been lately though. I want to talk to her about this, but as soon as I bring up the subject, she just starts shaking her head and if I don't drop it, she'll walk away and totally shut me out. I'm trying so hard to figure her out, but I'm stumped."

"Has Greg given any indication of what he's going to do?"

"No. I spoke with him last night. He had a meeting with some of the head people at Lenox yesterday. Today, he was having dinner with the same guys and a few of the other doctors on staff. He'll be headed back this way some time tomorrow. He said he's still praying about it. I get the feeling he's going to take it. He kept saying that something was pulling him in that direction and that he felt there was a destiny and purpose involved in him being offered this position. I need Mama to be prepared for me to be gone by the end of the month and she's nowhere near prepared."

Sherry sat quietly. Jessica watched her twirl her straw around in her glass and watch the ice cubes swim around in a circle in the flattened cola.

"What?" Jessica asked, seeing the thought-provoking look on her friend's face.

"I was just thinking," Sherry said. "I need to ask you something and I need for you to be honest with me."

Jessica agreed with a silent nod.

"I know it's been stressful around here for you lately with me and Ricky not getting along and everything. I know that I've irked you a time or two with my need to purge my feelings on Greg and I've even inconvenienced you with an overnight stay at your house."

Jessica wanted to break in and convince Sherry that none of that had been a problem and tell her how happy she'd been that they could be there for her in her time of need. But none of it would have been the truth. Sherry was right. Irked and inconvenienced was exactly what she'd felt at the time. Jessica remained silent and allowed Sherry to have her say.

"What I want to know is, does your willingness to leave have anything to do with you wanting to separate me from Greg?"

"What?" Jessica was stunned.

"It's just a question, Jessie. But I need an honest answer. I know how much you love Trinity College and how much you loved the fact that Ms. Mattie and Ms. Lena decided to move in together and live in Ms. Julia's house which was more convenient to where you and Greg's new home was than where either of them had lived previously. It was important to you to live close to your mom so that Julian could be close to his grandmothers. Now, all of a sudden, you're not only willing, but ready to move two hundred and fifty miles away and settle for seeing your mother twice a month. That's a really big change, Jessie."

"I can't believe you're making this accusation, Sherry."

"I'm not making an accusation, Jessie; I'm making an observation. I'm not telling you that this is what's going on. I'm asking you whether or not it is. I've been a thorn in your side lately and as much as I know that, I've felt like there was no place else that I could go. I didn't want my parents or siblings knowing what was going on because to do so would have put Ricky at an unfair advantage. He doesn't have the big family unit like I do and it would have felt like we were all ganging up on him. I knew Greg would be able to think clearly and be impartial. He's always been that way, so I went to him.

"I got selfish at times, I know. I disregarded your feelings when I knew I was pissing you off, and I'm sorry for that. But I don't want my actions to play at all into your desire to relocate. I'd hate to bear the burden that I actually ran you out of town because I wouldn't leave your husband alone. I would like to think you trust Greg more than that, Jessie, but I can't help but ask."

"Stop it." Jessica had harshness in her

whisper as she stopped Sherry's rambling. "I don't *want* to relocate to New York, but I'm *willing* to do it if Greg takes on this job. I never said that my choice is to move there . . . it's not. My choice is to follow whatever plan that God has for our futures and if that means moving to New York, then yes, I'm prepared to do that. This has nothing at all to do with me wanting to get Greg out of your reach. I admit that I had some issues about that, but Greg and I had a real heart-to-heart about it and I am reassured that both your and his intentions are pure. That's an entirely different matter that I'm not at all factoring it into the New York issue. And just for the record, it was never Greg that I didn't trust."

Sherry didn't readily respond. She stared into her glass for a while before reaching again for the sandwich that had by now lost all of its warmth. She took a small bite, getting more bread than meat and chewed slowly.

"I'm sorry," Jessica whispered.

"No, no, it's cool. I might have had that one coming, but make no mistake, girl: You are about the only one who I would take that from without snatching you across the table and busting you in the face."

"Geez," Jessica said. "Remind me to

always be your friend."

Sherry laughed. "I know, right? In any case, I'm glad to know that what happened doesn't play into your decision." Sherry sucked the last of her soda through her straw and then looked across the table at Jessica. "I have an idea of what we can do before picking up the kids at five."

"What?"

Sherry took a quick look at her watch and then said, "Ricky is in court again today. Let's peek in on him and see how the case is coming along."

Jessica was pleasantly surprised by Sherry's suggestion. She didn't grasp how an idea to do something that would most likely please Derrick evolved from what had just transpired, but it sounded like the perfect thing to do. "Sure," she agreed. "Closing arguments today?"

"No, but I heard him telling Mr. Wilson over the phone a couple of nights ago that he thought they could wrap it all up by Friday."

"Great," Jessica said as they both stood and counted out the appropriate amount of cash to cover their meals. "Greg will be home tomorrow. Maybe we can all be there for the closing arguments."

CHAPTER 22

An overabundance of thoughts traveled through Greg's mind as he sat and ate a catered lunch in one of Lenox Hill Hospital's many conference rooms. He'd been following the counsel of his pastor and had been praying about the offer that seemed too good to even think of passing up. Greg knew that he was making a connection to heaven and he had no doubts that God had been hearing his prayers — but why hadn't he received an answer? Was God saying, "You idiot! Do you need to be struck by lightning? How can you question whether or not this gift is from me?" Greg wished he knew the answer to that, but as sure as he was that he was going to sign on the dotted line, he was just as sure that he wasn't. Today, for the first time, he noticed that the tug that he felt towards New York only happened outside of the hospital walls. Inside, though he was welcomed and honored, he still felt like a stranger. The higher-ups at Lenox Hill seemed confident that they'd successfully done their job, but Greg was no closer to making a decision now than he was when he read the initial letter. So much was clouding his ability to see clearly.

According to Jessica, her mother was still holding strong to her fight against any mention of New York and Greg was becoming more and more inquisitive about his own mother's strange behavior. When he called her after speaking with Jessica last night, he learned from his mother-in-law that Pastor Baldwin had come by and picked Lena up again. They were still working towards finalizing the plans for Sunday's program. Greg's mother had always played an active role when it came to special events at the church, but she'd never depended upon anyone to get her there. She always drove herself. Now, lately, she and Pastor Baldwin seemed to do most of the church planning together. Then there was Derrick and Sherry. He'd received a glimmer of good news from Jessica that the two of them had at least carried on a civilized conversation following yesterday's hearing, but they had a long way to go to get back to the passionate and loving couple that they once had been.

Those were issues that Greg would have to address when he returned to D.C., but for now he tried to focus on the activities around him. Because it was the middle of the workday, all of the doctors on staff couldn't stay and sit for the lunch, but each of them had been invited to drop by and at least grab a plate. There was more than enough to go around. Doctors and nurses were in and out of the room constantly, acknowledging those who sat before returning to their duties. The hospital had gone all out, providing Greg and the others with a smorgasbord of choices to dine on. From roasted chicken Parmesan to finger sandwiches and fresh fruit, there was something for every appetite. It was nothing short of a celebratory gathering that had been labeled a corporate luncheon.

"There's some major butt-kissing going on up in here today. If one of these white folks go to tap dancing or shining your shoes, I'm gonna think we're in the *Twilight Zone*."

It took all of Greg's willpower to choke back the laughter that seemed to bang against the walls of his throat. He pursed his lips and turned to look at LaRon, who sat next to him inconspicuously bowing his head and repeatedly whispering, "Yes, suh,

Massah Dixon."

LaRon was only slightly overdramatizing the situation. Mr. Price and the senior staff members had gone beyond the call of duty to make a stellar impression on Greg over the past two and a half days. If one person wasn't inviting him to lunch, dinner or drinks, another was offering him prime-seat tickets to see the New York Yankees. He'd turned down most of the enticements for lack of interest, but he did take Dr. Tanner up on the baseball game last night. Secretly, the Yankees were the one New York team that Greg embraced and rooted for, even when they were up against his hometown Washington Nationals.

It was obvious that Lenox Hill desperately wanted to add the esteemed name of Dr. Gregory Dixon to their roster of capable physicians. As Greg had gone down the line preparing his plate, he even noted that the spread of food consisted of many of his favorites. It was highly improbable that the absence of red meat, the presence of grilled salmon and the abundance of fresh pineapples were pure happenstance.

"So, how's the wife, Dr. Dixon?" Mr. Price asked. "We can hardly wait to meet your family. You know what they say: Beside every good man is a good woman."

Montgomery Price's question broke Greg's previous thought flow and took him directly into another. Of all the recreational perks that the staff had offered him, none of them even came close to the enjoyment that he'd gotten from finally being able to fulfill his telephone fantasy with his Grace last night.

"I'm sure she's ready for you to get back home, but you be sure to tell her that we appreciate her letting us borrow you for a few days." Mr. Price's continuance snapped Greg back from the pleasure trip his mind had begun recalling.

"Grace is fine, Mr. Price. Thanks for asking."

"She's just as important to us as you are, Dr. Dixon."

"Butt-kissing." LaRon buried the words inside of a bogus cough so that only Greg was sitting close enough to understand.

"I appreciate that, Mr. Price." Greg somehow maintained his composure. "And I'll be sure to let her know that you asked about her."

Glasses half-filled with champagne had been placed at each table setting. Without Greg telling them, they knew he didn't drink and had instead given him sparkling white grape juice. Someone had done his homework. Dr. Tanner picked up his glass and raised it in the air.

"To Dr. Gregory Dixon," he said, smiling as the others grabbed their glasses and followed his lead. After a nudge from Dr. Clayton, Greg slowly reached for his as well. "May he *not* be able to fill the shoes of Dr. Joseph Armstrong because he, with so many formative years ahead of him, will need a much bigger pair."

It was three o'clock by the time the lunch meeting ended. With both his mind and his stomach filled to capacity, all Greg wanted to do was get back to his hotel room and rest up for his early morning flight back home. As he and LaRon parted ways in the hall, a woman stopped Greg's trek to the exit doors.

"Dr. Dixon, I'm Dr. Mallory Higgins. I don't think we ever had the pleasure of meeting personally, but I'm one of the physical therapists here at Lenox Hill."

"Good to make your acquaintance," Greg said, hoping this wouldn't turn into a long conversation.

"Do you remember Sergeant Evan McDonald? He's the man —"

Greg interrupted her. "Yes, I do. I remember him and his surgery well."

Dr. Higgins handed Greg a folded slip of

paper. "He was here for his therapy session while you were in the meeting with Mr. Price. He wanted to stay around and wait for you to finish, but he had to leave. Mr. McDonald asked me to give you this note."

Greg looked at the short note scribbled in pencil. As tired as he was, he smiled at the request from Sergeant McDonald that Greg come and meet him so that they could "catch up on things."

The ride to the policeman's home should have only taken twenty minutes, but with the inaccurate directions that Dr. Higgins had given him, Greg's route took nearly twice as long. As he pulled into the driveway of the modest brick home, Greg immediately spotted Sergeant McDonald petting the head of a large dog. It had begun barking from inside the fence at the strange vehicle that had approached.

"Close your mouth, Charlie!" Greg heard the sergeant say as he cautiously exited his rented vehicle. "That's the man that saved my life. Now cut that noise out and go sit down somewhere."

Greg couldn't help but laugh when the dog obediently sat on the ground beside Sergeant McDonald. Just so he wouldn't be mistaken for a wimp, Charlie growled one last warning as his master met the man who didn't look familiar to the dog's sharp eyes or smell familiar to his keen nose.

"Dr. Dixon, how are you?"

As Greg accepted his former patient's embrace, he noted that the policeman only used one arm. Despite that, his hold was tight and to Greg it felt as though he was hugging an old friend. Once again, he detected the strange tug towards New York.

"I'm fine, Sarge. You're looking well. How have you been?"

Before answering, Sergeant McDonald led Greg into his home and showed him into the living room. The house was nice and cool inside and the décor reminded Greg of how his home had looked when he was a bachelor. Sports memorabilia lined the shelf over the fireplace, and on the wall behind the couch Evan had a framed jersey hand signed by Michael Jordan. Greg gasped, not just because it was a signed jersey by his all-time favorite sports hero, but because it was a Washington Wizard jersey, not one from the champion Chicago Bulls team.

"I should have known that you'd like that." Sergeant McDonald laughed as he took a seat and left his company standing and admiring other items in his collection.

"Oh, man," Greg said, seeing all of the

wonderful pieces that had been collected over the years. "This is some awesome stuff." Greg's gaze had just fallen to a larger version of the photograph of the grand-daughter that Evan had showed him at the hospital when the policeman spoke up again.

"Look out that back window there," he told Greg. "What do you see?"

Greg looked into the fenced-in backyard and saw an old, but well-kept car. "What's that?" he asked. "A seventy-two?"

"Close." Evan seemed impressed. "It's a nineteen-seventy Chevrolet Impala."

"And it works?"

"Not a lick." The policeman laughed again, fishing a toothpick from a jar beside him and slipping it into his mouth. "But it was brand-spanking new when I picked up Hank Aaron in it some years ago. He was on his way to a practice session there in Atlanta, Georgia, and I had just drove Lou-ise off the lot."

"Louise?"

"Yeah, that's what I named her," he said with a chuckle. "Something happened to Hank's car and there he was, sitting in it on the side of the road. I stopped to help and he asked me if I could take him to practice. I was obliged, of course. I wished I had my camera with me that day, but I didn't. When I asked for an autograph, he took a permanent marker and signed the dash for me right before he got out of the car."

"You're kidding!"

"Nope. It was a surreal experience that I'll never forget. To this day, in my opinion, ain't no man done for the game of baseball what that Henry Aaron did."

"He signed the dashboard of your car? No wonder you won't get rid of her."

"That's a part of the reason," Evan said. "Hank wasn't the only person I had in that car. There's a reason I named her Louise."

Greg held up his hand. "I don't think I want to hear that story." He finally sat. "You didn't answer me before. How've you been?"

"I'm living and I probably shouldn't be, so I can't complain. Got my hair back too."

"I can see that." Greg nodded. "How's your therapy coming along?"

Sergeant McDonald used his right hand to lift up his left arm. When he let it go, there was only enough strength in the arm to hold it up for a few seconds before it fell into his lap. Then he wiggled his left fingers, using much less effort than he'd used when Greg had asked him to do it weeks earlier in the hospital. Greg smiled, not expecting

274

to hear the policeman's next words.

"I won't be going back to the force."

"But that's good, Sarge," Greg encouraged. "You've made progress. You're not giving up on it, are you? These things take time. Your therapy has only been going on for a few weeks."

"Oh, no. I'm not giving up. I still have my badge and I'm still a sworn officer of the law for right now. It's not about giving up. I aim to have every bit of my movement back before it's over. But even when I do, I don't have the heart for policing anymore. Some days I wake up and feel like there's one more 'big one' in me, but then I look at this arm and realize that it's just wishful thinking. Even if I recovered enough to get back out on the streets and go after more dealers . . . that might take years, and I don't have that long to wait. I'm fifty-six years old, Doc. I was planning to hang up my hat in another two to three years anyway. That baseball bat to the head just forced me to do it a little early.

"Since my accident, I've been getting the urge to travel or to go and spend some time with family. Maybe go visit my kids and my grandkid. Life is too short. I could go back, take the financial benefit and start with administrative duty, but why? In my heart of hearts, I know that's not really what I want to do and most times money isn't everything. They had this surprise 'Welcome Back' party for me last week. The doctor cleared me for the administrative position and the guys and gals at the station threw a party fit for a king. The chief of police said he knew he could get me a pay raise for my heroism. They gave me every reason in the world to come back, but I realized that my heart wasn't in it anymore. Am I making sense to you, Dr. Dixon?"

Greg smiled down at his open hand and nodded. "You make a lot of sense, Sarge."

The officer disappeared into the kitchen and returned with a glass of water for Greg. He went back for the second glass and then returned to his seat. Greg's first reaction was to feel sorry for what the severe beating had taken away from the man, but his limitations didn't seem impede him much at all. Seeing Greg watching his movements, Evan smiled, but chose to change the line of conversation.

"I was surprised to hear that you were in a meeting today at the hospital. Are you filling in for another doctor?"

Greg took a sip of his drink and then stared into the glass for a moment.

"It's peach flavored," Evan told him. "I

hope you like peaches."

"Actually, it's quite delicious," Greg said, taking another swallow before continuing. "Lenox Hill is offering me a fulltime job there. One of the head doctors is leaving at the end of the month and they want me to take over his position."

From his expression, it was hard for Greg to tell whether the policeman was happy or just surprised. He ran his hands through his silky brown hair and then displayed a broad smile. "Well, there's an opportunity for you, huh? Are you gonna take it?"

"I don't know," Greg admitted. "You're right, it would be an awesome opportunity, but . . ."

"But?" Sergeant McDonald repeated the conjunction. "What's your heart saying, son? Think about every decision you've ever made in your life. On those where you followed your heart, I'll bet you any amount of money that those are the ones you never regretted. The ones you make with 'buts' attached are the ones that grow to disappoint you."

Greg drank more of his water as he thought about the choices he'd made: his choice to attend Georgetown University so that he could remain close to his mother; his choice to accept Christ just as he was entering college; his choice to pursue Grace, even when Derrick hated her; and his choice to perform her aneurysm surgery at the risk of losing his job at Robinson Memorial. Evan was right. Each time that he followed his heart, he had no misgivings. Pastor Baldwin had preached a recent message of how God spoke to the heart. Perhaps he'd had his answer long ago, but just hadn't been aware of it.

"If I would have listened to my heart years ago, I probably wouldn't be living all alone in this house," Sergeant McDonald said. "The heart has a way of telling you which way to go and when you fight against it, you might win the battle, but you'll lose the war."

Greg still felt the fatigue stemming from his late night out at the ballgame, but at Sergeant McDonald's house, he sensed a certain level of comfort that seemed to come naturally. He leaned back on the soft pillows behind him and said, "Sounds like there's a story in there somewhere."

"You sure you want to hear it? It's about Louise."

Greg leaned forward long enough to place his empty glass on the coaster on the coffee table. "Sure," he said, leaning back again.

"Louise wasn't my wife, she was my

mistress . . . the other woman, in other words. I never saw her as such because my wife and I weren't together at the time and hadn't been in quite a while. Remember how I told you that I wasn't always a good cop and how I did stuff that was illegal in the name of getting back at my father's killer?"

Greg nodded. He remembered the story well and applauded Evan for being so open about his past life of racism and hatred.

"Well, while I was out picking up black hookers and sleeping with them to get back at black men, I messed around and fell in love with one of them."

"Louise?"

"Yeah. I don't know how in the world it happened, but it happened. I couldn't just walk away feeling smug that I'd bagged another black woman like I'd done with all the rest of them. Louise meant something to me from the first night I was with her. After being with her, I couldn't just drive down the street and pick up any old Jane Doe anymore. It had to be her. I even threatened to kill a man who was just getting ready to pick her up before I got there one night. I had the gun to his face and all. If Louise hadn't pleaded for his life, I would have shot him; I know I would have."

Evan settled back in his chair as if he'd closed the book and the story had ended, but Greg's interest had been piqued and he wanted to know more.

"What happened to Louise?"

A sad look crossed Evan's face. He hung his head and then shook it in sorrow. "I don't know. I made the mistake of leaving her and when I went back to try and find her, I guess she'd changed corners. For weeks, I combed all the areas where I knew prostitutes hung out, but I couldn't find her anywhere."

"Why'd you leave her?"

"Well, like I said, me and Nancy were separated during this time, but she suddenly came back into my life and wanted to put our marriage back together. I told Louise that I'd invested so many years with Nancy that it just wouldn't be right for me not to give it one last try. It was stupid of me to think such a beautiful girl would still be waiting there for me just in case the reconciliation didn't work out."

"And it didn't work out."

"No, it didn't. Truth of the matter was, as wrong as it might have been, I'd fallen totally out of love with Nancy in the two years that we'd been separated and my heart belonged to Louise. I should have followed my heart and just ended my marriage and given Nancy the chance at real happiness that she deserved and myself the chance with Louise that I really wanted. Instead, the last time I saw her she was crying uncontrollably and screaming at me for using her. Little did she know."

"You never told her you loved her?"

Evan shook his head in deep regret. "So instead of having Louise here with me, I got a car in the backyard that I can't get rid of because it's one of the last pieces of her that I have left. Like that old car out there, Louise ain't humming in that off-key way of hers, but she'll always be with me one way or the other."

Greg hated to leave. Sergeant McDonald was getting more interesting to him by the minute, but glancing at his watch, he realized that he needed to get back to the hotel for some overdue rest. It was nearing six o'clock now and Jessica would be expecting a call from him soon. When Greg mentioned to his favorite Lenox Hill patient that he needed to be on his way, Evan seemed as unprepared for him to leave as Greg felt about leaving. Greg could feel the bizarre tug, even as he followed Evan towards the door to make his exit. As soon as the door opened, Greg winced, startled by the grey cat that lunged from the front step directly into Sergeant McDonald's arm.

"Hey, Mat," Evan said, unfazed by the sudden bundle that purred over his shoulder. "Hungry?"

"You're an animal lover," Greg observed, stepping around Evan and putting space between himself and the cat. Greg was not at all fond of felines.

"Just Mat the cat and Charlie, that's all. It's all a part of a desperate, pitiful attempt to hold on to a past that never should have gotten away."

Greg was confused. "How so? Did Louise love dogs and cats?"

"Sad to say, I never got to know enough about her to say whether she did or not."

Greg fished in his pocket for his ringing cell phone as Evan kept talking.

"I named them all after her," he said. "The cat, the dog and the car; they all have pieces of her name. Louise's full name was Mattie Louise Charles. I'll never forget it."

Greg heard what sounded like frantic words from Jessica coming from his phone as soon as he flipped it open, but Sergeant Evan McDonald's words had temporarily frozen him. Holding the phone a distance from his ear, Greg stared at the policeman and said, "Wha . . . what did you say?"

CHAPTER 23

Sirens and flashing lights served as beacons that drew dozens of people to the brightly colored child-care facility with the painted wooden sign on the front lawn of a woman embracing a child. Cars carrying parents, who had just been notified of the mayhem, were still arriving. People seemed to be jumping out of the cars before they shut off the engines. Several television news stations had arrived and there were even news choppers flying above, capturing the devastation that panicky parents were enduring while police hindered them from getting any closer to the building. Inside, forty children and seven adults were being held hostage. Representation from every emergency force could be found on the grounds of Open Arms Day Care.

At the sight of a familiar Town Car, Sherry broke away from the tearful huddle that she and Jessica had formed and dashed across the lot towards Derrick, jumping into his reaching arms. Through eyesight blurred with tears, Jessica watched them embrace for a moment before Sherry grabbed his arm and led him back to where Jessica waited.

"Are both of them in there?" Derrick asked.

"Yes," Sherry said through sobs. "He's got both of them."

"What have they told you?"

"Nothing," Jessica said, trying desperately not to fall apart. "We were two of the first ones here. We were just coming to pick up the kids and saw the police starting to gather. They wouldn't let us in. We learned that there was a hostage situation after one of the other parents arrived. He had heard it on the news."

Both women watched as Derrick fought his way through the crowd towards the first policeman he could reach. At first, he asked for updates on what was known about the gunman or the condition of the hostages inside. All he got in return were repeated demands that he stay back and let the police do their job. After several more minutes of questioning and throwing out his title and degree, Derrick rejoined them, having accomplished nothing of value.

"They're not going to let us anywhere near the building," he said. "Has anyone called Greg?"

"Jessie did, about a half hour ago," Sherry told him.

Jessica nodded. "He said he was going to catch the first flight out, but even if he could have caught a flight the minute I called him, it still would be another hour before he lands, let alone the time it would take him to drive from the airport to here."

"I'm sure he had to get packed and everything," Derrick reasoned. "It'll be a while before he gets here. Did you call your mom or Ms. Mattie?"

"I called Pastor Baldwin right after I called you," Sherry said. "I thought it was best if he went by and told them rather than us telling them over the phone. I didn't want to worry them too much."

"That was good thinking, baby," Derrick said, rubbing his hand helplessly over his hair and looking around at the growing crowd of desperate parents and nosey neighbors. Mumbling almost as if talking to himself, he said, "We've got to get our kids out of there."

"There are a gazillion cops out here and it's only one of him," Jessica said in a burst of tears. "Why won't they just teargas him out of there?"

"Sweetie, there are kids in there that they have to be concerned with," Derrick said, hugging her close. "They've got to put the safety of our children first. They don't want the children to be hurt and neither do we. God knows if that man injures so much as a hair on Dee's head . . ."

Derrick never completed the sentence. He held one woman in each arm, trying to convince himself as he tried to convince them that their children would be fine. He continued to scan the crowd, not sure of what it was he was looking for. Then his eyes locked in on the officer he determined was negotiating with the man who'd barricaded himself in the building with the children. He'd seen scenes like this before only in movies and on the news. Situations like this could take hours to resolve and the endings weren't always happy ones.

More helicopters were hovering overhead now. Derrick wondered if any of them carried snipers, searching for a clear shot through one of the day-care windows to take the gunman down. He didn't care how they got him or whether he lived through the ordeal or not. Derrick just wanted to know that his daughter and godson were okay. He wanted all the children to come out of this in one piece, but there was no denying that Denise and Julian were the two he was praying hardest for.

Derrick took Jessica's ringing phone from her trembling hand and, recognizing the number on the display, he immediately answered. Jessica knew that it was Greg and she looked up at Derrick as he spoke. She listened while Derrick gave her husband an update of what appeared to be transpiring with the frightening nightmare that was unfolding in front of them. Just when she thought that Derrick was getting ready to end the call, Jessica watched a look of disbelief come over his face. Then, with no explanation, Derrick pulled away from both of them and excused himself for a private conversation with Greg. Jessica knew that there was apparently something that neither Greg nor Derrick wanted them to hear, but she reasoned that it had to do with circumstances surrounding the hostage situation. Derrick knew that anything negative said would send both Jessica and Sherry into hysterics. She was glad he'd walked away. She'd rather not face the downside of what the end might bring. Thirty minutes passed before they saw Derrick again.

"Where've you been?" Sherry asked, cuddling up to him as soon as he was within reach.

Derrick handed the cell phone back to Jessica as he spoke. "Two other calls came through. I talked to Pastor Baldwin. He's told both Ms. Lena and Ms. Mattie and they're all at the house now. He said he was trying to prevent them from watching the news, but neither of them would hear of it. They agreed to stay at home and not come here, but he said they are glued to the television. He also said they've been and will continue to be in prayer."

Jessica sank onto the grassy area where they'd been standing. Instinctively, Sherry and Derrick followed. The seven o'clock hour had just passed. The crowd wasn't getting any smaller, but much of the commotion had quieted. The police had threatened to arrest anyone who made an attempt to cross the yellow crime tape that had been connected to several trees surrounding the building. Parents and other relatives had conceded that law enforcement was doing the best they could to resolve the chaos, but the waiting was torture.

"Who was the other call from?" Jessica asked. "You said two other calls came through."

"It was one of your students from Trinity.

I can't recall her name . . . sorry. But she said she was watching the news and just wanted to know if this was the same Open Arms that Julian attended. She told me to tell you that she's keeping her fingers crossed for you."

"We're going to need a lot more than crossed fingers," Sherry said.

The seconds passed like minutes on the clock. At eight o'clock, a truck pulled up in the parking lot lit only by the headlights of cars and the lights that beamed down from the overhead helicopters that still loomed. Four police officers stripped down to their undershirts and boxers to carry in trays of burgers that had been ordered from a local Burger King. Someone in the crowd had a portable radio and according to the reporter, having the sandwiches delivered by the scantily clad officers was one of the demands that the offender had made. The reporter also said that there was indication that several of the younger children were getting restless and agitated at having to sit inside the building and now, so was the gunman.

"Oh, God," Jessica prayed softly with fresh tears spilling down her cheeks. Derrick's hand on her shoulder offered very little comfort. Julian had been attending the day care and learning center for most of his life. He was accustomed to the time that his mother would pick him up. Many times when Jessica arrived to get him, Julian would be standing by the glass door with his face pressed against it, waiting for her appearance. By now, he would be one of the restless ones.

Shortly after the meals had been delivered, relief came for several of the parents when ten of the children and two adult providers were released. Sherry and Jessica cheered along with the others when two infants, five toddlers and three school-age children safely cleared the parking lot and were delivered to waiting ambulances that would take them to local hospitals to be certain that they hadn't been harmed. Neither Julian nor Denise were in that number.

It would be another hour before Greg arrived, and when he found his way to the others, Jessica grabbed him around his neck as though her life depended upon how tight she could hold on. As uncomfortable as her grip was, Greg didn't fight it. He allowed her to cling as hard and for as long as she needed to until all of her tears had soaked both his shirt collar and his neck.

Jessica could hear him assuring her that it would all be over soon and that Julian would be fine, but the hour had grown late and her faith had begun to wane two hours earlier. Although spring was giving way to summer, the late night air brought lower temperatures. Greg removed his suit jacket and draped it around Jessica's arms and they stood, embracing and looking towards the dimly lit center where their son was being held against his will. Derrick and Sherry struck a similar pose just a few feet away.

"It's Mr. Miller!"

The sudden announcement came from someone in the assembly behind them. Jessica and Greg turned, as did others who stood close by. The man's voice had come from the darkness and they couldn't see his face, but he turned up the radio so those around him could hear the update that was being introduced as breaking news. What she heard made Jessica's knees buckle in astounding fear. Had Greg's arms not been around her, she would have fallen to the ground.

"Channel 9 News just reported that Hiram and Deloris Miller recently finalized a hostile divorce that left Mr. Miller with little more than his name. After several attempts by Mr. Miller to persuade his ex-wife to reconcile, sources say that he disobeyed court orders this afternoon by entering the child-care center brandishing a loaded gun and creating a deadly environment for everyone in his path. Though it has not been confirmed, it is believed that the former Mrs. Miller was in the center at the time Hiram Miller entered and she was not one of the adults released to police just a short while ago. Police say that no shots have been fired from them, nor the suspect and they are working towards a peaceful end to this frightening ordeal. According to Channel 9 News, Mr. Miller is now requesting that an unarmed officer come inside for a face-to-face talk and to discuss new demands. Due to the suspect's fragile state of mind, officers are hesitant to comply. The gunman has threatened to begin shooting hostages if his latest request isn't met within five minutes. We will keep you updated as new developments are received."

Gasps were heard throughout the crowd and Jessica's wails were not isolated ones. Greg's heart pounded in his chest upon hearing the last few words of the report, but he knew he needed to stay strong for his breaking wife. He closed his eyes as he cuddled her trembling body as closely to him as he could. Just as he started to whisper a prayer, Greg stopped, feeling a twinge of guilt for his selfish act.

"Let's pray," he suddenly said aloud. "Everybody that wants to join me in prayer, come this way. Our children need our prayers. Come quickly."

A few of those surrounding them stood back and chose not to participate, but most of the fearful parents and on-lookers didn't hesitate to gravitate towards where the shadowy figures of Greg and Jessica stood. Holding hands, they formed a circular fence and tears fell from nearly every eye as Greg led the group in a powerful heavenly plea for the lives of those inside.

"Let me holler at you for a minute," Derrick said to Greg shortly after the prayer had ended.

Greg hated leaving Jessica, but she seemed to be satisfied with embracing her best friend as the men walked away to a more private area where Derrick had parked his car several hours earlier. Derrick used his keyless entry to unlock the doors and both of them climbed inside. Once alone, Derrick leaned against the steering wheel, covered his face and sobbed quietly. Greg didn't touch him, nor did he speak. He knew what Derrick was thinking and he knew that the emotional display was one that he'd been holding in for the sake of Sherry.

"I'm such a jerk," he said, drying his eyes with the sleeves of his shirt. "A big, dumb, stupid jerk!"

"You're not dumb or stupid, Rick."

"But you agree that I'm a jerk, don't you?"

Greg shook his head slowly. "You're not a jerk. You do have jerk tendencies though. So I'm not saying you're a jerk, but you can be kind of jerk-*ish*." Greg's attempt to lighten the mood with his best Jamie Foxx impression failed.

"Man, if anything happens to my baby, I won't be able to forgive myself."

"Why? You didn't cause this mess."

"No, but I haven't hugged Dee-Dee in weeks. I've been so irate with Sherry about her giving me another baby that I've just totally neglected Dee. I think I was mad at her, too, in a way, you know? I know it doesn't make any sense, but I think I was. I wanted a son, Greg. I *still* want a son, but God knows I don't want one at the risk of losing my baby. What if God is punishing me for being stupid? What if He takes Dee-Dee away from us because of me?"

"He wouldn't do that, Rick."

"How do you know that? If you give Julian a gift and he throws it on the floor or shows no appreciation for it, wouldn't you think he didn't deserve it? Well, I'm a child of God, right? He gave me Dee as a gift and basically in the last month or so, I've just been throwing her back in His face. What if He takes her back? Wouldn't you take a gift back if your kid did that to you?"

Greg thought for a moment. He didn't know how he'd handle the scenario because he'd never been put in such a situation. But in the course of his thinking, his mind traveled back to a time when he was thirteen and he had scoffed at a watch that his mother had bought him for Christmas. He's asked for a watch, but the one she bought wasn't like the one that he'd pointed to in the catalog. Lena had snatched the package right out of his hand and that was the last time he ever saw it. She was so outdone with his lack of appreciation for the watch she'd saved for that he was graduating high school by the time his mother thought he had matured enough to get another one.

"God isn't like us, Rick. Just because I might do something like that to Julian doesn't mean that God would do that to you. We've prayed and now it's all in the hands of God. He knows your heart and He knows how repentant you are. Now if there are other people that you feel need to hear your apology, then you need to do what you've got to do. But God won't make Dee suffer for your mistakes."

Derrick found hope in Greg's words and he stared out the front window, looking at the backs of the people who made up the thick crowd. Turning the key to power up his car, his eyes locked onto the lighted clock on the dash. It was now almost eleven o'clock. Derrick turned on the radio and listened for updates. Music played instead and he lowered the volume.

"Tell me more about Jessie's dad," he said. "I still can't believe you actually found him and brought him to D.C."

"Think of how dumbfounded I was when I figured out who he was," Greg responded. "I had just found out he was her father when I got her call about this," he said, pointing in the direction of the day care. "At first, I wasn't going to tell him about Grace, but he insisted on coming with me when I told him about the phone call. He's such a cool guy, Rick. I knew he had to be told eventually, but it wasn't until I could think a little clearer on the plane ride here that I told him."

"How'd he take it?"

"Like a champ, actually. There was some shock and disbelief initially, but I think in some small way he was relieved. That man really loved Ms. Mattie and probably still does. I think knowing that she had his child brought him some joy. Now, how she's going to feel about him is a different story."

"Are you sure he's Jessie's dad?"

"Yeah, I'm sure. When I first saw him, I saw something familiar about him, but couldn't put the pieces together. It was all in his eyes and his smile. I kept thinking that maybe I'd seen him somewhere before, but really it was just the likeness of him that I'd seen. Grace looks a lot like him."

"He's white, right?"

"Very much so." Greg nodded. "He has dark hair and dark features, but he's white. I liked him from the day I met him, but I'm not sure how Grace is going to feel about him."

The chatter hushed and both men stared back towards the flashing lights that still surrounded the day care. Greg was always known as the levelheaded one, but he could feel his own anxieties beginning to soar as the time ticked away on the clock.

"Where is he now?"

"Who?" Greg asked.

"Jessie's dad. Did you drop him off at a hotel or something? Where is he now?"

Greg shrugged as he looked through the darkness around the car. "I don't know. I wanted to get straight here, so we didn't stop to check him in yet. I told him to keep his distance. I didn't want to upset Grace any more than she already was. Now's not the time to spring her father on her. But he's out here somewhere. I guess he's just —"

"Shhh!" Derrick turned up the volume on the radio.

"Reports have just come over the wire that more hostages will be released momentarily. Talks between the officer inside the building and Mr. Miller have been in progress for the last half hour. Sources say that police have just received word that for the exchange of a private chopper that will take him to the Mexican border, the gunman has agreed to let more of the children go."

Derrick shut off the engine as the reporter kept talking. He and Greg jumped out of the car and ran back to the area where their wives were waiting. They'd heard the news, too, from the portable radio that a man in the crowd had.

"He's letting more of them go," Jessica said as Greg and Derrick approached.

"We know," Greg told her. "We just heard it on the car radio."

"God, please let our babies come out," Sherry whispered aloud.

Ten minutes passed and then there were

sounds of an approaching helicopter. The small craft hovered closely over the ground, causing the trees to rustle, hairstyles to scatter, and dress skirts to rise. It soon came to a rest on top of the child-care facility. Moments later, four . . . seven . . . twelve . . . twenty . . . then more frightened children poured out the front door of the center. Policemen and other officials raced to cover them and to keep order among the parents, who pressed through the crowds to find the ones that belonged to them. After the children had cleared the door, then adults came pushing babies — some piled on top of each other in strollers — through the opening and towards the ambulances where they were directed.

Greg and Jessica were among the parents who were trying to get to the ambulances to see if their child had been freed. It was no use. About a dozen ambulances were packed with children and rushed, with sirens blasting, towards the medical centers.

"Oh, my God," Jessica cried. "Where is he? Where's my baby?"

"Let's go this way," Greg said, pulling her arm in a direction to clear them from the throng of other panicking parents.

They reached a clearing and Greg saw the last person limping from the doorway of

Open Arms Day Care and Learning Center. He held a child in one arm and the other arm rested by his side. Greg stopped in his tracks, causing Jessica to run into him from behind.

"What?" Jessica looked around, trying to follow the direction of her husband's eyes.

After seeing him pass the child to a waiting paramedic, Greg watched Evan, dressed in nothing but his underwear, rush to get as far away from the building as he could. The police stood back and waited for the suspect to come out. The helicopter still rested on top of the building and a small ladder, that would lead to his safe climb aboard, was lowered near the entrance door. When the inside of the day-care center, which had been dim since the sun went down, suddenly lit up as though it had been struck by lightning, everyone knew the terror wasn't over yet. Someone was shooting. The sounds of the chopper's turning propellers covered most of the magnified firecracker sound. There was still no certainty that everyone who was inside had been accounted for. Police officers, with guns drawn, began to rush towards the building. But before they could reach the front door, a second shot set off another incredible flash of light.

Frantic cries were echoing all around the

grounds where parents were still seeking answers and for any sign that their child was among the fortunate ones. Greg felt paralyzed with fear. Feeling the pressure of an unknown object fall at his feet, he turned to see Jessica passed out on the ground beside him.

CHAPTER 24

"You're sure? You're sure they all got out?"

"Yeah, I'm sure. Watch out for that truck."

Jessica woke up to darkness and familiar and unfamiliar voices. Her head felt heavy and she struggled to sit up. Focusing her eyes, she realized she was lying in the backseat of her husband's car and as he jerked the steering wheel to avoid colliding with another vehicle, she almost fell to the floor. She grabbed hold of the back of the driver's seat to keep her balance.

"Grace," Greg said, realizing she'd awakened. "Just sit back and hold on, baby."

"Where are we going? Who are you?" she asked the strange man in the passenger seat, who turned around and looked at her.

"I, uh . . ."

"He's a police officer, Grace," Greg interjected, knowing it wasn't the time for her to find out Evan's true identity. "We're on our way to the hospital to see about Julian."

"Why? What's wrong with him?"

Greg calmed her. "Nothing is wrong with him, baby. They took all the kids there for precautionary measures."

"So he got out?"

"They all got out, sweetheart." Evan's voice was shaky as he answered. He looked into the darkness of the backseat and saw a beautiful, feminine image of himself. "All the children did, anyway," he added before turning back to face the front.

Jessica wasn't sure how comfortable she was with having the strange man refer to her with such fondness, but she was too sidetracked with thoughts of Julian to be overly concerned. She looked out of the back window and saw a line of cars. Everyone's emergency lights seemed to be flashing. No doubt, they were all concerned parents, trying to reach the same destination as they.

"Where are Rick and Sherry?"

"About three cars ahead of us," Greg told her.

The nearest hospital to where the incident had occurred was St. Mary's. It was the hospital where Jessica had been initially placed six years ago after the deadly accident that she'd been involved in. She'd spent several weeks there before being transferred to Robinson Memorial where she met the man who would, through divine destiny, become her husband. Because her entire time in the hospital that catered to mostly the underprivileged was spent in an unconscious state, Jessica had no memories as she stepped through the sliding doors. She held her husband's hand and joined dozens of other parents who had arrived before them.

She searched the overfilled waiting room, looking for signs of Sherry. In doing so, she caught the stare of the strange white gentleman who had ridden in the front seat with her husband on the drive over. Briefly, their eyes locked, but Jessica pulled hers away, feeling a bit unnerved by his gaze.

"There's Rick," Greg said, tugging at her arm and leading her towards the opposite side of the room.

The four friends embraced and spent a few moments sharing notes, seeking for any updates that one another may have heard on the drive over. The radio in Greg's car had been turned off, but Jessica and the others listened as he gave them the firsthand account that had been passed along to him by Evan.

"No one was left inside when Evan left the building except Mr. and Mrs. Miller," he told them.

Derrick shook his head. "So the two shots?"

"If they were on target, most likely it's going to be ruled a murder-suicide. Sarge said he couldn't convince Mr. Miller to release his ex-wife and he said he was getting irritated with him for trying to. Evan didn't think he was going to shoot her though. According to Sarge, Mr. Miller said she was his insurance to get safely on the plane and across the border. He had no choice but to leave the two behind when Mr. Miller threatened to kill that last kid if he didn't leave immediately. With his handicap, Sarge was in no condition to try to take Mr. Miller on, so he left and hoped for the best. I guess something happened to make him change his mind about the escape."

"Mrs. Miller probably wouldn't cooperate," Derrick offered. "What a shame."

"Oh, my God," Sherry whispered. Over the years, she'd gotten to know Deloris Miller quite well. Denise had been attending the learning center since she was Julian's age. To have a kind woman die such a horrible death was almost unimaginable.

Although there were so many people inside that most of them were forced to stand, there was a quiet relief in the hospital's emergency waiting area. Some of the news cameras that had been at the school now convened out in the lot of the hospital. Administrative officials wouldn't let the cameras enter the already crowded facility.

Greg and Jessica stood together embracing and quietly giving thanks in a corner space. From over her shoulder, Greg could see Sergeant McDonald standing in the mix of others, watching their display of affection and support.

"Dixon!"

Breaking their hold on one another, both Greg and Jessica turned towards the familiar voice of Dr. Simon Grant. He maneuvered his way through the maze of people and hugged Jessica, who was waiting for his arrival with outstretched arms. Greg shook his hand and embraced him as well.

"Dr. Grant, what are you doing here?"

"I was watching the whole thing on the news, but I didn't realize that you were back in D.C. until I called Joseph Armstrong and he told me you caught an early flight."

Greg reached for his cell phone. "I guess I should call them. I didn't have time to explain to them why I needed to leave. I just told Dr. Tanner that it was a family emergency."

Dr. Grant reached out and covered the

top of Greg's cell with his hand. "I told Joseph while I was on the phone with him. He said that he'd be sure to pass the information along. That was a couple of hours ago, so I'm sure they know by now. I tried to call you on your cell earlier, but got no answer. I left a message."

Greg looked at the message indicator and saw that he had four waiting. "Sorry. I'd turned the ringer off during the flight and never did turn it back on."

While Greg stepped aside to listen to his stored messages, Jessica tried to accurately fill Dr. Grant in on all of what had transpired over the past several hours. Some of it he'd heard on the news, but Jessica's account was far more detailed. After the final message had been played, Greg closed his phone and tucked it away in his pocket.

"You look disappointed," Evan said, approaching Greg while glancing in the direction of Jessica and Dr. Grant.

"No, not disappointed . . . well, maybe I am a bit, but it just makes me realize even more that I'm making the right choice."

"What do you mean?"

"A few hours ago, the staff in New York was notified about the standoff here that involved my son. None of the messages on my phone were from them. Nobody called to see whether my son was living or dead. Nobody."

"I see," Evan said. "That does tell you something."

"That tells me a lot. When I was there, they told me how much I and my family meant to them, but their actions are speaking louder than their words. See that guy over there talking to Grace? He's from Robinson Memorial. I had a message from him on my phone, plus he's here at the hospital to check on us. He's one of the reasons that it was hard to even consider leaving Robinson to begin with. Dr. Grant is on duty tonight, but he took time away once he heard that the children were brought here."

"So, you've decided not to take the job at Lenox?"

Greg nodded. "Not because of this incident, though. I really came to the conclusion while I was at your house. Something you said made me realize that my place was here."

Sergeant McDonald was on the verge of responding when their attention was taken by new voices that had joined them in the waiting room.

"Stay here." Greg whispered the instructions before he turned quickly to meet the others as they headed towards Jessica and Dr. Grant.

Lena and Mattie were asking so many questions that it was impossible to answer them all. Greg calmed the excited women by telling them that the children were fine. From the corner where he'd joined the rest of the family, Greg threw a glance towards the direction he'd just left and saw Evan leaning against the wall in a manner that made it seem that he needed the support in order to stand. He'd caught a glimpse of the woman he'd left hurt, angry and unknowingly pregnant nearly thirty years ago. Greg repositioned himself so that there would be no chance that the women would spot the policeman, who was making no attempt to hide his presence in the room.

"Well, praise the Lord," Pastor Baldwin said after hearing how all of the children had been released. "We heard on the news that there was gunfire, but they didn't make it clear as to whether it was exchanged between the policemen and the suspect or what."

"It was Mr. Miller," Sherry told them. "He shot Mrs. Miller and then himself."

"Lord have mercy," Mattie said, shaking her head.

A commotion behind them caused all

heads to turn. Hospital attendants in white uniforms were beginning to deliver the children, most of whom were crying, to their anxiously awaiting parents. Greg and Jessica began pressing towards the double doors where several nurses were.

"Daddy!" It was Denise's voice and Greg only caught a glimpse of her before she lunged from a nurse's hand into Derrick's arms.

Jessica's hand tightened onto Greg's as they got closer to the front where parents were signing release forms. She looked at the bundles that several nurses were holding. None of them was Julian. Her heart started to pound. What if the policeman that rode in the car with them was wrong? What if Julian had somehow been left behind? The building had been so dark and the situation so tense that the caretakers could have easily overlooked one of the smaller ones when they were given permission to leave. What if Julian was still there now, wandering in the darkness, scared and alone? Jessica whisked away a falling tear from her cheek.

"I don't see him," she told her husband.

Greg spotted a familiar blue blanket. Julian hardly went anywhere without it. It was a blanket that Lena used in her only child's crib when he was an infant, and when Julian was born, she passed it along to him. Greg knew that beneath that blue blanket, in that nurse's arms, was his son. He motioned for Jessica to follow him.

"It's Julian!" she gasped after spotting the blanket also.

The closer they got to the waiting nurse, the larger the lump in Greg's throat felt. "I think you have something that belongs to me," he said as they stood directly in front of her. His hands trembled when he reached to pull back the blanket and Jessica's tears broke loose when they saw the confirming mass of soft, dark brown hair that was revealed.

Julian turned and broke into a wide grin at the sight of his father and immediately wriggled from the nurse's grip and wrapped his arms around Greg's neck, squeezing with all of his might.

"Now I see where he gets his good looks," the nurse said to Greg while draping the abandoned blanket over Julian's back.

Jessica would have to wait for her embrace. She didn't know if her eighteen-month-old son had any idea of the severity of the situation he'd just gone through, but he was holding on to his father with no signs of letting go. She buried her face into Greg's shoulder and wept, all the while wrapping her arms around both her husband and her son.

Walking back towards their waiting mothers and Pastor Baldwin, Greg noted Sherry in a kneeling position, rubbing Derrick's back as he sat rocking back and forth holding his daughter closely to his chest. Although he succeeded in hiding the flood of tears from those around him, the shaking of Derrick's body gave away the fact that his emotions were soaking into the cotton fibers of his daughter's blouse.

"Give me my baby," Mattie said, reaching forward and almost prying Julian from his father's arms before Lena could.

Greg once again took a quick look in Sergeant McDonald's direction. For the first time, the man saw what represented a whole slice of his life that he'd not had the opportunity to be a part of. It was a scene that was too much for him to endure any longer. Even from across the room, Greg could see reflections of light glistening from the tears that were streaming down his cheeks. Wanting to, but unable to stop him without the inquisition of his family, Greg watched Evan walk towards the exit doors and disappear into the night.

CHAPTER 25

It had been a long night for many families in D.C. Even those that didn't have children at the center sat up and watched the live updates that were given constantly over the airwaves. If one television news station wasn't reporting on it, another was, even to the degree of cutting into other programming to share the unfolding, nail-biting drama to all who were interested.

Greg raised the bar that night with his wife. It was more than lovemaking; it was like an advanced class in Loveology. Greg wanted to make her feel like she'd never felt before. He wanted the night to be, for his Grace, so memorable that if it were their last time together, she'd remember it forever. Life was fragile and, from this time forward, Greg vowed that he'd love his wife and son so much that there would never be any regrets should they be taken from him or he from them in an untimely way. Life had ended in tragic fashion that night for two people who had once loved each other and shared a life together. Mrs. Miller could not have known what her ex-husband was capable of. Greg knew he'd never do anything to harm his family, no matter what. But still, he had a heightened need to let each of them know how much he loved them. And Jessica was first on the list.

It wasn't until they were moist with perspiration and lying in each other's arms that Greg told her of his decision to remain at Robinson Memorial. Jessica tried not to be overjoyed, but Greg could tell that she was pleased with his final decision. He knew how uncomfortable she was with leaving her mother, but she'd been willing to go if that was his choice. He loved her for that. Now, somehow, he had to figure out a way to tell her just why her mother had been so adamant. Greg recalled that it wasn't until he'd mentioned his patient's name at the dinner table that Sunday that Mattie had become so irrational and almost overcome with fear. For years, she'd told Jessica that she had no idea who her father was. But now, the truth was staring her in the face and Mattie couldn't bear the thought of facing her own past, nor admitting the untruth that she intended to carry to her grave. Greg didn't know how it would all unfold, but he asked Jessica to allow him to be the one to notify everyone of his intent to remain in D.C. and she agreed.

The official word of the murder-suicide wasn't given until Friday morning and Open Arms Day Care and Learning Center closed its doors indefinitely. In a morning news clip of the story that was dubbed, "Tragedy at Open Arms," a close-up shot of the once lively day-care facility showed grim yellow tape still draped around the building and law enforcement officers still lingering, doing whatever it was that they did following a crime such as this one.

"Hey, guys, come look!" Sherry called out as she sat in her friends' living room waiting for them to join her.

Greg and Jessica rushed from the bedroom where they had been getting dressed for today's agenda and joined Sherry in front of the television where Channel 9 News was showing a clip of a brief interview they had filmed the night before right after the fatal gunshots had been fired. With Julian in her arms, Jessica sat next to Sherry on the couch. Unable to move any closer to the sofa after noticing the voice and image on the big-screen television, Greg stood and watched.

"Why did you so boldly volunteer to go into such a dangerous and unstable environment, Sergeant McDonald? As I understand it, you're an officer with the NYPD, so you certainly didn't have to do what you did. Why did you do it and how did you get the assailant to release the children?"

Evan's attention was divided as the newswoman pushed the microphone into his face. Because of the recent shots, the scene was turning chaotic as policemen and bystanders began running in all directions to find out what was going on.

"Something had to be done," Evan said, his words coming quickly. "I couldn't let the children stay in that situation. Whatever was the reason behind this senseless crime, it was no fault of the innocent hostages. I had to do what I had to do. My son-in-law and I got the news . . ." Greg held his breath as Evan paused to rephrase his words. "My grandson was in there. I couldn't just sit around and let something happen to him before I had the chance to get to know him." As he ended the sentence, Evan's voice broke.

"He was one of the younger ones?" the news reporter asked, not realizing the true depth and meaning of Evan's words.

"Yes." Evan was relieved for an escape

from could have been words that would have given his still-secret identity away.

"Gunshots were just fired inside of the school, Sergeant McDonald. That proves beyond doubt, the magnitude of how much danger you put yourself in. Any regrets?"

"My only regret is that I couldn't ensure the safe departure of everyone that was inside. I did what I thought was best for the sake of the children. My daughter still has her child and so do all of the other parents that were in fear of losing children. Sometimes in this business, you can't save everybody, but you just have to thank the good Lord for the ones you do."

Sherry gasped and placed her hand over her chest. "He's so brave. I wish to God I had a chance to hug his neck."

"Isn't that the man that was in the car with us?" Jessica said, pointing at the television screen and looking at Greg. "He's the one who saved the kids."

Greg nodded slowly and responded with a soft, "I know."

"Baby, why didn't you tell me?" Jessica asked. "I would have thanked him or something. I'll bet he thinks I'm the most ungrateful person he's ever seen. I was right there in the car with him and didn't thank him."

"It's okay, Grace. I thanked him for both of us. You were passed out, remember? He knew you were out of it, so it's no big deal. I told him how selfless he was and how much we all appreciated it."

Jessica still showed signs of disappointment, but she didn't press any further. The interview was over and they resumed their preparations to leave for the closing arguments of Derrick's case. Greg was relieved that his wife hadn't remembered the name of the patient that he told her he'd operated on in New York. Had she recalled, it would have been too much of a coincidence that this man shared the same name and was a member of the New York Police Department. There would have been too many follow-up questions for him to answer right now. Jessica had to know eventually, but the process to handle this delicate matter had to be planned with care.

To complicate matters, nothing had been heard from Evan since he disappeared from the hospital last night. Greg had no idea if he was still in D.C., or if he'd decided to make an escape back to his safe world in New York. On the flight to Washington yesterday, Evan agreed with Greg that their meeting had been ordained by God. He'd repeatedly said that he desperately wanted the chance to get to know his daughter and his grandson. If Mattie didn't want him to be a part of her life, he said he understood that and believed that it was a justifiable punishment for his mistake. But he desired to establish a relationship with his youngest child and her son. With his disappearance, Greg was unsure if he still felt the same way. Maybe Evan had decided that it was more trouble than it was worth. Perhaps seeing the whole family gathered at the hospital served as some type of wake-up call for him and he no longer had an interest in being an active part of their lives.

The first thing Greg noted when he pulled his car into his mother's driveway was the dark green pickup truck that had become a frequent presence at the house. He sat for a moment and looked at the vehicle after shutting off the engine. He wasn't stupid or naïve. More than church event planning was drawing Pastor Baldwin to the home, but right now, Greg didn't have the time to address it or deal with it.

Pastor Baldwin opened the door and greeted each as if he were welcoming them into his own home. Greg accepted his pastor's handshake, but was unsure of the unfamiliar feeling that engulfed him as he did. If the others were even remotely suspicious or concerned about the preacher being there on a weekday morning, they didn't show it.

"Lord have mercy, Jesus!" Lena exclaimed, taking Julian from Jessica's arms and planting a heartfelt kiss on his cheek. "Boy, do you know how blessed you are? That old no-good, snotty-nosed devil tried to steal your grandmama's baby from her, but he is a liar and the Lord sent him right back to the pits of hell where he belongs," she said to Julian, who grinned as if he understood.

She then turned to Sherry, who held Denise up for a kiss too. "Yes, Lord," Lena said. "The Lord delivered y'all, girl. You hear me? What did Grandma Lena tell you to say when the Lord do something for you?"

"Thank you, Jesus!" Dee-Dee screamed, with both her hands lifted high into the air.

Instinctively, Julian's hand shot up towards the ceiling too. He screamed something that was no doubt meant to echo the words of his playmate, but it sounded far more like gibberish. Even so, the display by the two children brought a roar of laughter from the adults who had the pleasure of witnessing it. Greg laughed, too, despite his ongoing desire to call his pastor out on whatever was going on between him and Lena. If the women weren't with him, he would have addressed it.

"Where's Mama?" Jessica asked, looking around the room.

"Girl, I don't know what's going on with that mama of yours. She always been crazy; I tried to tell y'all that from the day I met her. But now, she just acting like she's losing her mind."

Jessica looked at Lena in concern. "What do you mean? She's not here?"

"What Lena means is Mother Mattie has been a lot more emotional ever since you all told her that you were contemplating a move to New York. Now, any mention of the city seems to rub her the wrong way."

Greg swallowed. He'd heard what Pastor Baldwin said, but he'd heard even more *how* he said it. This was the second time that Greg had heard him refer to his mother by her first name. In all the years they'd been members of Fellowship Worship Center, Greg had never known his pastor to refer to his mother as anything other than "Mother Dixon," or most often, "Mother Lena." He took special interest in the fact that although he had just made reference to her by only her first name, he still put the church title on Mattie's.

"We were watching the news a little while ago and they were interviewing the man who got that gunman to let the children go. She was sitting here just acting normal, but when that news flashed on the screen and when them people said that that man was really with the police department in New York, she threw her hands over her mouth like she'd seen a ghost and then went to crying and skedaddled into the bedroom and ain't come out since," Lena said. "Now, I'll be the first to say that I ain't tickled to know that y'all might be moving either, but if you decide to, I do know that God is going to take care of me. I'll be all right."

When Greg tossed a look in Pastor Baldwin's direction this time, the preacher was already looking back at him. Their eyes locked and Greg felt as if a whole conversation was taking place, though no words were exchanged.

"I'll go talk to her."

"No, Grace," Greg said, breaking his stare with his pastor. "You help to get the kids settled. I'll do it."

There was no answer when Greg tapped on his mother-in-law's room door, so he took the liberty of turning the knob to let himself in. Seeing her posture, he eased the door closed behind him. Greg sat on the bed beside where Mattie knelt and got the sense that she was doing more crying than praying. When she slowly lifted her head and looked up towards him, he saw that he was right.

The texture of Jessica's hair undoubtedly came from the genes of her father, but the thickness of it could easily be a result of her mother's. The brief time that Jessica had allowed her hair to grow until it hung beneath her shoulders, it was full and she would get frustrated with how long it would take to dry after being shampooed. Greg had fallen in love with the short style that she had when they went on their very first date so ultimately, Jessica had Sherry cut it and allowed it to remain at a shorter, more manageable length.

Looking down into her face and her tear-filled, pleading eyes, Greg reached forward and smoothed down the top of Mattie's graying hair with his hands.

"Please," she said, her lips trembling with emotions that she could barely manage. "Please, Greg. I know it's asking a lot of you to turn down the kind of money that them folks are offering you. But please don't move to New York. Don't take Jessie and Julian there. If you don't do nothing else for me in your whole life, just do that for me. Please."

Greg didn't know what was eating at her more — the guilt of not telling her daughter the truth from the beginning, the fear that Jessica would move away and cross paths with her father, the pain of remembering her past life and the man who left her expecting, with no place to go or the anger at herself for living with the lie for so long that she had begun to believe it herself. Whatever the case, Greg had never seen her this way and his heart bled for her. He had to tell her.

"Hold on a minute," he whispered, digging his cell phone from his pocket and dialing.

Dr. Simon Grant had only asked one thing of him and that was to let him be the first to know, aside from Jessica, what his final decision was. Greg had already told Even, but he couldn't disclose it to Mattie before speaking to his mentor. Dr. Grant was elated and relieved to hear the words coming from Greg over the phone, but his joy didn't even compare to Mattie's. When she heard Greg's words to Dr. Grant, she, still in a kneeling position, grabbed Greg around his legs and held on, thanking him repeatedly between the falling of brand-new tears. After ending the call to Dr. Grant, Greg helped Mattie to her feet and then pulled her to a seated position on the bed beside him. He held her hands in his and looked her directly in the eyes as he spoke.

"Ms. Mattie, I have to be honest. I didn't just do that for you. I did it because it's what was best for my family and it's what God wanted me to do. I did it because my place is here. I did it because home is where your heart is and Robinson Memorial is where my heart is. I followed my heart."

"I'm glad you did, baby." Mattie wrapped her arms around Greg's shoulders and squeezed as hard as she could. "Thank you."

"I was honest, Ms. Mattie." Greg pushed her away and found her hands again, covering them with his. "Now, it's time for you to be honest too."

A look of confusion crept onto Mattie's face. She didn't understand what his words meant. Her perplexity only lasted for a moment because Greg's next words made her body stiffen with tension.

"I know about Evan McDonald." Greg watched her eyes fill with more tears, which immediately began to overflow and spill. Her body began to visibly tremble, but she said nothing. Greg continued. "Ms. Mattie, he is the reason that God had me to go to New York to begin with. I'm convinced of it. Right before I was leaving to head back here, I was at his house just to check on his progress and he told me the story of the prostitute that he fell in love with and how he made the mistake of letting her go. He kept calling her 'Louise.' "

When Greg said those words, Mattie pulled her hands from his and placed them over her face. She was sobbing heavier now, but still not loud enough for the others to hear in the living room.

"Ms. Mattie, he has a cat named Mat, a car named Louise and a dog named Charlie. When he told me that he named them all after the woman he never stopped loving and that her name was Mattie Louise Charles, I didn't know what to say or do. Why did you keep this from us? Why did you keep it from Grace? Don't you think she had a right to know?"

For several moments, all Mattie could do was moan, rock back and forth and shake her head. She removed her hands from her face, but almost seemed unable to speak.

"Ms. Mattie, please talk to me. It's just you and me in here. Nobody out there knows yet, but I need to know why." Still, a few more moments passed, but Greg sat and waited until she was ready.

"I sold myself for money, Greg," she

whispered. "What's that for a mama to tell her child — especially a daughter? I wasn't lying at first," she quickly added. "I really wasn't sure who her daddy was because Evan McDonald wasn't the only white man I'd sold myself to. He just was the only one I felt I had a real relationship with. He was the only one of any color that I felt I had a real relationship with. I stopped selling myself because of him. He gave me money, but it wasn't for sex. It was so I wouldn't have to sell to nobody else and I didn't. It was just me and him. For the first time in my life, I had somebody who was taking care of me and treating me like I meant something."

She stopped and used the back of her hand to wipe away the appearance of more tears. "Then one day he just up and left me. He was a married man, but he wasn't with her no more and he told me that it was all over with her. I soon found out that he was just making a fool out of me, 'cause the same woman he told me it was all over with, he left me to go back to her. I guess that was the Lord's way of whipping me for living that kind of lifestyle and messing with a man who was somebody else's husband."

"Sarge says you never told him you were pregnant."

"How could I? I didn't know myself until after he was already gone. I prayed day in and day out that the baby inside of me wasn't his, but I guess I knew all along that it was. I protected myself with just about everybody else except him. I just felt like if the baby wasn't his, then I could move on and forget him. You know, act like he was just another john. I had my gut feeling, but it wasn't until Jessie was five that I knew for certain that she was his. She came home from her first day at kindergarten and was showing me and her Grandma Agnes her drawings. She was so proud of her class-work and when she smiled that day, for the first time, I saw Evan."

Greg had to agree. His wife's smile was definitely that of her father's. He looked at Mattie and said, "I understand why you might not want her to know, Ms. Mattie, but you have to tell her."

"No. I can't."

"Sarge already knows about her and he knows about Julian. He's the one who saved the kids from the day care."

"No! How would he know? I know he saved the kids. I saw that on television, but how does he know about Jessie and the baby?"

"If you'd stayed and watched the whole

interview, you would have heard him say that his grandchild was on the inside of the building. Ms. Mattie, I told him about them. Once I knew the story, I couldn't keep it from him. He wants a chance to get to know them."

"No."

"Ms. Mattie, that's not fair and you know it," Greg said. "God gave you a second chance with Grace when you basically dumped her on your mother. You gave birth to her and knew about her and still opted not to care for her until years later. Sarge didn't know about her until yesterday. It's too late for him to be a part of her growing up, but he shouldn't be barred from being a part of her life now. Grace deserves to know her father. She's always had questions about him and his whereabouts. After her second surgery, she asked me if aneurysms were hereditary because she wondered if it were possible that they were a trait on her father's side that she'd inherited. I can answer the medical stuff, but I can't answer all the questions she has about her father, and neither can you. Only he can really fill the void that she has and I'm sorry, Ms. Mattie, but if Grace wants something and I can provide it, that's just what she's gonna get and you know that."

"I can't tell her about this . . . she'll hate me, Greg."

"If you don't, I will."

"Greg, you can't." Mattie was pleading again, but this time, Greg was unyielding.

"I can and I will. I want *you* to tell her, or at least have your blessings before I tell her. But one way or the other, she's going to know. Grace and I have never kept secrets and we aren't going to start today. She won't hate you. She might be hurt and you should be able to understand that, but your daughter is a strong woman and she loves you. Knowing about Sarge is not going to change that."

"Lord, help me." Mattie muttered the words while clasping her hands under her chin.

"This is a lot for you, Ms. Mattie, and I know that. You don't have to do it right now. We're on our way to see the end of Derrick's case. You don't have to tell her right now, but you need to get it together by Sunday. I go back to work on Monday and Sarge may have to get on back to New York —"

"He's still here?"

"Yes, ma'am. I believe he is. He agreed to keep his distance until we talked to Grace. I'll stand by you and give you all the support you need. I'll even do the talking if you want me to. But by dinnertime on Sunday, this can't be our little secret anymore. Okay?"

Mattie closed her eyes and lowered her head before nodding in agreement.

"Now, I need you to lie down," he said.

She raised her head and looked up at him, standing beside where she sat. "Why?"

"Because I don't need to be lying when I walk out there and tell them that you're okay now, but you're just resting."

Mattie obediently raised her feet onto the bed and laid her head against the pillows. The worry could still be seen clearly on her face, but at least the tears had subsided. Greg bent down and kissed her forehead, telling her that he loved her. Mattie forced a smile in return.

"I love you too," she whispered.

CHAPTER 26

The Honorable Justine Wilberforce had a reputation that preceded her. She was a tough, no-nonsense white woman in her fifties who was known to put brakes on arguments or testimonies that she deemed wasted both her time and the court's. Already, she had interrupted the prosecutor and several of his witnesses and now, she was about to be faced with Attorney Derrick Madison, who had already done an award-winning job during cross-examination.

All of the fears that Sherry had that the lack of a full night's sleep would somehow put Derrick at a disadvantage on this crucial day in Perry's case were quickly put to rest when the testimonies and interrogations began. She'd had no idea that he'd attained so much information. The reason she had been so clueless as to the progress her husband was making in his quest to find whatever it was that he suspected about the case was because of the distance that grown between them in recent months. Seeing him display his sharp wit and his refusal to yield because of the testimony of the witnesses for the prosecution, reminded Sherry of why she fell in love with him to begin with.

Last night, after Denise's safety was assured, was the closest they'd been as a family in quite some time. Sherry couldn't pry their daughter from Derrick's arms. She'd been forced to drive home from the hospital because he wouldn't put her down. He even volunteered to prepare her for bed and read her a bedtime story. His attentiveness to the little girl made Sherry feel a strong attraction to her husband that she'd thought was long lost in the midst of their fighting and bickering. While Derrick was spending time with Denise in her bedroom, Sherry took her shower, put on what she knew was his preferred fragrance and one of his favorite gowns and waited for him under the covers.

She was disappointed when he walked into the room with Denise on his shoulders and Derrick was disappointed with his own decision when he smelled the fragrant aroma that lingered in the air and saw Sherry lying in wait. He paused in the doorway and watched in heightened awareness as she gathered the bedspread and covered herself.

"I told Dee-Dee she could sleep with us," he said. "I'm sorry. I didn't know . . ."

"It's okay," Sherry said pulling her hair away from her face and tying it back into a ponytail with a hairclip she retrieved from her bedside. "Come on, honey," she called to her daughter.

Through eyes of desire, Derrick mouthed the words "I'm sorry" again as Denise nestled happily close to her mother. Sherry returned his longing stare and smiled while he kicked off his slippers and joined them. There was no need in being angry or even blameful. It had been a long time since they'd been together and she knew that knowing what she had planned for the evening would be punishment enough for him. From her seat in the courtroom, Sherry returned the smile that Derrick sent her way after completing his cross-examination of the opposing counsel's final witness.

Derrick returned to his seat and looked down at his notes. He glanced behind him to the area where Mr. and Mrs. Wilson sat. Mrs. Wilson was a woman of few words, but even after the stellar job Derrick had just done in his questioning, she still looked frightened for her son's future. Mr. Wilson, on the other hand, was confident. He'd hired the right attorney and the nod of approval that he threw in Derrick's direction told him so. He seemed almost more certain of his son's chances than Derrick felt at the moment.

The prosecuting attorney had done a good job and his witnesses had been thorough in their account of what had happened that day. The looks that the jury displayed when the other worker who had been in the store gave testimony of how Perry had shot the woman in the chest at close range was a clear indication that things weren't moving in the boy's favor. Derrick hadn't expected them to. Perry was guilty, just like they said; however, the folder in his hand would be the evidence that could at least get the boy a lighter sentence than expected. Mr. Wilson had told him to do what he had to do to help Perry avoid jail if possible and that was exactly what Derrick had done. Let the chips fall where they may.

When the prosecution rested, Derrick called the only person he would ask to testify in Perry's defense — Perry himself. He had told both of Perry's parents that he would not be able to avoid putting him on the stand. If there was going to be any pity felt by the jury, it would have to be through Perry's own testimony. The victim's survival was still uncertain. Even if she did pull through, she'd most likely need care for the rest of her life. Perry didn't want to testify and Derrick understood. His parents, Mr. Wilson especially, didn't at all like the idea of their son being put on the stand and Derrick knew why. Still, he had to put him there. The jury had to hear the full account from Perry's own lips. Besides that, he had no other witnesses. Derrick tossed away the idea of character witnesses. He had gotten a signed affidavit from one of the boy's teachers, as well as the school's guidance counselor, both of whom raved about the improvements in behavior and academics that Perry had made in the last year. He had one other affidavit from a close friend of the victim who was willing and ready to testify if called upon. Derrick didn't submit her name. If Perry didn't testify, all the court would have to go on was the vivid, horrid accounts given by the others who'd testified against him.

Understandably nervous, Perry tugged at the front of his suit coat as he took the stand and waited for the questions that he and his attorney had rehearsed. Only when the questions began, they weren't the ones they'd used during the mock court sessions that Derrick had orchestrated. Perry should have known that something was different when Derrick opened with his first statement.

"Perry, do you recall what we spoke about in the meeting that we had together? I told you that you had to be completely honest with me and if you did so, I would do all I could to help you. Remember that?"

Perry nodded.

"Perry?" Derrick's eyes reminded him that men didn't shrug and nod.

"Yes, sir," he said, swallowing hard.

"Okay, the same works here in the courtroom. I need you to be totally honest and speak the truth. Do you understand?"

The judge had already had enough. "The witness has already been sworn in, Mr. Madison. Were you not in the courtroom at the time? Please get on with something that the court would deem pertinent."

Derrick tugged at the hem of his suit jacket, but complied by getting directly to the point. "Why did you shoot Ms. Owens?"

"It was an accident."

"You went into the pawnshop with a gun, did you not?"

"Yes, sir."

"You pointed it directly at her, did you not?"

"Yes, sir."

"And you pulled the trigger, did you not?"

Perry paused. "Yes, sir."

"So how do you expect this court to believe that it was an accident?"

Perry looked in the direction of his parents and immediately Derrick moved so that his view was blocked.

"Perry?"

"I . . . I . . ."

"Speak up, Perry," Derrick said.

"I didn't know it was loaded."

"Did you load it?"

"No, sir."

"Who did?"

"I don't know."

"Where'd you get the gun?"

"From . . . a friend."

"So, you were not the only one involved in this crime, am I right?"

Perry looked down at his hands. Derrick thought of how far the teenager was from the nonchalant boy who had sat in his office playing the rehearsed tough-guy role just weeks earlier. Perry looked as though he wanted to jump from the witness chair and head for the nearest exit. He was frightened.

"Answer the question, Mr. Wilson," the judge spoke.

Lifting his eyes from his hands, Perry looked again in the direction of his parents, but instead he met Derrick's intimidating, yet trustworthy gaze. Leaning closer to the microphone, he said, "No, sir."

"Who assisted you with this crime, Perry?" Derrick asked.

"I can't say."

"Why not?"

"We show our loyalty by helping one another. We don't stab each other in the back."

"Who is it that doesn't stab one another in the back? Are you in a gang, Perry?"

"No, sir."

Derrick walked back to his table and retrieved the folder he'd been looking at earlier. "In my hands, I am holding the results of some tests that were given by court order to Ms. Marva Owens two days ago. A copy of these records was delivered by courier to opposing counsel's office on this morning." Derrick laid the open folder on the desk in front of Perry.

"What does the highlighted portion of this paperwork state, Perry?"

Perry looked at the words in front of him and his eyes widened before he looked up at his attorney.

"What does it say, Perry?"

Perry looked back down at the paper. " 'Pregnancy test results are positive. Estimated progression is fourteen weeks.' "

Gasps and moans ran around the courtroom, but quickly silenced at the sound of the judge's gavel. Tears rolled down Perry's cheeks as he stared at the open folder.

"Did you know that Ms. Owens was expecting, Perry?"

"No, sir." Perry's words were distorted by his attempt to choke back a heavier flow of tears.

"Somebody did, Perry," Derrick said. "Somebody knew Ms. Owens was pregnant and it's my conclusion that the person who gave you the gun is that person."

"Your Honor, I object." The prosecutor stood. "Counsel is grasping for straws. There is no evidence that his client didn't purchase or steal the gun himself. Authorities were unable to trace the gun's origin."

"Sustained," the judge agreed. "This isn't a reality show, Mr. Madison. There's nobody to vote off in your quest to find this mystery man that you're hinting at. It was your choice to have only one witness, so I suggest you make better use of him. You have evidence to prove a pregnancy, but the court doesn't have all day to endure your line of questioning. Would you happen to have any evidence to back your other theory, Mr. Madison?" the judge asked.

Perry continued to sob as Derrick walked back to the table to retrieve another folder. He turned and faced the judge's bench. "I thought you'd never ask," he said, returning her sarcasm. "In this folder are affidavits from two of Perry's school administrators that will vouch for the improvements he has made in the past year at his high school. I also have an affidavit from Kim Knowles, a personal friend of the victim who states that Ms. Owens came to her in confidence and told her about the pregnancy that the father demanded she terminate. She refused to comply. Therefore, it is my supposition that the father named in Ms. Knowles's affidavit is the mastermind behind this crime. The name in question is highlighted for Your Honor's convenience."

Judge Wilberforce shot him a glare, making him aware that she didn't particularly like his tone or his less-than-subtle sarcasm, but she said nothing.

Derrick spoke again. "Opposing council's own witnesses testified to the fact that although my client did pull the trigger, he was visibly shaken and even dropped the gun afterwards because he was shocked that the gun actually discharged. This coincides with Perry's testimony that he was unaware that the pistol was loaded."

The judge took the folder and glanced at the paperwork on the inside. She tried to hide the startled expression in her eyes as she looked over her reading glasses at Derrick, but he saw it and considered it a personal victory. After another moment to look over what she'd been presented, Judge Wilberforce removed her glasses and gave him permission to continue. Derrick walked back to where Perry sat with his face buried in tissues that someone had handed him.

"You may not have known that the gun was loaded, Perry, but the man who gave you the gun and sent you into that pawn-shop did. He *used* you to commit a crime that he wanted to be executed because this baby would have posed a problem for him. He gave you that watch, didn't he, Perry? I don't have evidence of where the gun was purchased, but I do have a receipt in my possession that will prove that the watch you've had didn't fall out of anyone's pocket, but was in fact purchased from an online jeweler. The same man that gave you the gun also gave you the watch to pawn and told you that it was worth a certain amount. Knowing full well that pawnshops never offer you what your item is worth, he told you that if she didn't offer you at least that amount of money, your job was to *frighten* her by pulling the trigger. All the while, he knew that if you pulled the trigger, you'd shoot her and likely kill her, thus killing the child.

"He banked on the fact that you'd be faster and stronger than he could ever be and you'd probably get away without being caught. But if you did get caught, he figured you could come to me and I'd get you off, because he thought that 'getting young black men off' was what I do. Then when he saw that that wasn't going to happen, he told you that if you played your cards right and didn't stab him in the back, you'd get a lesser sentence because of your age. It was your duty to make sure that it didn't come back to him, wasn't it, Perry? He saved you. Is that what he told you? He's used that tactic with you before, hasn't he? Three years ago, before you moved here for the inheritance your grandfather left, you'd do little petty-crime favors for him then, didn't you? You *owed* him these favors, didn't you, Perry? What did he tell you, you owed him for, Perry? Saving you from having to live in another foster home? Saving you from life on the streets? Saving you from starving to death? You're adopted, aren't you, Perry?"

Derrick waited for Perry to speak, but this time he accepted his nod in lieu of a verbal answer.

"The only man you've ever known as your father used the fact that he adopted you when you were ten and saved you from more years of being in the system, used your past to manipulate you into putting your future at stake."

From her seat in the courtroom, Mrs. Wilson burst into tears, screaming the words, "Say it's not true!" over and over as she swung her arms wildly at her husband. Armed officers removed her from the courtroom as the judge's gavel pounded numerous times to try to disrupt Derrick's speech.

"Your father did this, didn't he, Perry? The person who gave you the gun, gave you the watch, told you to go to the pawnshop, told you to stick to your story. It was your father, wasn't it?"

Degrading names and words were being tossed from every end of the courtroom, directed at Mr. Wilson, who sat with his head hanging and no defense to stand on. Perry pulled the tissues from his face long enough to look up. Derrick stepped aside so that his view to his father was unobstructed.

Perry could only look at him for a moment before he burst into tears again. Several louder poundings from the gavel finally brought some order to the disrupted audience.

Greg looked at his friend, who had taken off his invisible attorney garment and was now embracing Perry and trying to offer comfort to the distraught teenager. Greg had been on television and in the newspapers numerous times for the things he did in the operating room, but he knew that it was only a matter of time before the entire D.C. area, and beyond, knew about the courtroom skills of Attorney Derrick Jerome Madison.

Once complete order was restored, the prosecuting attorney told the judge that he had no questions for Perry and the boy was dismissed from the witness stand. Shortly after words from the bench, the judge ordered Mr. Wilson to be placed under arrest and delayed Perry's sentencing indefinitely. Mrs. Wilson quickly whisked Perry away in a waiting limousine to avoid the bloodthirsty reporters that were waiting on the outside.

"Wow," Jessica whispered as she and Greg watched Sherry edge by, dismissing onlookers on her way to her husband.

"I know," Greg agreed.

When Sherry finally reached him, Derrick was sitting at the desk with his face buried in his hands. Essentially, this was a victory for Derrick. No doubt, as long as Ms. Owens survived, Perry would spend no time in jail. But the case had drained Derrick, and Sherry knew that this particular victory brought him little, if any, desire to rejoice. He looked up when he felt her hand rub against the back of his neck.

"Congratulations, baby," she whispered.

Derrick shook his head. "I don't feel any celebration inside of me," he said. "Here's a boy whose father used him for evil. As a man who snatched a little boy from hopelessness, George Wilson had a prime opportunity to raise him in a loving environment and the resources to give him all that he needed, plus the stuff that he just wanted. How can a man influence his son in such an evil manner, Sherry?"

Sherry saw tears in her husband's eyes and her heart went out to him. She brushed her hand beneath his chin and kissed him softly on the lips and whispered, "Let's just go home."

"Yeah," Derrick agreed, packing his belongings in his briefcase.

"Maybe we can get Jessie and Greg to

346

keep Dee-Dee tonight." She paused when he turned and looked at her. "And maybe we can try making a baby."

Derrick's smile was weak and he looked as though he was going to cry. He pulled Sherry in for a hug and then released her after a kiss on her cheek. To her surprise, he began slowly shaking his head.

"What? You don't want to have a baby anymore?"

"I think I wanted to have a baby for all the wrong reasons. I'm not closing the door on it and if you really get the itch, we'll go for it. Right now, though, I'm content with my daughter and my wife. But it means the world to me that you laid it out on the table like that. I know that if you had a baby right now, it would be something that you'd be doing just for me. That means the world," he repeated.

Sherry breathed a sigh of relief, exhaling slowly so that her husband wouldn't notice just how thankful she was. "So, you don't want me to ask them to keep Dee?"

"I didn't say all that," he quickly said, slipping his arm around her waist and heading towards the exit doors where their friends waited. Clarifying himself, Derrick added, "I said I didn't want to make a baby. I didn't say I didn't want to make . . ."

He left the sentence open.

"I hear you, baby," Sherry said.

CHAPTER 27

The Spirit moved so mightily through Fellowship Worship Center on Sunday morning that it seemed Pastor Baldwin would never get the opportunity to preach his prepared Father's Day sermon. The congregation at the church was predominantly black, but there were enough members of other races for Sergeant McDonald to hide in the crowd. No one knew that the tears that fell from his eyes were a direct result of seeing and hearing his daughter sing for the first time. To Evan, Jessica glowed like an angel as she effortlessly belted out the lyric of Yolanda Adams's "Still I Rise." What a surreal way to spend a Father's Day that, six months ago, he thought he'd be spending alone.

On Saturday, he finally contacted Greg by way of Dr. Grant. The Dixons' home phone number was unlisted and Greg had never given Evan his cellular number. Therefore, the only means of connecting with him was to call Robinson Memorial and speak with Simon Grant. When Greg received the message, he called Evan at the hotel where he'd been staying and informed him of his talk with Mattie. The plan they devised called for the retiring policeman to be on standby this afternoon when Mattie finally told their daughter the truth. If for any reason Jessica chose not to meet her father, Evan agreed to leave without incident. From the seat where he sat observing the service, he prayed that her decision wouldn't be to send him away.

This Father's Day had a special meaning to any man in the city whose child had been held captive by a crazed gunman just three days ago. In a morning telephone conversation, Derrick had told Greg how amazingly content he felt now, just being thankful for the life of his daughter. A son was "no longer on the front burner," but he also made it clear that the idea "hadn't been totally removed from the stove" either. It might be something he and Sherry would consider in the next couple of years. Within himself, Greg thought that perhaps by that time, he and Jessica might be discussing adding to their family as well.

Mattie appeared to be at ease during most

of the services. But once they were all gathered at the "family house" for dinner, reality set in and she was quieter than normal while Lena fussed about a conversation she had after church with one of the ministers. Mattie mostly just listened as she helped her friend set the table for their waiting guests, who were snickering quietly at Lena's grievance.

"I tell you, some of these young men don't have no manners nowadays. It used to be a time when a man wouldn't ever come up to a woman and ask her age," Lena griped.

When Mattie didn't readily respond, Lena looked at her and huffed before returning to her task of placing silverware on the table and arguing. "Well, maybe this kind of thing don't bother you none, but there's just something wrong with the world when men lose their respect."

"Maybe he wasn't trying to be disrespectful, Lena," Mattie finally said. "Maybe he was trying to give you a compliment."

"That wasn't no compliment. He gonna look at me with his ig'nant self and say, 'Mother Lena, you mighty sharp today. You don't look a day over sixty or sixty-one.' "

"Well, what's wrong with that?" Mattie asked. "You are sixty-one."

"Most men, *if* they trying to compliment

you, will think of an age that's a few years younger than you really are, so you'll feel good about how you look."

"Maybe he thought he *was* giving you an age that was a few years younger," Mattie reasoned.

The laughter that rang from the living room saved Mattie from what was sure to be cutting words from her quicker-witted, sharper-tongued housemate. Lena glared at her from across the table, but chose to direct her words towards the thin wall that divided the kitchen from the living room.

"I know y'all not laughing," she warned. "Especially you, Gregory Paul Dixon."

Greg sobered quickly. "No ma'am, I'm not laughing." He knew full well that it was only a half-truth.

As was customary for Sunday dinners, Sherry and Jessica had already fed the children and they had been put in the playroom to share toys and watch the educational station until it was time to go home or until they fell asleep, whichever came first. Some days they played harmoniously and other days, the nearly three-year age difference was more apparent. Today was an amicable day.

The dining area returned to a quiet state, with only the sounds of dishes being arranged and rearranged on the table. Every now and again, Lena would begin humming a tune, but Mattie was working in silence. Greg knew what was going through her mind and he could feel the rapid beating of his own heart as the time neared. He had no way of gauging how Jessica would receive this news that until now, only he, Derrick and Mattie were aware of. His mind filled with things he could have done differently or ways that he could have prepared his wife for what was about to happen. Last night, after they'd put Julian to bed, they sat up and talked for hours. He should have worked it into their conversation. He could have asked her some vague questions to get a clearer understanding of where she stood as far as her absent father was concerned. In any case, it was too late now as the aroma of food radiated through the house.

The women were stalling and Greg's suspicions about the matter were confirmed when Sherry answered a knock at the door and Pastor Baldwin entered. He'd apparently gone home to shower and change from the clothes he'd drenched during the energetic presentation he'd given today from the pulpit, to a fresh blue suit that fitted him well. He spoke to each of them before making himself comfortable on the sofa and returning Greg's intense look. Greg knew right away that the keen pastor could sense the tension that had begun to brew between the two of them in recent days.

"Okay," Lena said as she joined them in the living room. "Dinner is served. Come on, Pastor."

It wasn't a new procedure. Every time Pastor Baldwin had come to dine with them, he'd always been given the respect of being seated first. It was an honor that all of them gladly extended. But now, with this different kind of relationship that, to Greg, was so obviously growing between Lena and the pastor, her call for him to enter the dining room first felt different. Greg was almost caught off-guard when his mother asked him to grace the food. He'd been prepared for her to summon Pastor Baldwin to do that too.

Chatter, as usual, started immediately at the table once the serving bowls began passing around. The early conversation was about the greatness of the service and the message that had been delivered. At present, Greg didn't want to admit it, but Derrick was right when he said that it was one of the best sermons he'd heard from their church leader.

"Well, Sister Jessica made it easy for me,"

Pastor Baldwin complimented. "That song of yours parted the Red Sea. Walking across on dry land was all that was left to do."

"Amen to that," Lena agreed.

"Mama, are you okay?" Jessica had finally noted her mother's uncanny silence.

"Why are you so quiet over there? I thought you'd be happier after finding out that we weren't going to New York."

Mattie stared into her plate for a moment, and when she lifted her head to try to speak, the words were moved to the side and tears took over. Jessica wasn't prepared for her mother's display and neither were the others who had been sitting and enjoying a genuinely peaceful family dinner for the first time in quite a while. Jessica slid her chair back to go to attend to her mother, but Greg stood first, motioning for her to remain seated. When he walked around the table and stood directly behind Mattie, Greg had the attention of the whole table.

"Ms. Mattie has something to say, but I don't think she's going to be able to express herself right now, so I'm gonna talk for her. Is that okay, Ms. Mattie?"

"I'm so sorry, Jessie. I'm so sorry," Mattie blurted out.

Jessica brought both hands to her mouth and immediately began to think the worst.

"Oh, my God," she whispered in a frantic tone.

"Calm down, baby," Greg said. "I'm sure it's not what you think. Your mother is fine; at least physically, she is. But there's a reason for her emotional roller coaster over the past couple of weeks that goes beyond our possible move to New York. It wasn't so much that we would be moving farther *away* from her as it was that we would be moving closer *to* someone else."

No one was eating anymore. Even Derrick, who knew most of the story that was about to unfold, was intently listening to Greg speak.

"What are you talking about?" Jessica asked.

Greg waited for a moment to see if Mattie was ready to speak. When she didn't, he took a deep breath and continued.

"Remember Sergeant McDonald, the man I was called upon to operate on at Lenox Hill Hospital?"

Jessica pondered the name for a moment, but soon put the pieces together. "That's the policeman that saved the kids at the nursery! How . . ." Her voice trailed off and was replaced by a look of utter confusion.

In a quick inner search for an easy way to disclose the information, Greg found nothing. He remembered Lena preparing to pull one of his loose teeth as a child and telling him that the most painless way for her to do it was to just grab it and snatch it out quickly. Pulling slowly, she told him, was only prolonging the inevitable and worsening the hurt.

"He was here during the standoff because I brought him from New York with me when I came back last week. That pull towards New York that I kept saying that I was feeling was directly related to him. God showed that to me. It wasn't about Lenox Hill or wanting to serve on their staff; it was solely about Sergeant Evan McDonald. I didn't understand it at first, but I visited with him during my trip last week and after talking to him for an hour or so, I came to understand my connection to him."

"Connection?" Lena was baffled. "Greg, what are you talking about? What kind of connection you got to that man other than the fact that you saved his life?"

"He's my father-in-law, Mama."

"What?" All of them seemed to speak in one voice. Greg had said the words, but no one straightaway grasped what they meant.

"He's your daddy, sugar." Mattie barely managed to look across the table and get the words out before breaking down again.

Complete silence blanketed the room. Derrick tried to look clueless as Sherry looked at him in shock. He didn't want her knowing that he'd known for three days and hadn't shared it with her. The feeling gave him a strange sense of supremacy. Usually it was the other way around. Most often, it was Sherry who knew something that Greg hadn't disclosed to him. This time, the tables were turned and Derrick couldn't deny his feeling of satisfaction.

Pastor Baldwin kept his eyes fixed on Mattie as if he thought he'd heard her incorrectly, and for the first time in a long time, Lena was speechless.

"What did she say?" Jessica whispered the words to Greg instead of directing the question to her mother.

"Sergeant Evan McDonald is not only a hero who saved our son, our goddaughter and thirty-something other children and adults from the Open Arms Day Care, but he's also the man who planted the seed that was to one day become Jessica Grace Charles."

Greg figured he'd leave out all the bad stuff that Evan had admitted to doing as an officer on the force. He'd let him tell Jessica about all of that himself, if he ever wanted her to know. "Grace," he added, when she still sat in disbelief, "he's your father."

Mattie's worst fears seemed to be becoming reality. Jessica was shaking her head in the same fashion that Mattie had done when they were trying to convince her that their move to New York wouldn't be a bad one. Tears pooled in her eyes.

"He can't be. You told me you didn't know who my father was."

Mattie hung her head in shame at her daughter's words. "I lied," she whispered. "Lord, forgive me, but I lied. I thought I was doing the right thing. I was trying to keep you from being hurt."

"For twenty-seven years, Mama? I could understand you thinking that way when I was a kid, but for twenty-seven years you were trying to shelter me from the hurt of knowing? Who else knew, Mama? Did Grandma Agnes know too?"

"No," Mattie said, using her napkin to wipe away tears. "I lied to her too. Mama went to her grave not knowing that I knew who fathered you."

Jessica stared at the woman she thought she'd known well, but now felt as though she'd only met three minutes ago. If she wasn't hearing it from her mother's own mouth, Jessica never would believe Mattie was capable of withholding such important details of her life from her. While it was true that Grandma Agnes had done most of her granddaughter's upbringing, Jessica felt that she and her mother had bonded beyond keeping secrets such as this one. The disappointment was evident by the near look of horror that Jessica displayed.

"How could you do this?"

Greg left his mother-in-law's side and returned to the seat beside Jessica to offer support as she and all the others heard the whole sordid story for the very first time. All of them had had their suspicions over the years that Mattie had been a prostitute, so that part of her story wasn't alarming. In the bits and pieces of her past that she'd disclosed at different times, that part had been assumed and Jessica had never held it against her. She also took for granted that her father had been one of her mother's many clients, but she'd never even given any consideration to the fact that Mattie had been living with the lie that the identity of her daughter's father was unknown.

After hearing the detailed version of the story from beginning to end, Jessica understood her mother's embarrassment of carrying on the relationship with a man who had not yet legally ended his two-year separation from his wife. Still, she couldn't comprehend a reason for her not sharing the information after so many years. Jessica felt that if she could move forward knowing what her mother did, she could certainly get beyond the knowledge of whom she did it with. Her whole life, she'd been robbed of a father because of her mother's selfish pride.

"And what about him?" Jessica asked, almost afraid of the answer. "Did he know too? Did both of you agree to keep this from me?"

"No," Mattie said. "I haven't seen or spoke to Evan since that day when he walked out of my apartment."

"I just told him about you, Grace," Greg said. "That's why he made the trip from New York. He wants to get to know you and Julian."

"He never knew?" Jessica asked the question as if needing verification.

Greg shook his head.

"Is he still here?"

"He's two miles away at the park," Greg told her. "Whether or not he comes anywhere near you is up to you, Grace. You say the word and I'll call him and tell him how to get here. You say the word and I'll put him back on a plane to New York. It's up to you."

CHAPTER 28

After the initial introductions, Greg stood back and watched the awkward meeting between Jessica and her father. They both cried and embraced immediately upon meeting face-to-face, but establishing a trusting relationship was going to take awhile. She allowed him to hold Julian, but the child wasn't fond of strangers and refused to stay with his new grandfather.

Pastor Baldwin had suggested, and they all agreed, that perhaps having Jessica meet Evan at the park was more sensible than giving the man, who was still a stranger in the pastor's eyes, the address where Lena and Mattie lived alone. Greg could sense that his real concern was with Lena, but it was a good idea still. With the exception of Mattie, who wasn't quite ready to see Evan again, they all loaded in their cars and drove to the park where the officer waited. Seeing them together, everybody agreed that aside from her skin's shade of brown, Jessica had gotten very little from her short, chubby mother.

She was only four inches shorter than her dad, who stood at the same six-feet-one-inch height as Greg. When Evan pulled family photos from his wallet and showed one picture of his deceased mother, who was part Italian, even Jessica's fuller lips and shapely figure proved to stem from the genes on his side. With her perfectly pecan-shaped eyes and her flawless smooth skin, Jessica bore a striking resemblance to her paternal grandmother. Even she could see the strong likeness and Jessica seemed touched to find that she had been partially named after her father's mother, whose name was also Grace. Mattie had never met Evan's mother, but she knew the woman meant a lot to him. Jessica couldn't help but think that Mattie must have loved him to pass his mother's name to her child.

Since no one had completed their dinner earlier, Lena suggested preparing plates and taking them to the park with them. They did and Sergeant McDonald seemed to feel at home, eating and getting to know his daughter's family. He seemed especially pleased when they all pressed him for police stories, including the details of the one that rendered him with a limp and limited usage of his left arm. He also told them about his unforgettable experience of seeing the destruction and devastation in the aftermath of the attacks on the World Trade Center.

Initially, Jessica was glad that Mattie had stayed behind. She was angry at her for years of deception and hiding behind a mask that disfigured the truth. Now, as only she and her father walked around the trail that coiled from one end of the park to the other, she had a clearer understanding. He was easy to talk to and Jessica jumped at the opportunity to ask all of the questions that she'd been forced to hold in for twenty-seven years.

Evan was being as honest with his daughter as he could. In his eyes, he owed her that and much more. Jessica listened while he told her his life's story: from the brutal death of his father to his misdeeds in his earlier years as a police officer. By the time they'd walked the half-mile trail, she knew about the dissolution of his marriage, his ex-wife's loss of her battle with cancer, his lingering love for Mattie, and all of what was going on in the lives of her half-brother and sister. They discussed the possibility of getting together for Christmas. Evan didn't think that his children would have any qualms about meeting Jessica.

"There's no way they won't fall in love with you just like I have," he said, embracing her and kissing her forehead.

"You okay?" Greg asked after they rejoined the rest of them.

Jessica whisked a tear from her eye. "I need to go and talk to Mama."

"I'll go with you."

Greg and Jessica excused themselves and drove two miles eastward. Mattie was sitting alone on the living room couch when they arrived. She had heard them enter the house, but she continued to stare at the open Bible in her lap.

"I'll give you two some privacy," Greg started.

Jessica shook her head and whispered, "I want you to stay."

Nodding, Greg stood with his back to the door and watched Jessica approach her mother and sit beside her on the couch. Mattie's eyes remained focused on the pages, but a tear could be seen making a slow trek down her right cheek.

"Mama, let's talk," Jessica said, sliding the book from her mother's lap and placing it in an empty space on the cushions beside her.

When Mattie looked at her, to Jessica she

appeared older than her normal self. Her eyes were red and puffy and the few wrinkles that she had in her skin seemed deeper and more pronounced. For the first time, Jessica looked at her mother and saw Grandma Agnes.

"Mama," she began."

"I'm sorry, baby. That's all I know to say is I'm sorry. In one sense, I feel like a burden that I been carrying around for all these years done been lifted off of me, but in another, my heart ain't never been so heavy. I didn't ever want to make you mad or make you hate me and I think that's why I just didn't want you to know everything."

Jessica reached forward and wiped the flow of tears from her mother's face. Then she said, "Mama, I don't hate you. I wish you would have told me a long time ago, but I don't hate you. I love you, Mama. And I'm not angry, not anymore, anyway. I just wish you had been honest with me."

"I do, too, Jessie. I wish I had done the right thing from the beginning, but I didn't and I can't change none of that now. I want to do something to erase your pain and make it all go away, but I don't know what I can do."

"Nothing, Mama. There's nothing you can do to erase all the years that I missed with my father. Those years are gone now, so if you're trying to think of ways to make that up to me, then stop. You can't."

"I'm sorry, baby."

"I know you are, Mama," Jessica assured her. "But listen to me. You can't do anything to rectify the past, but you can do something that would make going forward much easier for me."

Mattie looked up with hopeful eyes. While trying to keep things neat and tidy, she'd made a mess that had affected both her and her daughter's life. The least she could do was something to make the future better. Jessica deserved that much. She was more than willing to fulfill whatever her daughter asked. That is, until she heard the request.

"I want you to come to the park and talk to Evan."

"No, Jessie. I can't."

"Yes, you can, Mama. Now, I've spent the last hour and a half with him and he seems to be such a genuine and caring man. He told me everything, so I know that all the fault of this wasn't on you. He wants to be a part of my life, Mama, and I want him to be a part of my life. I need for you and him to make amends. I need you to talk and bring closure to all the hurt and ill feelings. I know he's willing, Mama. He wants to see you. Please do this for me, Mama. If you really want to make up for the past I was forced to have without my father, just help me with the future I want to have with him."

Mattie sat, staring at the flower arrangement on the coffee table in front of her. After a moment of saying and doing nothing, she shook her head, stood and walked out, disappearing down the hall that led to her bedroom. Jessica looked at Greg in helpless confusion. He walked over to the sofa, sat beside her and cradled her in his arms. His support felt good.

"What now?" Jessica asked, hoping that he wouldn't let go anytime soon.

"You have to give her time, Grace. All of us have to give her time. She went through a lot after Sarge left her. Hurt like that doesn't go away overnight."

"But it's been twenty-seven years."

"Twenty-seven years of her not dealing with it," Greg explained. "She's buried this away and never really dealt with it until now. This is like a fresh open sore to Ms. Mattie. Just be patient, baby. You go ahead and establish a relationship with your father and she'll come around when she's ready."

Jessica turned to face Greg. She really couldn't think of a time when he didn't support her. Even in those times when she thought he wasn't being supportive, he'd always been there. Looking at him and knowing who he was inside and out, she once again understood why women, including her best friend, Sherry, might look at him and long for a fraction of her man.

"What?" Greg asked when she continued to gaze.

Jessica shook her head and smiled. "Nothing. I love you. You know that, right?"

Kissing her briefly on her lips, Greg replied, "Yeah, baby. I know. But if you want to convince me a little more, I got a few ideas."

Jessica felt flushed, but didn't have the opportunity to respond before his lips found hers again, exploring her mouth deeper this time. She reached up and caressed his smooth-shaven head, causing him to groan. Greg slipped his arms around her waist and pulled her closer.

"Oh, cut that foolishness out and come on here. Ain't nobody got all day."

Mattie's voice startled them, causing them to move away from each other like two high school students who had just been caught making out by one of their mothers. Mattie had gone into her room and changed into a more comfortable dress and a pair of flat-heeled shoes. Jessica and Greg exchanged

glances and grins as they watched her walk
out the front door.

CHAPTER 29

Walking through the doors of Robinson Memorial on Monday morning, Greg felt like a new man. The past few months had proven to be trying for relationships within his family and within his intimate circle of friends, but they'd all survived and were stronger because of it. Where the future of his career as a neurosurgeon would be lived out had once been in question, but in praying and following his heart, Greg had no doubts that he'd made the right choice. Taking a moment, he looked around his office. It wasn't as big, bright or as beautiful as the one he could have been sitting in right now at Lenox Hill, but it was his.

Dr. Tanner and Mr. Price were stunned at the news that Greg was turning down their offer. Over the phone, Dr. Armstrong told Greg that in spite of his disappointment, his decision came as no surprise to him. He would have been more shocked had Greg actually taken the job. He knew how much respect Greg had for Dr. Grant and vice versa and he told Greg that he too believed he'd made the right decision.

"I've been working at Lenox Hill Hospital for a lot of years," Dr. Armstrong said. "Things are not always as they seem here, but you can bank on Simon any day of the week."

Greg didn't know exactly what his words meant, but the implication made him even more comfortable and satisfied with his decision to stay put. Lenox Hill had made a highly attractive offer. Undoubtedly, whoever their second choice had been would jump at the opportunity to serve there.

The New York mission that God had sent him on was complete — at least for now. Greg chuckled when he thought of yesterday's events and the reunion that finally took place between Mattie and Evan. The policeman's eyes twinkled when Mattie stepped out of the car. He couldn't have hid his delight if he'd tried, but Mattie wanted no part of it. Or, at least that's what she wanted him to believe. Greg and Jessica had caught her stealing looks at him throughout the gathering, but she avoided interaction with him at all cost. By the end of the evening, though, she was laughing at his funny stories of police bloopers with the rest of them.

Evan won a piece of Mattie over when he made a phone call to Chicago. He shared the news of his discovered child and after convincing his son that it wasn't some kind of joke, Richard accepted the invitation to come to New York for the holiday to meet her. Then, for a few minutes, Jessica and Richard conversed, bringing tears to Jessica's eyes. When he got the phone back, Evan bragged to his son of Jessica's extraordinary gift for song. Richard immediately pitched the idea that he get her to a studio to record a demo for him to present to a few producer friends of his. Jessica loved the idea, and so did Mattie.

A knock on his door disrupted his thoughts. "Come in," Greg called as he picked up his clipboard to look over his assignments for the day.

"Good morning."

Greg had expected Dr. Grant, but he'd presumed wrong. "Dr. Lowe," he said, placing the clipboard back on his desk. "Come in." He pointed towards a vacant chair, inviting his colleague to sit, but Dr. Lowe declined.

"I heard you were back in the office today and I just wanted to stop in and say hello. I worked the late shift, so I'm on my way out."

"Well, thanks for stopping by." Greg wasn't sure how to receive the unexpected visit.

"Listen," Dr. Lowe said. "I know things have been a bit strained around here between you and the rest of us. Pridgen, Neal and I were talking about it a couple of days ago. I think we all were a bit perturbed that Dr. Grant recommended you instead of one of us to fill in for Dr. Armstrong in his absence. We probably took that out on you in one form or another and I'd just like to apologize. I'm not sure if any of the others will own up to our conversation, so I hope you'll accept my apology as being one for all of us."

Greg was genuinely moved by the effort that Dr. Lowe had put forth to make amends. He reached out and took his offered hand and shook it firmly.

"For any part that I played in it, I'd like to apologize as well," Greg offered.

Dr. Lowe smiled and then turned to leave. He stopped just before opening the door, reached in his pocket and turned back to Greg again. Greg looked at the unmarked white envelope that he held out towards him.

"This is for you," he said. "The guys and

I made a bet that the attention that Lenox Hill was giving you had swollen your head. We all wagered a hundred dollars each that you'd never step foot back in Robinson Memorial again. We lost, and since we had no one who bet against us to pay the money to, we decided to give it to you."

"Lowe —"

"Please take it," Dr. Lowe said. "I don't care what you do with it. Put it in your kid's college fund, I don't care. But you deserve it."

Greg accepted the envelope, not sure how to respond. Dr. Lowe opened the door to exit and then turned and faced him again.

"Good to have you back."

"Good to be back," Greg said just before watching the door close behind him.

Walking around his desk, Greg opened a drawer and slipped the envelope inside. Once again, the clipboard became his prime focus and just as had happened before, a knock interrupted. Dr. Neal was the proudest of his three fellow neurosurgeons, so Greg figured that this visit would be from Dr. Pridgen.

"Come in." He was wrong again.

"May I have a moment of your time?"

It wasn't totally out of the ordinary for Pastor Baldwin to stop by his office on occasion, but he never stopped by this early in the morning and seldom on a Monday, which was generally Greg's busiest day.

"Sure," Greg said, after a slight hesitation. "Have a seat."

Pastor Baldwin always dressed like a clergyman, even during the week. He didn't always wear a suit or his ministerial collar, but he always looked presentable and projected an appearance that called for respect. Today he wore a dress shirt, a pair of slacks and a sport coat to complement it all. After he sat, Greg did the same. Having served in the capacity of counselor to many of his church members, Pastor Baldwin was no stranger to closed-door, one-on-one meetings and he wasn't one to bite his tongue, but today, he seemed uneasy. Even so, Greg was unprepared for him to put the ball in his corner.

"Is there something you want to talk to me about . . . ask me, maybe?"

In Greg's eyes, it was an unfair tactic. If anything, he should be asking that of his pastor. Greg respected Pastor Baldwin and always had, but he refused to be placed in the position where the preacher was trying to put him.

"No," Greg answered. "Should there be?"

Pastor Baldwin was not ready for the

answer he was given and he repositioned himself in his chair to try to mask his discomfort. His quietness was beginning to irritate Greg. He assumed that the preacher was using the quiet time to think of another way around the issue. Greg stood from his seat.

"I'm sorry, Pastor, but I have a full list of patients to check on. I need to start making my rounds."

"You don't approve of my relationship with your mother, do you?"

"I've not been told that you and my mother had a relationship other than that of a pastor and church member." Greg's tone mirrored the displeasure he felt in not being informed sooner and in a more proper manner. "How can I disapprove of a relationship that I've not been told about?"

"I understand your annoyance, Greg."

"Do you?" Greg challenged. "My father died nearly thirty years ago, Pastor Baldwin. The way I heard it growing up, people were flipping coins and making bets on Mama hooking up with someone else within the first two years, but she didn't. I've been taking care of Lena Dixon for nearly ten years now and although she's the parent and I'm the son, I should have known about this before now. Mama said no man could ever fill the place in her heart that my daddy left open. Are you telling me that you're doing that?"

"I'm not filling his place, I'm just trying to make my own," Pastor Baldwin said. "Lena wanted to tell you about this some weeks ago, but I told her that I should be the one to do it. I know how much you love your mama, Greg, and I'd never do anything to hurt her. I said nobody would ever take Clara's place too, but had those same people placed their bets on me that placed them on your mother, they would have walked away winners. It's not been two years yet, but Lena means a lot to me and I just want to see if I can have a chance at happiness again."

Greg turned his back to his pastor and took a moment to look out of his window at the landscape of the hospital grounds. This was a conversation that he never thought he'd have with any man, let alone one whom he'd viewed as a father for most of his life. Pastor Baldwin was a good man . . . a real good man and Greg loved him. Ironically, if Phillip Dixon was alive today, he and the preacher would be the same age. Greg didn't doubt the legitimacy of Pastor Baldwin's intentions, but still, there were questions and concerns.

He turned from the window and said, "You're an educated man, Pastor. You're a Morehouse graduate. Mother Baldwin was a Spelman graduate. My mother didn't get beyond the seventh grade before my grandfather pulled her out of school to work. Mother Baldwin was soft-spoken and shy. Lena Dixon has never held her tongue for anybody and if she's shy about anything at all, I haven't found out what it is yet."

Greg stopped talking when he noticed the smile broaden on Pastor Baldwin's face. It was as though the things he was saying were increasing the preacher's fondness for his mother instead of making him think twice about his affections for her.

"I loved Clara, Greg. God knows I loved that woman with my whole heart and soul. I thought I was going to die when she died, and although I know that the whole church was praying for me, I also know that it was Lena's prayers and her faith that pulled me through. It was her genuine concern for me that made me desire to live again. I'm seventy years old. I didn't think that at this age, I'd be thinking of starting over again with someone new, but that's just what I'm thinking."

He stood as he continued to talk. "All of those things you named are big reasons that

Lena has grown on me. She's definitely a feisty one and I've not had that in my life, but I love it. I love that she speaks her mind and I love that she's a take-charge, independent kind of woman. I also love that she's an upright, praying, giving woman; and the fact that she loved Phillip so much that she waited this long speaks volumes on her commitment to relationships. I still miss Clara now and I'm convinced that I always will; just like Lena will always miss your father. I love everything about your mother, Greg. One of her biggest selling points is you. I've always loved you and I know you know this. I have children and I love every single one of them. But without a doubt, I'm closer to you than I am to any of my own sons. To know that you accept our relationship is more than just important to Lena. It's important to me."

Greg sighed. He had no good reason to object to Pastor Baldwin's place in his mother's life. It was his insatiable need to protect her that was making it hard for him to accept. Essentially, Greg had been the only man in Lena's life for as far back as he could recall and maybe his hesitation wasn't about Pastor Baldwin replacing his father, but instead, accepting that the preacher would more accurately be replacing him. At one time, he'd thought that his mother would be lost if he ever became inaccessible to her on a daily basis. Now, just the thought of her moving on and him no longer being the center of her world gave Greg a misplaced feeling. The one thing he knew for certain, though, was that he was placing his mother in strong, capable, godly hands.

"Are you asking for permission to marry my mother?"

"Not just yet," Pastor Baldwin said with a hearty laugh. "I just want to be able to court her with your blessings. I don't want the relationship I have with your mother to build a wall between you and me. I want you to be able to see me as more than your pastor. I want you not to feel threatened by my presence in Lena's life, but to make room for me so she'll feel free to do the same. What you think means everything to her and I won't have a chance without your blessings. Am I asking too much of you?"

The fact that Pastor Baldwin wasn't asking for his mother's hand gave Greg some comfort, but he knew that it was only a matter of time. He reached out to shake his pastor's hand and instead, Pastor Baldwin reached out with both arms and pulled him in for a firm embrace. Just as they released one another, Greg's door opened and Dr.

Grant stepped in.

"Sorry," he said, visibly embarrassed by his unannounced entrance. "I'll come back."

"No, no," Greg said as he formally introduced the two men. "I seem to have a revolving door today, so just join us."

"Actually, he's all yours, Doctor," Pastor Baldwin said. "I was just leaving. Thank you for your time, Dr. Dixon. I'll see you Sunday, if not before."

Greg smiled and returned his wave and then looked at his newest visitor of the morning.

"I didn't want anything in particular. I was just wondering if you were here," Dr. Grant said. "I hadn't seen you on the floor yet."

"I haven't made it out there yet, but I'm on my way now." Greg picked up his clipboard for the fourth time. "I see we have a full house."

"Yes, we do," Dr. Grant said, opening the door as they both stepped into the hallway. "Actually, I have clearance to hire a new neurologist. They'd had a freeze on the hiring since Dr. Merrill retired and we haven't been able to replace him. Now we can and I think I'm ready to move forward."

Greg's eyebrows rose. "Oh?"

"Yes, I'm going to be posting the position

on Robinson Memorial's online job site. My preference is to get an intern and I'd like you to be his main teacher. Are you up for the added responsibility?"

Greg smiled as they came to a stop in the middle of the hall, forcing others to walk around them. "Not only am I up for it, but I can save you the trouble of job posting and interviewing."

He had Simon's complete attention.

"I met an intern at Lenox Hill Hospital who would be a perfect fit for us. He's bright, he's hardworking, he's energetic. He's just an all-around great guy."

Dr. Grant held up his hand to stop Greg's sales pitch. "If you're sold on him, so am I and if Lenox hired him, his integrity can't be in question. My concern is that if he's already on staff with them, will he be willing to transfer and move here to work with us? Lenox is a bigger and busier place than we are. Would he be interested?"

"I'm pretty sure I can convince him. I'll give him a call tonight."

"Great," Dr. Grant said with a wave of his hand. "Let me know something tomorrow."

Greg took a moment to scope his surroundings. He watched men and women in white coats walk towards one destination or another to care for those in need. He saw patients being pushed in wheelchairs by assistants and trays of empty breakfast plates being wheeled back to the cafeteria by orderlies. This was better than anything another hospital could offer him. This was home.

"Hey there, handsome, glad to have you back. We missed the motivational view."

Greg smiled at the compliment that came from a familiar female doctor whose name he didn't know. He waved back as she turned and sashayed down the corridor. Even the flirtations at Robinson sounded nicer to his ears than the ones the females at Lenox offered.

Smiling at the little, almost silly blessings that now played through his mind, Greg turned the corner and headed towards the room of his first patient. Just as he placed his hand on the door, his pager alarmed. With his clipboard tucked under his arm, Greg made long quick strides towards the O.R. Several feet ahead of him, he saw the back of Kelly's head as she entered the double doors. Lenox couldn't possibly have offered a better O.R. assistant than her. Approaching the doors of the operating room where a critical patient was awaiting his ministry, Greg stopped for a brief moment and looked at the instruments that had been divinely used over and over again.

"Guide these hands, God." He whispered the prayer before swinging open the doors.

CHAPTER 30

Journal entry: 1:06 a.m.: I know I'm late with today's thoughts, but the combination of fulfilling my duties as a doctor at work and fulfilling my duties as a father at home left me too physically drained for earlier journalism. The hot shower that I just took rejuvenated me. Now, I can write with a clear head. Don't get me wrong, I'm not complaining, especially about the latter. Julian is such an active boy and growing every single day. I cherish my time with him because I know these years will quickly pass. When I look at him, I see a miniature me and I pray that God will allow me to live to watch him grow into the incredible man that he is destined to become.

Speaking of incredible, such has been my day! The O.R. was busy and I was two for three. Sadly, I couldn't save the nineteen-year-old whose trigger finger wasn't as fast as the guy's was in the opposing gang. He was basically dead when they wheeled him into the hospital. My starting the incision on his head was almost a moot point. Patients like him make me both angry and sad. I'm angry that he chose such a violent way to live, thus sentencing him to a violent death; but I'm sad because he was still someone's child and delivering the news of a youngster's senseless death to his parents never gets any easier. I guess it's that same mixture of emotions that Rick feels when he defends a kid like Perry, only to find out that the real criminal was the boy's father: glad to put the true culprit in jail, but sad that doing so meant taking a husband from his wife and a father from his son.

On that note, it's good to see Rick and Sherry getting it together. I'll admit that they had me concerned. I tried to remain strong for both of them and for Grace, but that was the rockiest road they'd traveled in their marriage. It was a quite a rough patch, but love prevailed and they're back on track. I knew things were back to normal when I called Rick to chat before leaving the hospital and he told me he'd have to call me back because he and Sherry had "stuff to do." I hadn't heard that one in a while, but it was music to my ears. The baby thing, I'm sure, was a direct result of Rick seeing so many young boys growing up in the wrong environment, but I think he's learned to separate business from his personal life. It's a shame that all those boys he defends couldn't have fathers like him. Sometimes life seems unfair, but Mama always told me that God never makes mistakes. She also used to tell me that when God sends an opportunity a-knocking, you best hightail it and open the door. I guess she took that one and applied it to her own life.

I'm still trying to digest the fact that there is a man in her life. A real man! At sixty-one-years old, my mother has netted herself a degreed college graduate who is physically fit, a prolific orator and licensed clergyman. Who'd of thunk? Grace thought it was wonderful news when I told her. If it was any man other than Luther Baldwin, I'd probably disagree wholeheartedly. But I love that man and I can't think of anyone I'd rather call "Dad" more than him. I hope it all works out.

Ms. Mattie and Sarge, well that's one we'll have to wait and see about. There's no doubt that there's still a spark there, but Ms. Mattie said Sarge is going to have to call on Jesus before he could ever think of calling on her. We laughed, but all of us knew she meant every word. Sarge is a good man with a good heart. I think if he hangs around us long enough, he'll follow along. If Grace could see the day her parents actually became a unit, I think she'd be too ecstatic for words. I want that for her. Anything that makes my baby happy, I want it for her. Grace deserves every good thing that life has to offer and if I have my way, she'll get it. God, I love that girl!

All this talk about Grace is making me hungry, so I'm headed for bed. The shower has stopped running which means she'll be ready to turn in soon. I hear opportunity a-knocking.

Good night.

ABOUT THE AUTHOR

Kendra Norman-Bellamy was born in Palm Beach, Florida. She attended Valdosta State University and graduated with honors from Valdosta Technical College in Valdosta, Georgia. She currently resides in Stone Mountain, Georgia, with her husband and two daughters.

The employees of Thorndike Press hope you have enjoyed this Large Print book. All our Thorndike and Wheeler Large Print titles are designed for easy reading, and all our books are made to last. Other Thorndike Press Large Print books are available at your library, through selected bookstores, or directly from us.

For information about titles, please call:
(800) 223-1244

or visit our Web site at:
www.gale.com/thorndike
www.gale.com/wheeler

To share your comments, please write:
Publisher
Thorndike Press
295 Kennedy Memorial Drive
Waterville, ME 04901